The Last Victim

2nd Book

ROBERT SANDILANDS

Paperback: 978-1-961438-54-5
eBook: 978-1-961438-55-2
Library of Congress Control Number: 2023914386

Ordering Information:

Prime Seven Media
518 Landmann St.
Tomah City, WI 54660

Printed in the United States of America

CONTENTS

CHAPTER 1

*N*ew shoes made to measure, cost a fortune, why are they so bloody sore to walk in? He sat on the park bench and slipped them off. The relief brought a smile to his face. Something caught his eye: a ball flying towards him. He was too slow to catch it, and it hit him on the chest. A rough, hairy dog ran up, stopped, and sat down at his feet, looking up at him and whining. Fisher tossed the ball back the way it had come. The hairy beast bolted after it.

"Sorry about that," a woman said, waving at him and smiling before chasing after her pet.

"No problem!" Fisher shouted after her, long blonde hair blowing in the breeze. *Must be about five feet six, in her late twenties, a right looker, shapely hips in her tight jeans, a fit-looking girl—wonder who's sleeping with her.* He fumbled with the blade in his jacket pocket, savouring the feel of the cold steel, the honed edge, and the needle-sharp point. He edged his feet back into the shoes and stood up, watching her disappear behind a clump of rhododendron bushes rich with scarlet blooms. What an ideal setting—couldn't happen in a more desirable place.

He took time to look in all directions. The only people in sight were playing sport a few hundred yards away. Their screams and shouts could be heard, and that was good. His new shoes slipped on the wet grass, but at the last minute, he regained his balance. The dog reappeared, chasing past him, almost brushing his leg before it snatched up its ball and retreated to the other side of the clump of bushes. Fisher followed the animal, confident that it would lead him to its owner.

The dog stopped at the young woman's feet, dropped the ball, and let it roll towards her. She picked it up and tossed it away, laughing as her pet scampered after it. *Now,* Fisher decided when she was distracted and her back to him.

He took three long strides and gripped her in a stranglehold. He pulled the knife from his pocket and plunged it into her back between her shoulder blades. At the first stab, she fought back, and he dragged her to the ground, where she lay facing upwards, her eyes bulging with fear as she gazed into his. He continued ramming the knife into her chest and stomach. When there was no more fight in her, he dragged her into the rhododendrons. "You were a pretty girl, too pretty for your own good," he said aloud, grinning at his work. He felt proud of his achievement as he struggled out of the bush into the open. The dog was standing in front of him, panting and looking down at the ball. He picked it up and tossed it away in the direction of the group playing sport. This time, the animal didn't give chase but sniffed at the trail of blood left by its owner.

"No, Eddie," his mother shouted from the kitchen, holding up his blood-stained coat. "You promised you would stop."

"It's not my fault. Why do you always blame me? They flaunt themselves and ask for it. It makes me sick the way they lust over me."

"One of these days you're going to get caught, and then what will happen when they lock you up? I'll have to walk down the street, knowing that people are staring at me and whispering to each other. I know what they will be saying."

"Don't worry, Mum. I won't get caught, and this time, I promise not to do it again. I mean it."

Nancy Fisher crumpled up the coat and put it in the washing machine, closing the door and turning it on. She returned to the living room away from the noise and sat across from her son. "What makes you so sure you won't get caught?"

Eddie turned away from the television and smiled at her. "Trust me, Mum. I know what I'm doing." He returned his attention to the film he had been engrossed in but couldn't concentrate on it. He jumped up from his chair and began pacing the living room, the way he had always done when she was angry with him.

"The police know what they're doing," Nancy replied and lit a cigarette.

Eddie stopped pacing and looked down at her. "I don't like it when you're angry with me. I know you're going to punish me and won't let me sleep with you." He got down on his knee in front of her and took hold of her hand. "Please try to understand. I find it difficult to stop, like dad used to be with his gambling."

She pulled her hand away. "Well, you know where that got him— so much debt we had to sell our home, and even that didn't square it up. He was so much of a coward. Took the easy way out … He should have done it sooner." She turned her head away, her eyes brimming with tears, not wanting him to see she was crying.

Eddie had known from a young age they weren't his biological parents; his drunken father had always let him know and cursed the day they had taken him as their own. Every time his adopted father got a big win at the horses, he would come home drunk, beat his wife, and then turn on Eddie. At the age of five, Eddie began sleeping in the same bed as his mother. She protected him, and he gave her the love she was deprived of.

"Please don't be angry with me." He took hold of her hand again, kissed it, and held it to his cheek.

She was a beautiful woman and didn't look her age of forty-one, more like in her late twenties. Eddie was nine the night the police came to tell her that her husband had driven his car over an embankment on the motorway and landed in the river; he'd been dead when they found him. Eddie had been relieved at first and had thought his mother would feel the same, but he was shocked to see her break down. It aroused a hidden rage inside, something he'd never known was in him. He'd wanted to lash out at her. He didn't like her having feelings for anyone else—she was the only one he loved.

Nancy jerked her hand away. "I'm not angry with you." She stumped her cigarette out in the glass ashtray she kept on the small table beside her seat. "And I'm not going to stop you sleeping with me. It's just I get frightened when you're not here. I don't know what you're doing or if you are committing another murder. I don't know the minute the police are going to knock on that door and arrest us both." She chose her words carefully, not wanting to upset him. Although he had never threatened her, she didn't want to push her luck.

Eddie stood up and started pacing. "We should move away from here, to where people won't know I'm your adopted son. We could live as a couple."

"I would like that, but you have to stop."

"I've told you I won't do it again." He rushed over, knelt in front of her, and took both her hands in his as he looked into her blue eyes. "I promise."

Nancy frowned, forced a smile, and leaned closer to his face. In his blue eyes she could see that he meant what he had said at that moment. In a day or so, she knew, it could be a different story. She had known him all his life—his mood swings, character changes. He could be the most loving person she could ever dream of, so gentle and kind, always considerate of her and respectful. Never at any time had he as much as raised his voice at her. But she had detected a dark side in him at an early age, though she'd kept it to herself, never letting her husband know how she felt. On his seventh birthday, she had presented him with a puppy, and to this day she remembered the look on his young face, as if he had just bitten into a sour apple. A week later, the puppy had disappeared. She withdrew her hands and sat back.

"I know how you feel about me, Eddie, and I feel the same way, so please for our sake, keep your promise."

He got back onto his feet. "Would you like a tea or a coffee or something stronger?"

Nancy nodded. "If we do move away, you'll have to stop calling me Mum."

"What will I call you?" he shouted from the kitchen.

"I don't think I need to answer that one," she said.

She picked up the television remote to start flicking through the channels, though her mind wasn't on it. Eddie had only been nine at the time of her husband's accident, but she suspected he might have tampered with the car in some way. Or was she being paranoid? Surely a nine-year-old wouldn't know how to. This argument had haunted her since the old couple they had once been friendly with had been brutally murdered. Eddie had come home that night with his clothes covered in blood.

"I've made you a cup of lemon tea, just the way you like it." He handed it over, smiling. "Enjoy it, *Nancy.*" He returned to the kitchen and came back with a can of lager. He sat back down on his chair, crossed his legs, pulled the ring on his can, and admired her perfect features. Her long, flowing blonde hair hung loosely over her shoulders, hiding most of her long, slender neck. She wore a small, tight-fitting woollen top that didn't quite meet the waistband of her jeans, exposing her naval. Eddie felt his heart begin to race and gulped the cold lager in an effort to calm himself. Of course, it didn't work—it never did—but he felt that this wasn't the time to let his emotions take control.

She took a sip from her cup and nodded in approval. "What would I do without you?"

"You will never be without me."

"That's why I'm begging you to give up doing these things. I couldn't stand being without you."

"Please believe me, Mum … er, Nancy. That was the last one."

She laughed lightly at him correcting himself. "I want to believe you. Honestly, I do. Prove to me that you have, and we'll move away from here as you suggested."

"That's not a problem. You can start planning to move."

"It'll take about six months to get things sorted out. If in that time you've proven you have kept your promise, then we will move."

CHAPTER 2

Billy Benson climbed out of his chauffeur-driven limousine and entered his country mansion to find his wife and three police constables sitting in the lounge. His wife had her head in her hands. It was obvious she had been crying. They all looked up as he entered.

"What's going on here?" he asked.

The female constable rose and approached him. "I'm sorry, sir, we have bad news. Would you like to sit down?"

Billy shot his arms up in the air. "What bad news? What the hell are you talking about?"

His wife got up and rushed towards him, throwing her arms around his neck and sobbing. Her tears ran onto his neck. "It's Amanda," she sobbed.

"What about her?" He gripped his wife's shoulders and gently pushed her out to arm's length.

The female constable stepped closer. "I'm sorry to inform you, sir, but your daughter's body was found in St James's Park, earlier today. It appears she has been murdered."

Billy drew his wife closer and hugged her. They both cried their hearts out. When he managed to pull himself together, he asked, "Do you have any idea who was responsible?"

She slowly shook her head. "Too soon to know. Her body was just discovered an hour ago."

"Any witnesses?"

The girl shook her head again. "Haven't found any yet, but it's too soon to tell. I'm sure somebody must have heard or seen something. People are frightened to come forward. Don't want the hassle of going through a lengthy court case."

At six thirty the next morning, Billy was in his office. Only the security guard was in the building. This wasn't unusual, as he quite often turned up unexpectedly at any time day or night. This guard, Richard Barton, was the reason he'd come in this morning. Billy knew this man well, knew he had exceptional talent.

"Sit down, Richard," Billy said, gesturing for the guard to take a seat in front of his desk.

Barton got himself seated. "What can I do for you, boss?"

"You've met my daughter, Amanda?"

Barton nodded with enthusiasm. "A lovely girl. Yes, I've seen her about and said hello." If he had been honest, he would have said her fancied his chances with her.

"She was found murdered in St James's Park yesterday. The report says she had been stabbed multiple times and dragged into bushes. It was her dog that got some walkers' attention. Otherwise her body may have lain there for days."

"Bloody hell, I'm sorry, boss. You must be gutted."

Billy nodded. "I am. You've no idea how much. Her mother and I have been up all night. We cried and hugged each other until we could cry no longer. We've decided to get the bastard who did this, knowing full well the police will take forever to find whoever it was. I need you to find this killer."

It took Barton a few minutes to believe what he what he had just heard. "I don't think I'm the right person for that job. I don't have any experience in investigating."

"That's not what I've been told." Billy stared into Barton's eyes and leaned forward over his desk. "My information is that you tracked down a bomb-making gang."

"That was pure amateur bungling and luck."

Billy grimaced. "That's exactly the talent I need."

"I wouldn't know where to start."

"As you know, I run a large gambling organisation. It generates a lot of hate when punters lose a lot of their hard-earned money. I strongly believe that the motive for her murder could have been revenge. That being the case, I have a list of people who have fallen into that category in the past few months." He pulled out a drawer at the side of his desk and produced a thick Manila envelope, which he pushed across the desk. "You'll find a number of names in there. That's where you start."

"Say by good luck, I find this person. What then?"

Billy sneered. "You bring that person back to me." He got stiffly up from his seat and removed his thick-lensed glasses. Then he pulled a smaller envelope from his inside jacket pocket and tossed it on the desk. "That should cover most of your expenses."

Richard Barton scooped up both envelopes and stood up. He held out his hand, and they both shook. "I'll do my best."

"You'll do beyond your best, if you know what's good for you."

CHAPTER 3

arton got home to his rented flat late that morning. Normally he would be in by eight, but it was after ten when he crawled into bed. He had examined Billy Benson's list of names and addresses and then sat on the sofa for over an hour wondering where to start. In the end, he'd decided to start at the top of the list and work his way down. After an hour of fitful sleep, he got up, showered, got dressed, and decided to head out to find the first name.

Billy had had the presence of mind to include the post codes on his list, which made the job easier. Barton lost no time in finding the first address on satnav. It was a bloody great block of flats. The area looked rough. Most of the windows had been boarded up, and wheelie bins lay toppled, their contents scattered over the parking area. An abandoned car propped up on wooden blocks sat on the front lawn. He entered the double doors, which were also boarded up where glass should have been. The lift was out of order, so he took to the stairs. Three flights later, he stepped out and was faced with a long corridor with numerous doors on both sides. Most of them were blocked off with galvanised steel sheets.

He found the correct flat. A thin, white-haired woman answered after several thumps on the door. Barton stepped back when the smell of damp clothes and body odour hit his nostrils. He guessed she was about fifty. Her long, curly white hair hung unkempt over her face, and her red eyes peered through the strands. A half-smoked cigarette hung loosely from her toothless mouth, the ash ready to fall off as she sucked at it and blew the smoke at his face.

"What the fuck do you want?" she croaked.

"I'm looking for Raymond Gibb?"

"Well, when you find him, tell him I want my fuckin' money."

Barton restrained himself from bursting into a fit of laughter. "Have you any idea where I could find him?"

"What are you, the law or something?"

Barton shook his head. "Nothing like that."

"Why do you want him?"

"I found a credit card with that name on it. I just want to return it and make sure he is the right owner."

She burst into a gritty laugh, spat the cigarette out on the floor, and coughed her lungs out. "That bastard with a credit card? What stupid cunt would allocate one to him? If you want to know where he's most likely to be, it's in the nick."

Barton nodded his thanks and walked away, glad to be away from the smell.

"If you want a good time, just knock. I'm not expensive," she shouted as she closed her door.

"I'll give that some thought," he replied and quickened his pace. He took the stairs three at a time and was glad when he reached the bottom and gulped in fresh air. He wasn't convinced that that old witch was being honest, so he sat in his car for half an hour watching the door.

He shot a quick glance at his timepiece and decided to start up and try the next address. Just then, however, a hoodie passed his car and headed for the door. Barton wound down his window and shouted. The figure stopped, turned, and ran around the back of the building. Barton quietly grinned to himself and thought, *Typical.*

He drove out of the park and hid his car behind a high hedge. Then he got out and sprinted back. He caught the hoodie opening the door. He gripped the man's arm and pulled him to the side, away from prying eyes.

"I'm looking for Raymond Gibb."

The hoodie jerked his arm free. "I've never heard of him."

"I know he lives in this block of flats, so if you see him, tell him I've found something he lost. I know he'll want it back."

Eddie stood at the door until the big guy disappeared at the end of the road. He sighed. He'd thought he had been caught. He darted inside and rushed up the stairs. Nancy was in the living room with a newspaper in her hand.

She looked up at him. "What's wrong? You look as if you had seen a ghost or something."

"It's nothing. Just got a fright. A big guy jumped on me asking for that creep Raymond who lives next door, I thought the guy was a policeman."

She slammed the paper onto the coffee table next to her seat. "I see a woman has been murdered in St James's Park. Please tell me that wasn't you."

"Relax, Mum … er, Nancy. It wasn't me, I can assure you."

"It happened yesterday. You came home yesterday with blood all over your coat."

Eddie laughed and sat on the sofa. "I'm not stupid enough to do that so close to home."

"Who's this Raymond guy that man was looking for?"

"I think he stays with that woman next door. I'm not sure. Haven't seen him about for a while."

Nancy got up. "I'll make something to eat. How was work?" She looked down at his close-cut red hair and couldn't help but admire his blue eyes and freckled complexion. He wasn't as tall and broad as her husband had been, but there was a strange similarity between them, the same red hair and freckles. When Eddie had been a young boy, people had often commented on how much he looked like his father.

Eddie got up and followed her into the kitchen. He put his arms around her waist as she leaned over the sink. "Have you thought any more about us moving?"

She turned, put her arms around his neck, and shook her head. "I don't know where you want to move to. We have to make that decision together."

"I would like to go up north somewhere."

She withdrew her arms and stepped away from him. "We can talk about it after dinner."

Eddie went back into the living room and switched on the television. The local news was about the murdered girl in the park. He felt proud that the police had no clues as to who the perpetrator was. *Stupid bastards have no idea what they're doing,* he thought. *Just keep changing the modus operandi and carry on.* When Nancy entered with his meal on a tray, he quickly changed the channel.

She stood shocked for a moment. "Have you been watching about that girl who was murdered in the park?" She stood there motionless with the tray in her hands, staring wide-eyed at him.

"Not particularly. I switched it on, and the news happened to be on. Didn't fancy watching it, so I turned it over."

CHAPTER 4

Four addresses later, Barton was about to give up for the day, not having gotten any response from banging on all the doors. At least the latter districts were a bit more upper class than the first. A black Volvo pulled into the driveway of the house in front of him. Two women got out. One stood to the side while the other lifted a child out of the rear. Barton approached them as they were about to enter the house.

"Sorry for the intrusion," he said with his sexiest smile and glances. "I'm looking for a Mr John Bank. I believe he lives here."

The woman carrying the child grimaced. "Are you his lawyer?"

"No, nothing like that. I found something in the park that belongs to him. I just want to return it."

"What was it you found?" she asked, looking more interested.

"I really need to speak to him in person."

"Well, the creep doesn't live here anymore. He pissed off with his fancy piece."

"Any idea where he lives now?"

"If I knew that, I'd go round there and smash his windows in."

The other woman interrupted. "I feel sorry for the girl he moved in with. Her body was found in St James's Park yesterday." She turned to look at her friend and saw her eyes widening in shock. "Oh! Marlin, I'm sorry. I thought you knew."

If Marlin had known she showed no signs of it. In Barton's opinion, she looked quite smug about it. Almost elated. If he had been the police and had discovered a connection like this, she would be his prime suspect. He felt pleased about being a step closer. He was beginning to think this was going to be a lot simpler than he'd first thought.

"What progress are you making?" Billy asked Barton at the office door.

Barton walked in and sat down in front of his desk. He waited until Billy turned and got into his own seat before speaking. "I suspect that the person responsible for your daughter's murder could be a woman. I'm not a hundred per cent certain, though. It's too early to be sure."

Billy shook his head. "It has to have been a man. Amanda was a fit, strong girl. Kept herself in good condition. She could have fought off any woman."

Barton leant closer. "Did you know she was having a relationship with a married man?"

"No way," Billy said, almost jumping out of his seat. "Where did you get that information?"

"According to John Bank's wife, her husband was the man Amanda was living with."

"Do you think it was this wife? She would have good reason. If she is strong and fit like Amanda, she might have been able to overtake her if she caught Amanda when her back was turned."

"It could also have been her husband," Barton interrupted. "The police will want to interview him."

"You have to get to him before they do."

"We could already be too late for that, but give me your daughter's address. This guy Bank might still be there."

"You go and find this John Bank tonight. You might get lucky. I'll get somebody to cover your shift. I'll be at home. Phone and let me know how you get on."

Bank wasn't at Billy's daughter's address. Barton could only assume he was at the police station being interviewed. He started up his car and decided to try Bank's wife again, a bit of an odds- on gamble. If John wasn't there, maybe he could learn a bit more about the woman's estranged husband.

Marlin was quick to open the door, and when she recognised Barton, she was equally quick in trying to close it. He pushed at it, sending her backwards.

"I need a few words with you," he said and walked in past her.

She slammed the door and ran after him. "I'm going to call the police!" she shouted.

"I would advise you not to." Barton gripped her wrist. "You and your husband are their number-one suspects in that girl's murder."

"Let go of me!" she screamed and jerked her arm free. "How could I be a suspect? I never knew her. Didn't even know where she lived or even her name."

The pressure Marlin had used to free her wrist from his grip told Barton she was strong, and by the look of her, she was in good physical shape. "You keep yourself fit, do you?"

"What's that got to do with it?"

"That girl who was murdered was a fitness addict, and only another fit girl or a man would have been able to take her down. You understand what I'm saying? That is the way the coppers will see it, and you have a strong motive, with your husband leaving you for her. Murder of passion, they call it."

"What are you, some kind of blackmailer?"

Barton shook his head. "Nothing like that. Believe me, if you or your husband are responsible for that girl's murder, the police will be the least of you worries. So, my advice is to you to tell me how I can get in contact with your husband."

"I don't know about that creep," she said, ushering him back to the door, "but I can assure you I had nothing to do with that woman's murder. The day she was found in that park, I was in Wales visiting my sister, and I can prove it."

"I hope so for your sake. So, prove it." Barton resisted being edged towards the door.

"What, now?"

"Well, when do you propose to?" Barton said, holding his hands out.

"The only thing I can do is phone her."

"Do that. And put your phone on speaker."

After listening to her sister on the phone, he was satisfied with her alibi.

"Now, tell me how I get in contact with your creep husband."

"As far as I know, he was living in her flat."

This time, Barton found himself on the step when she banged the door in his face. He was about to shout through the door that he had already been there but decided it was a waste of time and effort.

From his car, he phoned Billy and informed him that he had eliminated the woman from his suspicions but that so far, he hadn't located the husband.

"Well," shouted Billy, "you can eliminate him. The police had him in custody. He had an alibi, and they let him go."

"So, we're back to square one," Barton said.

"You've got the bloody list I gave you, so get on with it." Billy cut the connection.

Barton drove back to the block of flats he'd started with and decided to eyeball the place for an hour or so. Maybe this Raymond guy would turn up. He had just pulled on the hand brake when the hoodie walked past. Barton hadn't had time to duck down and wasn't sure if the guy had noticed him. When he looked in his rear-view mirror, the hoodie had disappeared. How the hell did he manage to get out of sight so quickly? Where had he gone? He felt a cold shiver run up his spine. Creeps in a place like this would bash your head in for drug money. He had never been one to back down from a fight, but when the enemy was unseen, that was when fear took over. He got the car started up and shot out of the car park.

As Eddie approached the door of the building and opened it a crack to see if anybody was walking about, a car drove in and stopped. Eddie opened the door an inch wider. He had a good view of the vehicle, which had just parked at the near end of the parking area. This was nothing unusual, as a few residents had cars, but this one was a strange car. He pulled up his hood, covering most of his face, and decided to investigate.

The driver ducked down into the footwell, but not far enough. He was too big a man to get down any farther. Eddie recognised him as the big man who had stopped him earlier. There was no mistaking that long black hair tied back in a ponytail, the huge shoulders inside the leather jacket, or the overgrown designer stubble. He'd never seen the man's eyes, not even when they'd been close together earlier. He anticipated that the driver would watch him through his rear-view mirror and ducked down behind the rear of the car.

He decided that this was too big a man to bring down and a knife would be useless. He'd need a gun for this one, or he could sneak up behind and use the crowbar he had hidden in his wardrobe. It had been the ideal weapon against the old couple last year. With a blast of exhaust smoke, the engine fired up, and the vehicle shot away, leaving Eddie crouched on his knees. He remained there until the car was gone.

CHAPTER 5

Barton woke after only a few hours of fitful sleep. He felt like he had a hangover and couldn't face breakfast. After half an hour in the shower, the feeling hadn't lifted. All night the hoodie had kept appearing in his broken dreams—that white freckled face with its little blue eyes, a slightly built youth about five feet, five inches tall. Certainly not the picture he had formed in his mind of Raymond Gibb. Based on Billy's description of his daughter, she would have been able to fight this person off. Barton decided this wasn't the guy on Billy's list. There was only one thing for it. He had to go back; only this time, he'd park the car out of sight and walk there. It was just after 5 a.m. Too early. That was the trouble with constant night work; the body clock needed time to adjust.

A musical chiming sounded. He had heard it before, but in that moment of semi-consciousness, it sounded unfamiliar. He jumped up, realising he had dozed off on the chair. It was 7 a.m. He was feeling better. He had another shower, had something to eat, got dressed, and was in his car and on the move by 8 a.m.

He parked up on a safe-looking side street and legged it to the block of flats. He found the place deserted. He didn't expect many people living in a place like this would be up to go to work, so they all must have been lying in bed, sleeping off the effects of booze or drugs. His expectations were dashed when the little hoodie dashed out the door and into a car. Barton jumped behind one of the few upstanding wheelie bins. He noticed a woman walk towards the same car and get in the driver's seat. She didn't rush. He had to admire her; she was quite tall with long, flowing blonde hair. She didn't wear too much make-up had a nice figure, like she kept herself fit. Just his type of woman. He wondered if she could be hoodie's mother. Surely not. Too young. Maybe a sister? Hopefully not her lover. He rushed to his car intending to follow them.

By the time he got into his car and drove to the main road, however, they were gone. He stopped at the side of the road and phoned Billy. "That Raymond Gibb, is there any way of finding out if he is in the nick?" he asked.

Billy came back saying he'd try to find out.

St James's Park was mobbed with onlookers. The police still had it cordoned off with blue and white tape.

"What's going on here?" Barton asked one of the spectators at the tape.

The tall, grey-haired man looked at him. "That's where that girl was found." He pointed at the clump of Rhododendron bushes. "It's a bad day when people can't walk in the public park safely."

Barton edged his way back through the crowd to the street, where a squad of police vehicles were parked. He noticed a familiar face talking to two other men. Billy was a lot smaller than the other men and seemed to be doing most of the talking. For some reason, he glanced round and straight into Barton's eyes. He strutted towards Barton looking rather irritated, leaving his associates standing open mouthed.

"What are you doing here?" he demanded.

"I was about to ask you the same question."

Billy caught Barton by the arm and steered him out of hearing distance. "These two guys are detectives, asking all sorts of questions. I think they suspect that I might take the law into my own hands, the way I did when my brother was murdered."

Barton was taken a back for a moment. This was something he hadn't known about. Finally he managed to say, "Were you charged for it?"

Billy shook his head. "They couldn't prove it, but my name is still on their records. They'll be keeping an eye on me, so no more phone calls." He turned and walked towards the detectives.

With Billy turning up at his daughter's murder scene, it was no surprise the police suspected him of once more taking the law into his own hands. If the law got wind of Barton snooping around and asking questions, it would only be a matter of time before they made the connection.

Barton sat in his car wondering what his next move was going to be, now that contact with Billy was out of the question. The woman he'd seen getting in that car with the hoodie came to mind. If he was honest with himself, she had hardly been out of his thoughts since he'd set eyes on her. He wondered what the chances would be of seeing her again if he went back to that car park the same time the next morning? Maybe then the hoodie wouldn't be with her. It was worth a chance, he thought. He could stop her and ask if she had seen Raymond Gibb, get chatting with her. Who knew where it might lead.

He was about to start his car up and pull away when a knock came on the passenger's window and Billy's face appeared there. Barton wound it down.

"What's wrong?"

"Raymond Gibb is in the nick. Has been for six months, for selling stolen goods."

"Another dead end."

"Not entirely. I heard a policeman tell one of his mates that whoever the killer was could be a regular visitor to the park."

"Any idea what makes them think that?"

"I don't know, maybe a witness or something. Anyway, you hang about. Keep an eye on all the visitors. You know what they say on telly: the killer always returns to the scene of the crime."

Barton nodded. "Worth a try, but you can't always believe what they say on telly."

"Be careful. I think they're following me. They saw me talking to you, so mind your back."

"How do I get in contact with you?"

"I'll get one of my boys to contact you. You'll recognise him; he'll be wearing a green trilby."

Barton locked up his vehicle and headed back to the park. He noticed a group of men standing close together near one of the park benches. One of them stepped over to a spot on the grass and pointed down at it. The rest joined him, and they entered a lengthy discussion. Barton edged over, all ears. He heard one of them talking about shoe prints and saying that they must be new, only a size seven. Was he now on the hunt for a small man or a female? Not wanting to be noticed by these men, he made his way back out of the park and into his car. There were still a few names on Billy's list, and he decided to try them.

The first house he tried turned out to be an elderly couple. He made the excuse that he was lost and asked them for directions to a street name he made up. Three addresses later, he finally got a reply from a squeaky-voiced little man with thick-lensed glasses smoking a large pipe that smelt like smouldering rags. "I'm looking for Mr Collin Walters."

"That's me. What can I do for you?"

"An item was found in St James Park a couple of days ago with your name and address on it. You have to prove it is yours and that you were in the park at the time."

"What was found?" Walters asked, taking a step back.

"What time were you in the park on Monday?"

"I wasn't in the park on Monday or Tuesday. Too many police about asking questions."

"So, this item can't be yours, then."

"Doesn't look like it. What was it?"

Barton grinned, turned, and walked away. He heard the door being slammed behind him. Another name crossed off the list for the time being. Something about that little man gave him an uneasy feeling. He drove along the street a short distance and stopped to see if Walters would come out of his house. A few seconds later, the little figure stood at his gate, eyes squinting in all directions like somebody with something to hide. Barton snatched out his mobile phone, took a few photos of him, and drove away.

All the way back to his flat, Billy's last words about maybe being followed rang in his mind. He made a few detours, constantly glancing in his mirrors, but he detected no following vehicles. Still, he didn't relax when he arrived home. He gathered up three jackets and a couple of baseball caps and packed them into a plastic shopping bag. He left again, locking up his flat, dumped the bag in the back seat, and drove back to the park.

The crowds had dispersed, and most of the police had left. Only a handful hung about, and they were looking bored, probably desperate for a break. He avoided them as much as he could but still wanted to get close to the crime scene to look for someone acting suspicious but with a smug victorious look about them.

He knew not to stand too long in the same place, and after a short period of walking about, he went behind a bush, dug into his plastic bag, changed his jacket, and put on one of the caps. He resumed his walking and stopping. This time he ventured a bit closer and saw the woman he'd seen earlier at the block of flats looking at the Rhododendron bush. Before approaching her, Barton searched for the hoodie. He was nowhere in sight. He walked up behind her and stopped a few feet away.

"A terrible thing to happen to a young woman."

She swung round, looked into his brown eyes for a moment, nodded, and walked briskly away without a word.

Barton admired her swaying hips and the flowing blonde hair sweeping gently over her shoulders. She held her head high, full of confidence. He was on the verge of following but stopped himself. It dawned on him that she was a fit looking woman, certainly fit enough to murder another fit woman if she had attacked her from behind with a knife. The report he'd seen on telly said the victim had been stabbed numerous times and dragged into bushes. He would have to play the lost credit card ploy. He chased after her and caught her as she was about to get into her car.

"I noticed you searching about near that park bench. I found a credit card here on Monday and was wondering if that was what you were looking for?"

She stepped into her car, closed the door, and wound down the window. "It's not mine. I haven't lost my credit card, and this is the first time I've been in that park." Once again she delayed a moment, gazing into his brown eyes. She could feel her heart give a flutter and couldn't control the smile that spread across her face. At that moment, a vision of Eddie appeared, and the fear returned. She started up her car and drove off, regretting every moment of it. She wanted to get to know this stranger but knew that had better not happen.

Barton delayed a while longer at the kerbside, watching her car disappear amongst the traffic. His instincts told him she was interested, and he wondered if she had a husband. Or was that hoodie her husband or partner? Seemed a bit too young, but some women preferred that. Maybe the hoodie wasn't as young as he appeared. All Barton had noticed was his face and some of his hair. He remembered watching him and the way he carried himself in his rear-view mirror. He'd had that youthful gait.

Barton returned to the park. He couldn't see the constables and guessed they must have decided that it was no longer necessary for them to be there. He sat on the bench where Eddie had sat and looked at the same scenery. He could almost picture what had happened. His instincts kicked in, telling him this could have been the place where the killer had sat waiting for his victim. Billy had decided that it must be a revenge killing by one of the punters who had lost a lot of money in his gambling establishments. If that were the case, the killer would have planned it, discovered that Amanda was Billy's daughter.

Barton studied the park visitors as they walked past, trying to read their body language as most of them delayed at the crime scene, passed opinions to each other, and walked on.

CHAPTER 6

Eddie was excited. This was going to be a good day. He had travelled by train into Bristol, sat in his seat, and waited till all the passengers had gotten off before following the young girl that had sat across from him. *Still in school uniform. Maybe going home for the weekend and hadn't time to get changed. Your misfortune*, he mused as he walked behind her. *Hope nobody's waiting for her outside.* His luck held. She jumped on a bus, and he followed her, sitting two seats behind. The bus was full, and passengers got on and off at every stop, but he kept an eye on her. It was almost empty when she got up. After a few seconds, he rose and stepped off behind her. Another man followed them along the street, and Eddie held back until the man turned off and walked down another street.

Up ahead, he saw a tree-lined pathway. He willed her to turn into it, and she did. Overhanging branches cast dark shadows as she walked under them. After a good look round, he could see they were alone and quickened his pace. He pulled the nylon cord from his pocket, having already tied it into a slip knot on the train. He rushed up behind her, slipped it over her head, and pulled her behind a tree with it. She lay on her back at his feet, her tongue swollen and protruding from her mouth, her brown eyes popping out like golf balls. He stamped his foot on her chest, held it there, and pulled at the cord until he heard her draw her last breath. He loosened the nylon cord, wound it up, and put it back into his pocket. Then he walked away towards the bus stop, a good day's work accomplished.

Nancy was playing with her mobile when Eddie opened the car door and slipped in beside her. She looked at him and forced herself to smile.

"Have you had a good day?" she asked, switching off her phone and dropping it into her pocket.

"An excellent day," he replied. "Everything went according to plan. The seminar went well, everyone went away happy, and the boss was very satisfied with my lecture."

Nancy didn't know whether to believe him or not but was too afraid to contradict him. It's not that he had been in any way violent to her, but she couldn't hold back the fear that developed in her when he was close.

"That's great. We could celebrate with a special meal." She started up the car and got it on the move.

On the short journey home, her mind drifted back to the man she'd met in the park. She couldn't understand the feeling that had come over her when she'd looked into his brown eyes or why she was attracted to his physical appearance. It was like some kind of schoolgirl crush. *Best put it out of your mind,* she thought. *It can only bring trouble. Probably won't ever see him again.*

"You're looking kind of distant," Eddie said as he opened the door to their flat. He smiled as she passed him in the short hallway. "What was your day like?"

"I don't know why you ask that," she replied taking off her jacket. "I haven't done anything out of the ordinary, just another so-so day."

"Have you been out somewhere?"

"Did a bit of shopping, that's all," she studied him taking off his jacket, trying not to make it obvious. She saw no blood on his white shirt and felt the tension ease from her body. She knew that these seminars only lasted a few hours and always started in the afternoon. He had left early and would have had a few hours to occupy himself before attending. She worried about how he passed that time.

"Bloody shoes are still pinching," he moaned as he sat on the sofa and eased them off. He smiled as she picked them up and dusted them off. "Looking for traces of blood? Well, you won't find any. I've kept my promise."

"I hope so, Eddie, for both our sakes. I don't want them to take you away. I don't know what I'd do."

"Don't worry, Mum … sorry, Nancy. That's never going to happen."

CHAPTER 7

St James's Park had been created on the side of a hill. In front was the huge clump of Rhododendron bushes where, Barton had learned, the girl's body had been found. The slope from the footpath was quite steep. This would have been an advantage for a small man or a woman; they could have rushed down and attacked the girl from behind, knocking her off balance with the sheer force of their momentum. Barton could understand why the killer had not been witnessed. At the bottom of the incline, another path ran parallel to the one he was sitting beside, making it easier for visitors to use that one rather than climb the hill to this level. Getting up here himself had taken a bit of effort; his breathing was laboured.

A familiar odour made him stand up. He looked down at the footpath below and saw the source. It was the little bald Walters, belching smoke from his large pipe. Maybe now that the police had left the park, he had decided it would be safe to return to the scene of his crime. There was one drawback to his theory:

if this little man were the killer, why weren't the police on to him? Could it be too soon? They could be building a case against him, collecting evidence, watching him. If that was the case, Barton should make himself scarce. He didn't want to be another suspect by hanging around the crime scene.

He moved his car into a position where he could see the park entrance without arousing suspicion from any police or wandering detectives watching the area. He could wait there for Walters to exit without fear of the man noticing him. He couldn't just point the finger at the little man without being positive he was the killer. Billy wouldn't hesitate at the slightest hint to drag him to wherever it was he intended to take the person who killed his daughter.

An hour dragged by, and Walters still hadn't shown at the entrance. Perhaps there was another way out that Barton hadn't noticed. He started his car just as a knuckle knocked on his passenger's side window, giving his nerves a jolt.

A constable bent down and gazed in. Barton wound the window down.

"Can I help you, Officer?"

"There's been a bit of trouble in this area, sir. Noticed you have been parked here for some time and was wondering why."

Barton nodded. "Sorry about that. Can you tell me if there is another way out of this park? My friend may have gone out that way if there is."

The constable grinned. "A stranger in this area, are you?"

"A bit, yes."

The constable walked to the front of the car and jotted the registration number down. That done, he came back to the window.

"Can I have your name and address?" He stood poised with his notebook and pencil.

As Barton was about to give his details, two other constables came out through the park entrance. Between them with hands cuffed behind his back was the little bald man, his thick glasses hanging precariously at the end of his nose, pipe still in his mouth.

The constable at Barton's car, closed his notebook, tucked his pencil in his top pocket, and said, "OK, sir, move on."

As Barton drove past, he saw the constable join his two fellow officers. He let out a sigh of relief at not having to give his details, but he was disappointed that he had not collard Walters before the police had gotten to him. Now, somehow, he had to get in contact with Billy. Should he risk phoning him or hope that the contact with the green trilby would turn up soon?

The tall gangly man wearing a green trilby stood at Barton's door, smoking. He handed his mobile over and said, "Billy wants a word."

"Hi, Billy," Barton said into the phone before Billy got a chance to speak.

"What's happening, Barton?"

"I've had words with a woman who seemed interested in the crime scene, but it turned out to be idle curiosity. Another man I suspected got nabbed by the law before I had a chance to grab him. I'm not sure if it's connected with this crime. His name is Collin Walters, a creepy-looking little man. He was on your list, so you must have his details on file. I saw him in the park walking about as if looking for something or someone."

"Why didn't you jump him when you had the chance?"

"He was too far away, and there were too many people going about. I decided to wait for him in my car outside the gates, but when he appeared, he was being escorted by two constables."

"I'll get him checked out and let you know what he's all about."

The call ended, and Barton handed back the man's phone. The man nodded and walked away. As

Barton entered his flat, his mind was drawn back to the woman he'd seen at the park. What was the attraction? Why had she affected him in this way? He knew he was a lady's man and found it difficult, sometimes impossible, to resist most women, but this one was different. He hadn't worked out why. The hoodie came to mind, and he wondered what the relationship could be between them. That aside, he had to get to know her, one way or another.

After a quick microwave dinner and a shower, he sat down to study Billy's list. Out of the ten names, he had managed to eliminate two. Walters was still a question mark; he looked a dodgy character, but would he be capable of murdering that fit young woman?

"You go and shower, Eddie. I'll make us something to eat," Nancy said on her way into the kitchen.

He got up off the sofa. "I could do with one after the busy day and all that travelling." He headed for the bedroom and shouted, "Do you want to join me?"

"You go ahead. I'm busy with supper."

Nancy had no intention of cooking, but she made some noise with some dishes and pots. She gave him time to get in the shower and then soft-footed her way to where he had left his jacket. She extracted the nylon cord from the first pocket and stared at it in horror. When the shower stopped, she plunged it back in and rushed back to the kitchen. She heard him pad his way back to the living room on bare feet and switch the television on. The signature tune for the evening news played, and she walked in on time to hear the report about a schoolgirl being found dead on a quiet public walk in Bristol.

She screamed at him, "What have you done?"

Eddie jumped up off the sofa with only a towel wrapped around his waist. It slipped to his ankles. "That wasn't me," he shouted, gathering up the towel. "Do you see any blood on my clothes?" It was at that moment that a police inspector came on saying the girl appeared to have been strangled.

Nancy pointed at the television. "You don't get blood on you when you strangle someone."

"Honest, Nancy, it wasn't me. Please believe me."

There was no doubt in her mind that it had been him. She felt sick and rushed to the toilet. When there was nothing left to bring up, she washed her face and returned. He was sitting back on the sofa with a can of beer in his hand. The expression on his face was that of someone who had just achieved something great. He smiled at her and patted the cushion next to him.

"Come here, honey."

"I'm in the process of making something to eat." She turned and went back into the kitchen, relieved to be out of the same room as him.

Trying to hide her fear was getting more difficult. She realised the only way to do it was to stand up to him but not push it too far. It had taken her years to know how far to go. A wrong word at the wrong time was all it would take for him to go out and find another victim. This, she was sure, was his way of punishing her. What had she said to make him go and murder that woman in the park and the one in Bristol? These were the ones she knew about. How many others were there? She couldn't help but feel she was to blame. She dreaded what would happen if he found out she was thinking about another man. *Try to forget about that stranger. Put him out of your mind. You'll probably never see him again; just give it time.* She saw movement out the corner of her eye and jumped at the suddenness of his appearance. Eddie was standing in the doorway—how long he had been there she had no idea. The towel was gone. He was naked.

"You look deep in thought," he said and grinned. "What have you decided to make?"

Not quite recovered from the shock, she said, "I wish you wouldn't creep up on me like that."

He laughed and edged closer, putting his arms around her waist. "Honest, darling, I had nothing to do with that girl's death."

Whatever little doubts she had in her mind about his guilt had just been wiped out with that one word; the only time he called her *darling* was when he was lying. She swung around out of his arms, stared into his blue eyes, and forced a smile.

"What would you like to eat?"

"I'll eat anything you care to make."

"You go finish your drink and watch the telly. I'll soon rustle something up."

CHAPTER 8

This time, Barton parked his car a few streets away and walked to the block of flats. He timed it so as to arrive there at the same time as the previous morning in the hopes that he would see her again. Just one glance would be enough to make his day. He didn't hide behind the wheelie bins this time, instead wandering around the parking area as if searching for something. In case the hoodie appeared first, he had put on another jacket and a baseball cap, tucking his ponytail up inside it. Barton almost missed him. He came out the door behind a group of other people, this time without the hooded jacket. He was wearing a blue suit, shirt, and tie and carried a leather briefcase. The only features Barton remembered about him was his white completion and the freckles, otherwise he would have passed without detection. The man walked with a confident swing and long strides and got into the same car that the woman had driven yesterday. Barton contemplated following him but dismissed the idea and cursed himself for parking his vehicle so far away. He hung about the parking area long after the dapper little man had driven away, hoping she might appear, maybe on her way to work or to do shopping. What Barton was unaware of was that he was being watched from one of the flats above.

Nancy had gone to her kitchen window to watch Eddie drive away in his car. Her heart almost jumped into her mouth when she saw the stranger standing there looking about. Although she didn't want to, she stepped back in case he happened to look up in her direction and see her. She feared for her own safety and that of this man, knowing what Eddie's reaction would be if he detected even the slightest hint of her involvement with another man.

Reluctantly, she went into the living room and sat on the sofa. Her mind was in turmoil. She wanted to get to know the stranger, wanted to know what attracted her to him, but at the same time, she was frightened to get involved. Finally, she jumped up and rushed back to the kitchen window. She couldn't hold back any longer, had to see him again, even though it could be for the last time. She froze, and her heart sank. The stranger was nowhere to be seen. Had he walked away from the car park, or had he entered the building and was already climbing the stairs? She wanted the latter but dreaded the consequences. She creeped down the short hallway and stood behind the door listening for his footsteps. When after five minutes they never came, she didn't know whether she was relieved or disappointed.

Barton made up his mind that she wasn't going to show up, so he walked back to his car, got inside, and studied Billy's list. He decided to go back to some of the addresses where no one had answered the door. At the first one, he stopped at the gate and walked up the gravel path. Something at the window caught his attention. Was that a slight movement of a curtain, or was he imagining it? He gave the door a good thump with his hand. After a minute with no reaction, he was about to turn and walk away when the handle turned, and the door opened a few inches. An attractive blonde woman looked through the gap.

"I'm looking for a Mr Bridge."

"Can I ask why?" she said, smiling.

"I might have something that belongs to him."

"What might that be?" Her smile broadened. She flicked her eyelashes seductively as she opened the door a bit wider, exposing her figure through a skimpy negligee that stopped just short of her crotch.

Not again. He could feel his heart going into overdrive. Barton forced his eyes away from her swollen breasts and the tuft of pubic hair her he could see through her negligee. "I really need to speak Mr Bridge."

"Well, he's not here." Now she opened the door completely. "You can come in and wait for him if you like."

Not having the strength to resist, he stepped inside. "When will he be here?"

She ushered him into the lounge and indicated for him to sit on a huge sofa. "Would you like a drink while you wait? Mr Bridge won't be home for a while."

"Just a tea or a coffee will do fine. I'm driving."

"You can surely have one small drink. Mr Bridge might away for a days. By that time, the drink will have worn off."

The one small drink turned into quite a few large ones. His head was thumping in the morning. He made to get out of bed, but she pulled him back down.

"Don't go yet. We're only just beginning," she said sleepily.

Barton's resistance was at a zero reading, and he obliged without a fight. One strenuous hour later, they both fell into a deep sleep only to be woken by a loud voice shouting at them from the bedroom door. They both sat up to see a tall, thin man standing there glaring at them.

"What the fuck's going on here?" the tall man shouted.

Barton made to jump up out of the bed, remembered he was nude, and wrapped the duvet around himself, leaving the woman lying there naked. She grabbed the corner of the duvet and pulled it back. Barton grabbed his pants and struggled into them.

"Hi, Dad," she said. "You're back early."

"Who the fuck are you?" he shouted at Barton.

Barton now had his jeans secured. "I'm a very close friend of your daughter's."

"Then you'll know she's only fifteen."

"No, I didn't know," Barton replied, shocked, pulling on his T-shirt.

"Then there's two ways we can do this: I can phone the police, and she'll say you forced your way in here and raped her, or to keep me from doing that, you can pay me to keep my mouth shut."

Barton looked at her and got another of her smiles.

"Looks like your dick has gotten you in trouble," she said. She jumped out of bed still wrapped in the duvet, giggled, and ran out the room.

By this time, Barton was fully dressed. He jumped at the tall thi man, grabbed him by the throat, and pushed him against the wall.

"You think I'm stupid enough to fall for that old trick? If you do, then you're the stupid one. You said she was only fifteen? Don't make me laugh. She's well into her twenties. Is this how you pay your gambling debts off?" Barton released his grip on Bridge's throat, caught him by his right arm, and threw him onto the bed.

"What do you know about my gambling debt?" Bridge croaked, rubbing his throat between his fingers and thumb.

Barton ignored him and walked out of the bedroom. He met the girl coming out the toilet. She was wearing only the flimsy negligee.

"Please help me," she pleaded. "Help me get away from him." She grasped the sleeve of his jacket.

"Is this another one of your dirty tricks to extract money?" Barton asked, releasing her hold on his jacket. Her tear-filled eyes looked over his shoulder. Barton followed her gaze. Bridge was standing in the open bedroom doorway pointing a gun at them, a wide grin on his face.

"Let's see how big a man you are now," he said. He aimed the gun at Barton's head and prepared to fire.

The girl stepped between them. "Not here, Stewart. The neighbours will hear the shot."

"You can shut up. I heard you asking him to help you get away from me. You're going down with him."

Barton pushed her to the side. "You going to kill the goose that lays the golden egg? I don't think so. Is this another part of the act?"

"This is no act," the girl assured him. "He's totally mad. He has held me hostage for months, forced me into doing this. He said he would kill me, cut my body up, cook me, and eat me if I didn't do what he said."

Barton decided the only way out of this was to bluff it out. "We have been watching you for a while. Had a tip off at what you were up to." He pointed to the girl. "This is not your first victim, is it? At this very moment, a marksman has a bead on you. You've got five seconds to drop that gun. What's it to be, Stewart?"

Stewart Bridge burst into laughter and waved his gun around. "I don't see any widows in this hallway for a marksman to get a bead on me."

"The weapons we have don't require a window. When I grabbed you in the bedroom, I placed a small device under your skin. The armour-piercing round we use can fire through brick or even stone. The shooter doesn't even need to aim his weapon; the round will seek out that device."

Bridge stopped laughing, an uncertain expression dawning across his face. After a moment's thought, he began to laugh. "There's no such thing as a rifle with device-seeking bullets."

"Are you sure about that?" Barton asked.

"Why hasn't it hit me? You said five seconds; nothing has happened."

"Oh, it will! The moment you fire off a shot, that shooter will hear it."

"You're just inventing all this shit. Anyway, I never felt you inserting a device under my skin."

"You're not meant to in case you try to pull it out."

Bridge started rubbing the back of his neck and the side of his head. Barton took advantage of the few seconds' distraction. He grabbed the girl by her upper arm and pushed her into Bridge. They both fell backwards onto the floor, grappling to get up. Barton ran to the door and was out running to his car when the shot came. He scrambled into the vehicle, fumbling with the keys. When he finally got it started, he rammed it into gear and charged up the street.

Eddie recognised the big stranger but ignored him and walked past, hoping that this big man hadn't detected his act. Why should he, without the hood? Grinning, he got into his car and drove a few streets way and then parked to wait and see if his vehicle passed. He couldn't remember the registration number but was certain he would know the car.

He waited a bit longer than expected. He began to wonder who the stranger was and what interest he had in that block of flats. If he were the law, surely he would know that Raymond Gibb was in the nick, so what could his interest be? The stranger's car went past following a coach. Eddie almost missed it and had to wait for a gap in the traffic to get out onto the main street. He thought he had lost it. He wondered if the big man had turned off somewhere. But then he got a red light just after the coach turned off, and there it was, just a few cars ahead.

He followed the stranger's car into an estate with bungalows of different ages, all with finely cut lawns and trimmed hedges on either side of the road. The vehicle stopped at the gate of one of the houses. The stranger got out and walked up to the door. Eddie continued slowly and stopped where he could see what was happening without making his interest too obvious.

A young woman came to the door wearing a see-through negligee. Soon after, the big stranger entered. Another good day coming up. Eddie laughed. Do the woman, and then go after the big guy. The problem, though, was where to get a gun to kill him. He couldn't see the woman being a problem.

It began to look as though the stranger was living there and had no intention of coming back out the house that day. *Be back tomorrow, big guy,* he thought, grinning to himself, and started up his car.

The big stranger's car was still parked in front of the house. Eddie pulled up at the same spot and saw the door burst open. The big man rushed out as the gunshot sounded shattering the silence he watched him jumped into his car, started it up, and screeched past. Before Eddie could get his own car in motion, the neighbours were at their front doors rubbernecking, eyes all over the place as they yapped excitedly to each other. *Time to get out of here,* he decided, *but don't rush it. Don't want to draw attention.*

His lateness didn't bother any of his work colleagues. They were used to seeing Eddie turn in at any time. He was, after all, one of the senior advisers and may have been working from home or visiting a customer. He got settled at his desk and booted up his desktop. He usually marvelled at his own ability to turn off any personal problems the moment he gazed into than that monitor, but not this time. He couldn't get the stranger out of his mind. That gunshot had come from inside that house; he was certain of it. Must have been that young woman who'd fired the weapon. Or—and he didn't want to believe it—there was someone else in that house. He needed to go back there and watch for evidence of another person living there. He would have to be careful, that gunshot would have been reported, and the police would be all over the place.

He realised he was on his own. All the other staff had left, their desks empty, computers shut down. He checked the time on his monitor—1:05 p.m. Where was everybody? A female voice from behind him soon answered his question.

"Mr Fisher, there is a meeting in the boardroom. Would you please attend."

He shut down his computer and followed her, admiring her shapely hips in her tightly fitted skirt and the swaying of her dark ponytail across her slim shoulders. She opened the door, and he walked in on front of her. He almost jumped out of his skin at the sound of applause and cheers that greeted him. The company director came towards him with his hand outstretched.

"Congratulations, Eddie. You've been elected the most productive and popular employee of the year."

Eddie took his hand and thanked him and all his colleagues. Champagne corks popped, and noisy cheers burst out again. The whole office staff came forward and shook his hand. Some of the females kissed his cheeks and gave him a light hug. This was a good day, although not the kind he had wanted. There would be more good days ahead. One good thing had come out of following that stranger: he now knew where to get his hands on a gun.

Eddie only had one drink. He knew better. He couldn't control his mouth under the influence. He decided to discreetly leave the party, making the excuse to the director that his mother was ill.

Barton was worried. He had been sitting in his car outside his flat for a good half hour trying to work out who had fired that shot. Had one of them been injured or even killed? Bridge had been holding the weapon when he left. Maybe when they'd struggled to get up, the gun had gone off accidently. He hoped nobody had witnessed him running away and gotten the registration of his car.

Billy's man with the green trilby was standing outside his door again, smoking. He pulled out the mobile, and Barton took hold of it and held it to his ear. He had to hold it back away when the shouting started. After things quietened down, Barton brought Billy up to date with the events. Billy came back at him telling him to go back to Bridge and collect £5,000 in unpaid gambling debts.

"He or maybe that woman could be dead," Barton shouted back at him. "The place will be crawling with police. I heard that shot, and so did most of the neighbourhood."

The mobile went dead. He handed it back to Green Trilby, who smiled, tossed his cigarette end away, and sharply departed.

Barton sat at his kitchen table with a microwave meal in front of him that he didn't fancy. His mind was racing. The big question was, why did Billy want him to collect unpaid debts? Surely, he must have a team of heavies to do that. He left the meal sitting untouched and sat down on the sofa in the living room, turning on the television to the news. A woman newscaster was saying that a woman had been injured in a shooting incident and had been taken to hospital. Her injuries were serious but not life threatening. He had missed the part saying where the shooting had taken place, but he was certain it was the same one he'd been involved in. He wondered how he could find out her name and what hospital and ward she could be in. He flicked through other channels in the hope he might find one that had just started broadcasting the news but had no such luck. He would have to try to catch the late-night edition.

He scanned through Billy's list again. There were a few addresses he still hadn't tried; that was what the shouting had been about. Billy had wanted to know what the holdup was. Barton had tried to explain but knew his explanation hadn't been listened to. Most people would be at home at this time, so he decided to try to cross a few other names off the list. He still suspected the little bald Walters, but what could be done if the police had him in custody? He'd try a few other names, and if there was time, he'd pay a visit to the block of flats. He might get lucky, get her outside, maybe on her way to their car, if the red-headed little guy was not around.

He set his satnav to the post code of the next address on the list. It turned out to be a good half hour's drive. Bloody satnav took him a long way round. When he pulled up at the address, it was beginning to get dark. *This'll be the last one tonight,* he decided as he rang the doorbell. A large, barrel- chested bald man opened the door. He glared into Barton's eyes.

"I'm looking for a Mr Barrie Patterson," Barton said hesitantly.

"What do you want with him?" the big man's voice boomed.

"I've found something that belongs to him. I think he might want it back."

"I'm Barrie Paterson. What have you found?"

"For security reasons, could you ID yourself?"

The man opened the door wider and dug his hands into his jeans pocket. Barton wondered how they managed to stay up; the waistline was below his crotch. He drew out an overloaded wallet and produced his driver's license.

"Is that enough?"

Barton studied the license and nodded. "That proves that it is you on the document, but I have to know you were at the place where this item was found. The name is quite common. So, could you tell me where you were last Monday around 2 p.m.?"

The man's eyes began to bulge, and his face became scarlet. "Fuck off, yah wanker," he roared and slammed the door in Barton's face.

Barton stared at the door for a while, grinned, and threw up a mock salute. "I can get proper sex anytime," he shouted through the letter box. "Can you?" He didn't score Barrie Paterson's name off the list. He looked strong enough to overcome that girl and weird and mad enough for anything.

Back at the block of flats, he counted thirteen floors, but very few were lit. *Must be about ten flats to a floor,* he reckoned. *A lot of empty homes in there. This might make it easier to discover which one she lives in.* There were only three streetlights, well separated from each other, creating a lot of dark places where a person could be well concealed in the car park. He had parked beside other cars, so that his wouldn't stand out. Before entering the car park, he had turned off his lights, and he'd let the vehicle crawl in at a tick over pace. He had lost track of time just sitting in his car, gazing up at the flats that had lights on and wondering which one was hers. A flash of light suddenly appeared as a car raced in and stopped at the entrance to the flats. Three men and a woman got out and rushed inside. A moment later, a police car raced in, blue lights flashing. Soon after, two more vehicles came racing in, lights flashing.

CHAPTER 10

Eddie and Nancy were at their kitchen window looking at the action down in the car park. They were in time to see a squad of constables rushing in the main door. Nancy could feel her heart pounding. A chill ran through her body; she was sure they were there for Eddie. She was on the point of passing out when he caught her.

"Relax," he said, pointing down at the police escorting a group of drunks into their vehicles. "They're not here for us." He helped her into the living room and sat her on her seat. "I'll make you a cup of tea."

Eddie put on the kettle and had another glance out the window. He saw the police cars drive away and sighed in relief, but his relief didn't last long. He noticed the big stranger standing beside some parked vehicles and stepped back quickly out of sight.

"What's wrong?" Nancy asked from the kitchen door. "What made you jump back like that?"

His heart skipped a beat at her sudden appearance. "It's nothing. Thought I saw someone sneaking about in the car park."

She stepped around him to the window, and her heart also skipped a few beats. The stranger was looking straight up at her. He caught her eye, and she stepped back. Now her heart started again. She ran into her bedroom, head in her hand, and lay down on the bed, burying her face in the pillow.

Eddie walked in carrying cups of tea and placed them on the bedside cabinet. "What's the matter with you?" He kneeled at the bedside and put a hand on her shoulder. "What's come over you? I've told you there's nothing to worry about."

She quickly turned around and stared into his eyes. "Nothing to worry about?" she shouted, swinging her legs over the other side of the bed. "I know what you've done, and suddenly a squad of police rush into the building. What more do you expect?"

"I've told you they'll never catch me."

"What makes you so sure of that?"

He stood up, lifted one of the cups to his lips, took a sip, and smiled. "I know where a nice bungalow is. I've enough money for the deposit. We can go and have a look tomorrow. If we like it, we could be out this shithole in a month."

"Do you think moving is going to solve the problem?"

"What problem? There's only one problem: the people around here have somehow gotten to thinking we are mother and son. When we get away from here, we can live as husband and wife or partners."

"No! Eddie, you're the problem. When I saw the blood on your coat, I knew you hadn't stopped. That young girl in Bristol? I know it was you. And after you promised."

He threw the cup against the wall. "I told you that wasn't me. Why don't you believe me?"

They watched the remainder of the tea run down the wallpaper, pieces of the shattered cup scattered over the carpet. She darted around the bed, got on her knees, and started lifting the pieces of broken cup. Eddie stomped past her out of the room and slammed the door. When she had collected all the pieces, she sat on the bed and let the memory of that big stranger drifted into her thoughts. Could he be her escape from this relationship? She jumped up, not wanting to dwell too much on something that could never happen. She went into the kitchen and dropped the remains of the cup in the rubbish bin.

Eddie was flicking though the television channels. He stopped at a late-night news flash about the shooting on Greenside Road, where a girl had been taken to hospital with a gunshot wound and a man was in police custody in connection with it. He heard Nancy in the kitchen, and quickly changed programs. He realised he had made a mistake. He should have charged into that house, killed the man and the woman, and grabbed that gun. Now he'd have to begin the search for another one.

Nancy came in and sat heavily on her chair. She watched the program he had selected but found she couldn't concentrate. The shock of seeing the police charging into the building hadn't subsided. Then to add to the problem, the stranger standing next to the cars had looked straight up at her.

Without looking at her, Eddie said, "Did I tell you what happened at work today?"

Nancy ignored him. She guessed that no matter what he told her, she would have doubts whether to believe him.

"They elected me the most productive and popular employee of the year."

He turned around to see her reaction. She had a deadpan expression on her face, as if she hadn't heard. He repeated it, this time much louder. All he got back was a blank stare and a false grin. She never looked in his direction.

"Are you not going to congratulate me and tell me how proud you are?"

"I'm going for a shower and then going to bed. Had enough of this day."

"I think I'll join you," he said and stood up beside her.

"No," she said, pushing him away. "You can sleep in your own bed tonight."

"Why? I've kept my promise. It's not my fault you don't believe me."

"I need some time to sort this all out, need to sleep on my own just for tonight."

Because the light in her house was behind her, Barton couldn't read the expression on the woman's face. Some strange instinct told him she was experiencing the same vibes he was. He hoped she would give him a signal, like a wave or even a nod, but instead she turned away and was gone from view. Could be that freckle face was in there with her. That would explain why she turned away so quickly. That brought back the question of what their relationship was. Was he her son? Her lover? What?

He was hoping that Green Trilby would be standing at his door and felt disappointed when he wasn't, not that he welcomed him. He just wanted to ask Billy why he wasn't sending his team of thugs to collect the debt from Bridge. After the night spent with the honeytrap girl, Barton felt he needed some female company. He phoned a few of his ex-girlfriends, but they were all partnered up. *Time to find another,* he decided. After a quick meal, he showered, got into his best jeans and jacket, and headed out for the nightlife.

The woman next to him sat up so suddenly that Barton almost fell out. He had spent the last few hours in Cloe's single bed trying to get some sleep. Her flat was only a few metres from the motorway, and the double glazing wasn't very good. Plus she'd snored in his ear, and her breath smelled of the pickled onions she had devoured earlier when they'd gotten in. He had sat down close to her in a bar and started talking. He'd bought her a few drinks and later driven her home, and she had invited him in for a drink.

Now she seemed to be wondering who this man was lying beside her in bed.

Barton smiled up at her. "Good morning, Cloe."

She grinned and looked at her watch. "Fuck! I'm late for work."

She rushed out of the room. A few minutes later, he heard the toilet flush, and then she was in the room struggling to get dressed.

"You get up and get to fuck," she shouted and threw his clothes at him.

He dropped her off at her job. "Would you care to share another night sometime?" he asked as she got out the car.

She sighed and shook her head. "My boyfriend's coming home later today." She closed the car door and walked away.

Green Trilby was standing, waiting again at his door.

"You been here all night?" Barton asked.

"You have to call into the boss's office today."

"Any idea what for?" Barton dug his keys out his pocket.

The tall man shook his head and walked away.

"You really are a chatter box," he shouted after him.

Billy jumped out of his seat when Barton entered his office. "That guy Bridge, I see the police have him. Do you think he is our man?"

"He's one of my suspects," Barton replied. "He's capable of it, but for £5,000, would it be worth the risk?"

"That girl, did you get her name?"

"She never gave her name. I don't think they were related. It would be a waste of time going to the hospital when we can't give the name of the person we want to visit."

"It's too risky," Billy agreed. "The police will be hanging around wanting to question her." He settled down on his chair. "They've let Walters go. According to what I've heard, he was nabbed trying to chat up some underage girl. Seems they have been watching him for a while."

"I knew there was something weird about that guy, but I'm not sure he's a murderer."

"He's not paid his gambling debt of two grand, so go back and scare him. Tell him he has two days to come up with the cash or you'll be back."

"I thought you had a team of collectors."

"I'm not asking you to collect, just threaten him."

"Why did you ask me to collect from Bridge?"

"That's a long story."

"Was it because you knew he had a gun?"

Billy ignored the question and grinned. "How far down that list are you?"

"Still got about half a dozen to do."

"They still haven't submitted Amanda's body to us yet. Her mother's distraught over it all. We both are."

Barton thought he noticed a slight quiver in Billy's bottom lip as he dropped his head.

"I'll get the list completed. It's a slow process; nobody's going to admit they were in the park at the same time that your daughter was murdered. I've been trying the old credit card trick or saying I have something valuable with their name on it. So far it hasn't worked."

Billy raised his head. "Keep trying. I know you won't give up. That's why I asked you. I need to get my hands on that bastard before the coppers do."

"I want to as well. I knew Amanda, thought she was a nice person."

Billy leaned over, his eyes blazing. "How well did you know her? I've heard all about you."

Barton held up his hand. "Not *that* well."

Walters opened his door a few inches, and Barton was looking at one eye through a thick lens.

"I want a word with you," he said, and he kicked the door in on the little man's face, knocking his glasses off. He pushed in past Walters while the man was fumbling on the floor, searching for his spectacles. Barton pulled him up by his collar and dragged him into the nearest open door. He found himself in a bedroom where a frail- looking woman with a mop of frizzy white hair was propped up by pillows on a bed.

"What's going on?" she screamed. "Not the bloody police again. Why don't you leaves us alone?"

Walters put his glasses back on. "It's OK, Mum. This man wants a word with me. He's not the police."

"Why has he got you by the scruff of the neck?" she asked, putting her glasses on.

"Don't you worry, Mum. It's just a misunderstanding."

Barton loosened his grip and pushed Walters into a chair by the bedside, glancing at the old woman. "Sorry for this intrusion, but it's important I speak to your son."

"It had better be, or I'll call the police," she croaked.

Remembering the way Walters had been dragged out of the park by the police, Barton almost burst out laughing. "This will only take a minute."

"What's this all about?" Walters asked.

"Billy Benson wants his money." Barton leaned closer to his face. He could smell the pipe tobacco on Walters's breath.

"Who's Billy Benson?"

"He's the head of the bookmaker organisation you gambled with."

"Wasn't me. Somebody's been using my name. I've never been to a bookmaker, and I don't gamble."

"You've got two days to come up with the money, or I'll be back."

Barton turned, nodded to the old woman, and left. Before he closed the outside door, he delayed a moment and could hear the old lady shouting at Walters. Something about him promising to stop gambling. Barton grinned and walked out, slamming the door to let them know he had heard what had just been said.

Before getting into his car, Barton had a good look at the house. It was a solidly built, two-storey, old-style manor house. It did not have as large a garden as would have been the norm for a building its age. It was rather unkempt looking, with ivy almost blocking the windows. The hedges around the perimeter needed cutting back, and the grass had gone to seed. It would still be worth a couple hundred grand, though, so Walters wasn't short of cash, he decided. He got into his car and headed for the block of flats to chance his luck at seeing her.

CHAPTER 11

Eddie had overslept. He was about to jump out of bed when he realised it was Saturday. He didn't work weekends. He turned to caress Nancy, and it dawned on him that he was in his own bed. She was next door. He wondered if she was still asleep. He couldn't hear her in the kitchen or moving about the living room. He got up and opened her room door. He could hear her breathing. So, he crept into bed beside her.

She woke the moment his hands touched her, jumped out of the bed, and scrambled into her housecoat. "I told you I wanted to sleep on my own."

Eddie smiled at her. "Well, you have. It's morning and time to get up."

"I'll get breakfast," she said and shuffled out the room.

"Can I have mine in bed?"

"You can make your own and lie in there all day if you want. I'm off to do some shopping after I have a cup of tea," she called from the kitchen.

"Can I come with you," he shouted back.

"You know I don't like you with me when I shop," she said, entering the room with a cup in her hand and a cigarette in her mouth.

He held out his hand. "Come on in here beside me."

She turned, walked out, and slammed the door behind her.

She walked slowly towards her car. She could feel Eddie's eyes on her. He would be watching from the kitchen window. Without making it obvious, she looked for the stranger. She wanted him to be somewhere close yet dreaded what would happen should he approach her while Eddie was watching. She dared not think of the consequences if that happened. Sitting in her car, she knew Eddie couldn't see her. She took advantage of that and had a good look around. The stranger was nowhere to be seen. Maybe he was in St James's Park. She started up the vehicle and decided that was her first stop.

Wearing his off-work clothes, Eddie pulled the hood up well over his head so that it almost covered his eyes. He could sense something was not right with Nancy. She seemed to have gone into her shell again. He decided it was time follow her, see if there was anything outside their life that was distracting her. He watched her drive out of the car park from the main door of the block of flats and then sprinted over to his own vehicle to chase after her.

He pulled up behind her car on the road that ran past St James's Park. This sent a rush of panic through him. Why was she here? What was she looking for? Was this murder scene the distraction? He got out his vehicle and walked in through the gate, taking to the high track where he had killed that stupid woman with the ugly dog. He approached the seat he had sat on then, stopped, and looked around. There were a lot of dog walkers and joggers going about but no sign of Nancy. At the edge of the path, he surveyed the people walking and talking on the lower footpath. He noticed one girl on her own, a likely target. Lucky for her, this place was too near his last victim. It was a big temptation one he must resist. He didn't want the police to make the connection and start hunting for a serial killer.

So far, he had left no similarities, always mindful of using different methods in different areas, seldom killing two people of the same sex or the same age in a row or using the same weapons. It had been almost ten years since his first victim, and the only person who knew about it was Nancy. Even she knew just a few of them. Lately she had been acting strange, though, and he was getting concerned about her conscience maybe taking control. He knew she couldn't report him without incriminating herself as being his accomplice by not reporting him sooner and covering up for him.

Nancy had decided to have a coffee in the cafe across the street from the park gate. It was by pure chance that she glanced out the window and noticed Eddie parking his car behind hers. She watched him get out and enter the park. *He's followed me*, she thought. She finished her drink, got up, walked to her car, and drove away. Now the fear was escalating inside. *I've never known him to do this before. What's he up to?* Over the past few days, she had noticed that distant look in his eyes. She had seen it before. It would happen soon after a murder had been reported, always in the area where his job had taken him. At first, she'd thought it must be a coincidence, as at that time, only two murders had been committed. When a third one happened, however, she couldn't hold back any longer and confronted him. She remembered him laughing, telling her not to be so paranoid. She had smiled with him and relaxed, and they'd shared a bottle of wine while watching a movie on television.

She pulled into the car park as close to the main door as possible, for easy offloading of her groceries. She dumped the bags on the step and then rushed to park her car. Normally Eddie would be keeping a lookout for her arrival and would come down and carry them up, but he wasn't in. So, she had to get back soon, or the bags would be gone.

"Can I help you?" a man's voice said from behind as she was about to lift the bags.

She jumped at the suddenness of it and jumped even more when she came face to face with the big stranger.

"I'm fine thanks," she stammered.

This was the last thing she needed: to be standing talking to this man when Eddie drove in. Yet she enjoyed his closeness, didn't want him to leave. Still, she knew what the consequences would be for both her and this man.

"Honestly, I'll manage." She picked up the bags and could feel his eyes on her, knowing she was struggling to hold all the bags at once.

"Let me take some of these bags from you. It's no problem."

Nancy nodded. "OK, thanks, but you must leave as soon as we get to my door."

Barton walked up the stairs behind her and could hear her breathing heavily. He wanted to take more of the bags from her but didn't want to push his luck too far, thinking she might tell him to drop the ones that he had right there. When they got to the level where her flat was, he realised this was the same one he had been on before when he was looking for Raymond Gibb. She stopped at the door next to Gibb's and told him to drop the bags. She dropped hers and dug into her pocket for her keys. She unlocked her door and thanked him. He stood there and watched her manage the bags inside.

As she was about to close the door, he said, "Would you like to go out for a drink some time?"

She smiled, showing a perfect set of white teeth, and her blue eyes sparkled as she flicked her long blonde hair away from her face. She shook her head and closed the door.

End of that experience, Barton decided, and he headed back the way they had come. Along the second-to-last flight of stairs, there was a window. He couldn't help but look out of it; the light coming in drew the eye. It looked down onto the car park. The hoodie was walking towards the building, his head bent forward, hands dug deep into his jacket pockets. Barton darted through the door of that level. He didn't want this character to know he was here in case he was her husband or partner. He had enough enemy's without adding another one to the list. The door to this floor had at one time had a glass panel, but now it was boarded up, so he was unable to see the hoodie pass. He would have to depend on hearing his footsteps and hoped he wasn't wearing trainers or soft shoes. Just when Barton decided the hoodie must have passed, the door flew open, hitting him in the shoulder. He jerked back with the impact and caught himself looking straight into the little blue eyes.

"You!" the hoodie cried. "You were here a few days ago. I saw you hanging about. What do you want?"

"This isn't private property, is it?" Barton barked back at him. "I happen to be visiting a friend, if you must know."

"We'll see what the police have to say about that." The hoodie got his mobile out of his pocket and held it to his ear.

Barton caught him by the wrist and pulled the mobile away from his ear. "If you don't put that phone back, I'll ram it up your arse."

His small blue eyes widened, and he dropped his phone back into his pocket, turned around, and ran up the stairs. When he reached his level, he shouted down, "I'll call them when I get inside."

Barton hadn't heard him. He was already well out of the building and heading to where he'd parked his car. He got in behind the wheel and sat there, looking up at her window, willing her to look down at him. She never did. Instead, it was the hoodie who came to the window and began twisting his head in search of him. He resisted starting up the engine, knowing that it would surely draw the man's attention. A few minutes passed before the hoodie turned away and disappeared into the room.

Barton grinned to himself. He could imagine what the conversation would be about in that house. He got his engine started up and slowly drove out of the car park. It was almost dark because of the black clouds that threatened a thunderstorm. He resisted putting on his lights until he was on his way along the main road. Just in case the hoodie had called the police, he kept a regular eye on his interior mirror. He headed back to the Banks' house, thinking that maybe to police had let him go. John would be their prime suspect, with him being Amanda's partner. Only the black Volvo was in the drive, however, and there was no other car parked in front of the house. He'd been hoping with Amanda out of the way that John might have returned to his wife. After some serious thinking, he decided to give Bank's wife a visit and see if she thought he might return.

"He better not," she readily replied to Barton's enquiry. "Anyway, what's it to do with you?"

He shook his head and smiled. "Nothing really. I just thought you might like a night out."

She returned his smile, opened her door wider, and nodded her head for him to come in. "I don't know about that."

Barton squeezed past her into the hallway and stood looking at her. "Have you something better to do?"

It was her turn to shake her head. "I need to get a babysitter."

She ushered him into the lounge and invited him to sit on a huge white leather sofa that occupied the length of one side of the room. He sat facing a television screen that took up half of the opposite wall. She looked down at him, and he watched her eyes taking in every inch of his body. He could almost read her thoughts, knowing the reason she'd so readily accepted his offer was to get her back at her estranged husband. That didn't bother Barton. He wanted her to talk about the man so he could try to discover if he might be capable of murdering the woman he had been living with.

She sat on the sofa three cushions away from him and clasped her hands, resting them on her knee. She gazed into his brown eyes and said, "Do you have a name?"

"Richard."

She reached out her hand. "Hi, Richard! I'm Marlin. Would you like a drink of something?"

Barton took her hand and held it for a while longer than normal. "Do you have a phone number I could call when you think you will be ready?"

"I think it would be best if you gave me your number. I'm not sure when the babysitter will be free to come."

He slowly withdrew his hand and dug into his pocket for his mobile. "I can never remember this number."

She laughed and said, "I'm the same." She moved to the cushion next to him. "What do you do, Richard? Are you some kind a freelance investigator?"

He grinned and shook his head. "No, nothing like that. I told you, I found something that belongs to your husband. I'll be honest with you, the moment our eyes met, I felt an instant fascination I can't explain. It has never happened to me before."

She turned her head away and seemed to be focused on something on the floor in front of her. "If we're going to be honest, I'm sorry I don't feel the same way. You're a good-looking feller. I'm sure there must be hundreds of women out there who would go out with you in a minute."

A long moment of thoughtful silence passed as they both seemed to be focused on the same spot on the sheepskin rug at their feet. Suddenly, the front door burst open, and heavy footsteps came charging up the hallway. A man stood in the doorway, his eyes glaring fire at them.

Marlin jumped to her feet. "What do you want?" she shouted at the intruder and rushed towards him with arms swinging, fists balled, battering at his chest and face.

Barton stepped between them and managed to push the man backwards against the wall. He could feel Marlin still swinging her arms and had to restrain her as well.

"I take it this is your husband," he said.

"Let me get to him," she yelled.

Bank slipped down the wall, landing on his haunches on the floor. "Please help me, Marlin," he sobbed with his hands over his eyes. "I've been in police custody for days. They kept asking me the same questions over and over, kept accusing me of Amanda's murder."

She reached around Barton's body and slapped Bank on the side of his head. "That's better than you deserve, you bastard. They were at me as well, saying I had a motive."

Bank moved his hands away from his eyes and stared up at Barton. "Is this your new boyfriend?"

"That's nothing to do with you," Marlin shouted from behind Barton. "You pissed off with that woman and abandoned me and our child, so now you can fuck off."

Barton grabbed Bank by the arm and pulled him up. "I think it would be a good idea for you to go away and come back when she's calmed down."

Banked jerked his arm away and stepped back. "I don't know who you are, mate. Don't tell me to go away. This is my house." He pointed at Marlin. "That's my wife, and my son is here as well."

"Not anymore," Marlin shouted, hooking her arm around Barton's. "This is my man now."

Bank lowered his head, turned, and walked towards the front door. He slowly opened it, but before he stepped out, he looked back at her. "I've got a right to see my son." With tear-filled eyes he left.

Barton was feeling quite sorry for him, but in truth, Bank had brought it all on himself, judging from what little he knew about this couple. When he turned to Marlin, she had gone. He found her lying on the sofa, crying her eyes out. He went over to her and put his hand on her shoulder.

She swung around and punched his hand away. "You can fuck off as well."

He grabbed both her arms and pulled her up so that she was just a few inches from his face. "Look, Marlin, I can see you still love the man, so why don't you forgive him and get back together for the sake of your son."

She punched him away. "If that woman hadn't been killed, he wouldn't have come near here. He's using our son as an excuse to get back with me."

Barton shrugged his shoulders. "Well, you know him better than I do."

"Oh, I know him well enough. He's an evil, spiteful person, and you better be careful. He'll be plotting something up for you."

"Do you think he's evil and spiteful enough to have murdered that woman?"

CHAPTER 12

Eddie admired Nancy's shapely buttocks as she cleared the dishes from the table. "That meal was delicious," he said when she reached the kitchen and placed the plates and cutlery into the hot water in the sink.

"Glad you enjoyed it," Nancy replied, but she wasn't glad. Far from it, she was scared. She didn't know what was going through Eddie's mind. He had mentioned bumping into the big stranger on the stairs but hadn't commented much on it. He had almost knocked her cooking out of her hand in his rush to the window.

Out of the corner of her eye, she saw him get up from the table with his mug in his hand and go into the living room. She knew exactly where he would sit and start playing with the television remote. She took her time with the dishes, giving herself a moment to maybe work out what was on his mind, but she couldn't shake the thought of that stranger and the effect he had on her.

As she had predicted, Eddie was in his usual seat with the remote in his hand. She laid her cup on the small table at her side and watched the television being flicked from channel to channel. Anything to avoid glancing in his direction.

Eddie wasn't paying much attention to the television either. He had too many questions to ask her but wasn't sure where to begin. That stranger had been hanging around for too long, almost every day now for over a week. What was the attraction? It couldn't be that creep Gibb next door; the stranger must know by now that Gibb was doing time. Then the possibility he didn't want to think about entered his mind: could the attraction be his Nancy? She hadn't been the same since he'd shown up. The more he thought about it, the more sense it began to make. Had they been meeting when he was away at work. Had it been going on since before the stranger had begun to show his face around here? He looked at her out of the corner of his eye. *I can't lose you. I won't lose you. I'll get a gun somewhere and make that stranger my next victim. Getting him away from this neighbourhood will be a problem, and that's if I can obtain a gun. First get the weapon; then start plotting.*

Nancy could sense his eyes on her. She hastily got onto her feet and went back into the kitchen. She went straight to the window, opened it slightly, and lit a cigarette. She jumped when his hands touched her shoulder. When she turned, his face was only an inch from hers. She drew back but found she had no room to move; she was jammed against the window. She felt his hand move to her throat.

"What's wrong with you, my love? You seem a bit on edge," he said, his hot breath mingling with the cigarette smoke. He slowly moved his hand up behind her ear, combing his fingers through her hair.

She looked into his small, blue eyes, faked a smile, and said, "What do you think's wrong with me? First that old couple; that was terrible what you did to them. Then the girl in the park; you can't deny that that was her blood on your duster coat. And the one in Bristol? Strange how you were there at the time."

"I told you I had nothing to do with that murder in Bristol. How can I convince you?"

It was on the tip of her tongue to ask how many more he had murdered, but she knew it was best not to. Doing so could set him off in a temper she knew he had been supressing all these years. Instead, she eased herself around him and headed back into the living room. He was right behind her and slumped back onto his seat on the sofa. He didn't lift the remote and didn't slouch back the way he always did.

"Are you going to tell me what's going on with you? I've never known you to be so preoccupied."

"I've told you what's wrong. Do you not think that's enough to make anybody be preoccupied? I know you're going to get caught. That time when the police charged in after that gang of drunks, I thought they had come for you. I haven't got over that shock yet."

"How many times do I have to tell you? That will never happen."

"I wish I could believe that. Don't you see that the police have all the resources to find criminals? You are on your own. Sooner or later, they'll come for you."

Eddie shook his head vigorously. "Not unless somebody tells them it was me, and you're the only one who knows."

"How are you so sure nobody witnessed you that day in the park?"

"I made sure nobody was near enough to see what was going on."

"It's a bloody public park. The weather's been good. People would have been out in their droves. Somebody must have seen you, even though you didn't see them."

He grinned and sat back. "Relax. Nobody saw me."

He was beginning to relax himself, now he knew that what was upsetting her had nothing to do with the big stranger. But just to be on the safe side, it would be better to get rid of him. That way he would know for certain. Maybe he could use his work computer to explore the Internet for illegal sales of weapons. He had heard of people doing it to get prohibited items

Marlin wiped her eyes and looked up at Barton. "I'm sorry. I shouldn't have taken it out on you. I know John has a vicious temper, but I can't be certain that he would go as far a murder. But to go as far as to say I still love him?" She shook her head. "Not anymore. If he can leave me for another woman, he can't have much love for me or his child."

Barton eased her back onto the sofa and sat beside her. "I agree with you; he can't have much love for you. But are you sure you don't still love him?"

"We've been together for six years, married for four. Throughout that time, I've been finding traces of him being with someone else."

"Why did you stay with him, then?"

She shook her head. "I don't know."

"Did you know he had gambling debts?"

She sat up and pulled back from him. "So that's why you're here? A fuckin' debt collector?"

"No, that's not why I'm here. I told you why I came back, and I'm not a debt collector."

"How did you know he was in debt?"

"A friend of mine goes into the same betting shop as he does. When it hit the news that his girlfriend had been murdered, my friend happened to say that he knew John and that they'd talked about gambling and what they owed the shop."

She studied him with a doubtful look, trying to read his mind, searching for the truth in his eyes. "That's more than he ever a spoke to me about it. I knew he liked to bet on horse racing and what have you, but he never mentioned he was in debt."

She seemed more relaxed from talking about it and settled close to Barton. He gently put his arm around her, and she responded by laying her head on his chest.

"I hope you meant what you said about why you came back." She looked up into his eyes. "I've been hurt enough in the last few months to last a lifetime."

Barton pulled her in closer. "Have no fear about that. I meant what I said. And don't worry about getting hurt."

They had spent the night on her sofa. It was not the easiest place to make love; the leather cushions had kept sticking to their sweat- soaked skin and falling to the floor. This had happened so often that they'd ended up making love on the floor on the sheepskin rug.

She lay on the floor now watching him get dressed and admiring his solid, muscular frame. "You must spend a bit of time in the gym to get your body in that shape."

As he tightened his belt, he smiled down at her. "You look pretty fit yourself."

"Not as fit as I used to be. Haven't got the same time now with the child."

He zipped up his leather jacket. "I've got work to do, but I'll be back as soon as I'm finished. Do you still want to go out, maybe for a meal and a movie?"

"I'll see if I can arrange my babysitter. What time, do you think?"

"Whenever." He grinned and bent over and kissed her. Then he waved as he opened the door and left. His mood soon changed when he discovered his two front tyres were flat. *So is this your childish little game?* he thought. *I'll soon get you sorted out, mate.* He contacted his breakdown service, and they told him it would take half an hour to get to him.

Marlin was at the door with her child in her arms before he had a chance to knock. "I saw you looking at your front tyres and guessed what he had done. He has done that to me as well."

She made breakfast while Barton played with the baby. He surprised himself at the amount of fun he was having with the child. He guessed he must be about nine months old—the age where they smile at you, kick their feet up, and wriggle … and, if they have no nappy on, they pee all over you. Marlin rushed through with a box of paper tissues. She took the baby from him and put him in a baby walker, looking embarrassed while at the same time laughing and apologising.

"Scrambled egg and toast and the necessary pee, my favourite. You really know how to please a man," Barton said, and they both burst out laughing. After he had managed to stop, he reached across the table and took her hand. "It's good to see you laugh."

She smiled. "It's been a long time since I last laughed."

"Well, get used to it, because if you want me, I'll be around for a while."

The moment was disturbed by the sound of the breakdown truck driver blasting his horn. Barton glanced at his watch, got up from the table, and kissed Marlin.

"I need to go. I'll see you as soon as I get this job done."

She walked with him to the door, they kissed again, and then he met the driver.

"I think they're only flat, mate. Just need blowing up, I hope."

"Some idiots let them down on you?" the driver said shaking his head.

Barton nodded. "And I know which idiot did it. You can be sure he'll not do that again for a while."

CHAPTER 13

The man was standing at Barton's door again, this time without the trilby.

"Somebody nicked your hat?" Barton asked.

A smile broke on the man's long hatchet shaped face. "It bloody blew away in the wind yesterday." He handed over the mobile, this time a different one, and had to show Barton how to use it.

Barton informed Billy that he had a strong suspect. "That guy who lived with your daughter," he said. "I think he is still living in her house."

"Not anymore!" Billy shouted. "I bought her that house; I'll have him out of there pronto."

"Give me the address, and I'll pay him a call and bring him to you."

Billy seemed to hesitate and then said, "What makes you think it was him?"

"Just a few things I learned about him. I think he's capable. I know the law had him in, but for some reason they had to let him go."

Billy gave him the address and said, "Bring the bastard here. My boys will get the truth out of him."

After trimming his beard to a designer stubble and showering, Barton was on the move again. He set his satnav to the address Billy had given him. When he arrived, Bank wasn't at home. The house was a two-storey end-of-terrace four-in-a-block. Barton created such a din knocking on the door that the neighbour was out looking over the hedge.

Barton waved and said, "I'm looking for the guy who lives here. Any idea where he might be?"

The neighbour shook his head. "Didn't know him that well. He only moved in with that poor woman a few weeks ago. I've seen him leave in the mornings—for work, I think."

"I don't suppose you know where he works."

A shake of the neighbour's head was all Barton got. He went back to his car and decided to come back later. Just then, however, a red Volvo pulled up behind him. Barton recognised Bank instantly through his rear-view mirror. Bank got out and bounded up the short drive. Barton followed and caught him before he managed to get the door open. Bank had just gotten his key turned when Barton pushed him inside. Bank stumbled and fell on the floor in the passageway.

"What's going on?" he cried, but he shut up quickly when he recognised who his assailant was.

"You like letting people's tyres down, do you?" Barton shouted. He jumped on top of Bank, grabbed him by the throat, and landed a succession of punches to his face.

Bank yelled and tried to fight back but was well pinned down by the heavier man.

"It wasn't me," he cried.

"Don't insult my intelligence," Barton shouted, and he landed a few more punches.

Bank stopped moving. Barton guessed he was unconscious. He lifted him up in a fireman lift and carried him out, dumping him in the boot of his car. When he slammed the boot door, the neighbour was at his gate looking worried.

Barton grinned. "Too much booze."

Billy was on the phone when the receptionist showed Barton into his office. He waved the man into a chair at the front of the desk.

When Billy put the phone down, Barton said, "I've got that package you wanted."

"Where is it?"

"In the boot of my car, but bear in mind that I'm not a hundred per cent sure he's the one who killed Amanda. So far, he's my strongest suspect, though. According to his wife, he's evil and spiteful and has a temper."

"I'll get the truth out of him." Billy picked up the phone, said a few words into it, and replaced the receiver. "I've got a couple of guys to help you. They'll show you where to take him."

The two men were standing at the outside door of one of Billy's gambling establishments. One was a large black man, about Barton's own size and build. The other was much smaller, with thinning blonde hair; he was wearing dark glasses.

Billy stepped out of the door glanced at the men. "You two, go with Barton. I'll meet you there." He jumped off the step and headed over to a silver Mercedes.

The black man got into the front passenger seat of Barton's car, and the other got in the back. A ten-minute drive later, Barton was directed into a narrow lane barely wide enough to accommodate his car. He cringed as he heard the bottom of his car scrape in the deep ruts. They pulled into an opening, and he was ordered to drive around the back of an abandoned warehouse that stood at the far side. Trees and shrubs had long ago taken over, with branches growing out of the bare windows.

"You sit still," the man in the back said.

Bank was conscious when they pulled him out the boot. Billy's men fought him to the ground and secured his wrists. The smaller blonde man told Barton to make himself scarce. At that moment, the silver Mercedes drove in and parked behind him. Barton saw Billy get out and walk towards the two men. Barton put his car in gear and drove off.

He was glad when he got his car back onto the main road, though he wondered if any damage had been done underneath. As he drove back into town, he listened for any sounds that would indicate something had been damage. He stopped at the first cafe and had a mug of tea and a burger. As he was wolfing his food down, his mobile sounded. He hadn't yet entered Marlin's name in his directory, but instinct told him that it was her.

"Hi, Marlin. Something wrong?" he asked before she could speak.

"No," she replied, "just wondering what time you were coming back so I could tell the babysitter."

"Try around six. How are you? Had any more trouble with you- know-who?" Barton knew well that she hadn't but had to cover himself should

Billy's hoods go too far and kill her estranged husband.

"Have you changed your trousers?" She giggled. "The little bugger. I was so embarrassed."

"Yes, I went home and had a shower. Looking forward to spending time with you tonight. Bye."

Barton went back to his car and had just gotten seated behind the wheel when his mobile sounded again. He saw Billy's name on the screen.

"What's wrong?" he asked.

"What's wrong?" Billy roared. "That guy you brought, we got some ID from his pocket, and guess what? He's a fucking copper. A Detective Constable Bank."

Barton almost dropped his phone. "I didn't know that. What have you done with him?"

"He's on his way to the canal wearing a pair of concrete shoes. Couldn't let him go and get us all done."

"When he doesn't turn up for his shift, they're going to start enquiring and call around to his home asking why."

"I think the law will have been round to his wife already, and she would have told them he no longer lived with her. When you called me about him last week, you said she didn't know his address.

He owes me fifteen thousand, his girlfriend has been murdered, his wife doesn't want him, and I told him to get out that house. That would drive a lot of people to commit suicide."

"So, I keep searching?"

"Yeah! But next time, do more checking on your suspects."

CHAPTER 14

Barton drove into the car park next to the rest of the vehicles and manoeuvred his car about so he could see the window of her flat. After half an hour, she hadn't appeared. He was about to drive away when the hoodie pulled the main door open and headed in his direction but jumped into a car at the end of the row. Barton was glad of that, knowing he hadn't been spotted. He ducked down as far as he could and watched hoodie drive away. He hoped she would come to the window to watch him leave, as she had the last time. Barton got what he had hoped for. She stood at the window until the hoodie was gone. He got out his car and glanced up, but she had moved away. He held back, slowly walking about until he could no longer resist the urge. He rushed at the door and bounded up the stairs. He knocked softly on her door, and as if she were expecting him, it opened instantly.

She smiled and stepped back to let him in. "I noticed you walking about the car park. Expected you to knock." She led him into the living room, and they both sat on the sofa. "What's your name?" she asked.

"Richard," he replied, smiling.

He was feeling quite nervous, which was unusual for him with women. He wondered why. What was it about her that was affecting him this way? She was no doubt a beautiful woman and looked as though she had taken care of herself. She had wide-set blue eyes and long blonde hair that hung down the front of her shoulders.

"What's your name?" he asked.

"Nancy." She held out her hand, all the while staring into his brown eyes.

Barton took her small hand and held it. When she didn't pull it away, he moved up closer to her and could hear her sudden intake of breath at his physical closeness. He knew she wanted him as much as he wanted her. But as if an ice-cold shower had rained down on her, she suddenly withdrew her hand and moved along the sofa away from him.

"I'm sorry, Richard. I want what you want but not at this time. Please give me more time to get to know you."

He leaned back on the sofa held out his hands. "That's OK with me. Take all the time you need, but try not make it too long."

She smiled, leaned over, and kissed his cheek. She then slowly got to her feet and looked down at him. "I've got things to sort out first before I can get involved. As soon as I can, I'll let you know. Give me your mobile number."

Barton stood up beside her, towering over her. "What is it, husband problems?"

She shook her head. "Nothing like that, trust me. I'll be in touch. Just don't ask any questions; I'll explain when I've got it all sorted."

They kissed passionately at the door before he opened it.

"I'll wait for your call if it takes a lifetime," he said, and when he left, he noticed her eyes were full of tears.

He walked smartly to his car and looked up at her window before he got in, but she wasn't there. He started his car, glanced at his watch, and discovered he had only ten minutes to get to his date with Marlin. He cursed himself on the way. He'd wanted to get a shower and change first. Hopefully she wouldn't mind coming to his flat to wait for him.

She was dressed and ready to go and opened her door before he had a chance to knock. He was sure his eyes would pop out his head at the sight of her. He felt his heart skip a few beats. She was stunning.

She was wearing a low-cut red dress and must have spent hours on her long hair, which hung down over her shoulders in loose coils. It took all his will power not to push her inside and back onto her sofa.

"Sorry I'm late. I haven't had time to shower and change, so if you don't mind, we'll go to my flat, and I'll get ready. Won't take me long."

She smiled, "You're not all that late." She turned around and lifted a jacket from a peg behind the door, putting it around her shoulders before stepping out beside him. She hooked her arm in his. "Where are we going?" she asked as she began walking with him to his car.

He drove to the city centre. They found a restaurant and then had to rush to the cinema. They watched a film Barton had seen numerous times, but he still enjoyed it. He was sure she was softly crying at the scene where the horse got tangled up in barbed wire covered in mud and the soldiers from both sides came to cut it loose.

When they got back home, they got out the car and walked arm in arm to her front door, where she stopped, looked into his eyes, and shook her head.

"Thanks for the lovely evening, Richard, but last night was a mistake. I'm sorry. I've been thinking over what you said about forgiving John for the sake of our child. I'm going to call him in the morning, and we'll meet somewhere to talk it over."

This sent a chill through Barton, knowing what Billy's thugs had done to her John. And he was guilty of delivering him to them. He stepped back from her. "I understand, but if it doesn't work out, you have my number."

She reached up, put her arms around him, and kissed his cheek. Then she turned without another word, unlocked her door, and stepped inside, closing the door and locking up behind her. In disbelief, Barton stood staring at her door, struck by her sudden change of mind and the problems it was going to cause. The neighbour that had witnessed him dumping John into the boot of his car would now have to be dealt with. As he climbed into his car, he thought about that neighbour, a strange-looking character. He wondered if there was bad blood between him and Amanda that could have escalated when a man moved in with her. Jealousy could make a person do things they normally wouldn't think of doing. Maybe he'd had designs on her, had fantasies involving her. There was one way of finding out, and it'd be the first job he did in the morning, nice and early when the neighbour would still be half asleep.

The tall, hatchet-faced man was standing at his door, smoking his lungs out, as usual.

"People about here are beginning to wonder if we are lovers," Barton said as he approached.

Hatchet Face smiled. "I'm up for it if you are."

"You can fuck off," Barton snapped at him, and he held out his hand for the mobile, putting it to his ear. "What's so urgent that you need me to call at this time of night?"

"I'm glad I finally got you, Barton," Billy came through loud and clear. "A little bird told me that the guy who lives next door to my daughter has reported to the coppers that he saw a body being carried out her house and dumped into the boot of a car.

Billy and his favourite saying. It was his way of not giving away any secret. *A little bird told me* meant his police informant.

"I'll go back and have a word with him. By the way, he is also one of my suspects. I think he may have fantasised about what he would do with her, waiting for the right moment, and when another man moved in with her ..."

"I get the message," Billy shouted. "Bring him to that old building. Let me know when, and we'll be there."

"I can tell you now when that will be: about six in the morning. I'll drag him out of bed and catch him half asleep."

"At that time, I'll be fully asleep. You can take him there and bind him up so he doesn't escape. We'll be along later. As soon as you've done that, you can go."

Eddie got up from the sofa, stepping over Nancy's outstretched legs to carry his empty mug into the kitchen. Outside was cloudy and dull, and the evening was wearing on. He didn't turn the lights on to give him the advantage of observing the car park without being seen. He was lucky he hadn't turned on the light, or else he wouldn't have recognised the big stranger's car pull up and shunt about next to other vehicles parked there. Eddie rushed out the kitchen, saying he had just had a call from his boss and had to go into town to meet him.

"At this time?" Nancy cried after him as he ran to the door, struggling into his jacket. The only response she got was the slamming of the door. She slipped into the kitchen and watched him drive away in his car. Like Eddie, she hadn't turned on the light. She delayed at the window a while longer and noticed the stranger come out from the parked cars, heading for the main door.

Time to find out for sure, Eddie decided as he got out his car. He had parked it in the next street, out of sight from the high flats. He listened to a few songs on the radio, giving the stranger time to get up the stairs and knock on her door if that was what he was hanging about for. The kitchen was in darkness; he couldn't tell if she was there. Normally if the living room door was open, he would be able to see her from the light coming from there. There was no sign of the stranger, so he crept over to the man's car and found it empty. He'd wait a few more minutes, give them time to get settled. He hid behind the cars, keeping an eye on the main door. He didn't have to wait long. The stranger barged out and rushed to his car. Eddie ducked out of sight till he heard the car start up. After all the trouble he'd gone through, Eddie still couldn't draw any conclusions. There was still that element of doubt. He had been hoping to see the stranger at the kitchen window with her. There was only one way of getting peace of mind, and that was to get rid of the stranger.

CHAPTER 15

Barton didn't make it to the neighbour's by six o'clock as intended; he woke up at seven and discovered there had been a power cut during the night. Cursing his own stupidity for not using his mobile as backup, he jumped out of bed and was starting his car fifteen minutes later.

It was no more than a ten-minute drive, and he was soon banging on the man's door. Nothing happened. After several more attempts, there were still no results. When he got back to his car, he heard the man calling from his window.

Barton walked to the gate and shouted up, "Can I have a word with you? I've found something I think you might have lost. It has your address on it but no name."

The man nodded and slammed the window down. Barton was at the door a while before he heard the key getting inserted into the lock. That was the last thing the man did before being knocked back by the impact of the door, sending him back onto his rump. Barton grabbed the back of his neck and bodily lifted him back onto his feet. A few sharp punches to the man's chin and he was out cold. He wasn't a tall guy but was heavily built. It took Barton a great deal of effort to get him jammed into the boot of his car.

Barton was surprised to see Billy standing at the door of the old building. His two goons appeared from the open door, and within a few minutes, they had the man out the boot and onto his feet, dragging him in through the doors. Barton marvelled at the efficient way they handled the dumpy little body.

Billy approached. "Hope this isn't another copper." He jabbed his thumb over his shoulder. "Have you checked him out?"

Barton shrugged his shoulder. "Take my word for it, that creep's not a copper. He's just a dirty, lecherous shit bag."

Billy chortled. "And you say he's not a copper."

Barton watched Billy enter the old building. He was about to start his engine when his mobile sounded. He recognised the number from her previous call.

"Hi, Marlin! Did you contact your husband?"

"I phoned the police station where he works," she replied, "but they told me he called off duty sick yesterday and hasn't reported back."

"Do you have his mobile number?"

"No, he must have changed it when he left me."

"You could call round to the place where he's living," Barton suggested, being extremely careful in his choice of words.

"I don't know where he is staying. The police think he's still living here. Maybe that friend of yours, the one you said knew him from the gambling shop, will know."

It was a last-minute memory jog that saved him from saying *what friend.* "Oh, yes, I'll call him and see if he knows. Maybe your ex has decided to make a quick exit. Think of his situation: First, he's in debt to a gambling and maybe drug cartel. Second, he has lost his family. Third, his girlfriend has been murdered, and he was questioned by his own colleagues, making him a suspect. I think I would want to get myself lost somewhere."

There was a long pause. Finally she said, "Maybe you're right. He always was very unpredictable. I wouldn't put it past him to abscond. Well, if he can bugger off from his family, what more can be expected of him?"

Barton started up his engine and said, "I'll give that friend a call, see if he knows the address. Either way, I'll let you know." He was tempted to suggest coming round to her house to talk about it, but at the last moment, he decided it was too dangerous. One wrong word is all it would take, as he had discovered that she was a rather clever woman, street wise and quick to come to the right conclusions. He said his goodbye, cut the connection, and headed back to his flat for a deserved shower and a good Sunday-morning breakfast.

Early-morning rises were not Barton's forte, and soon after breakfast, he fell asleep on the sofa clad only in a towel wrapped around his waist. His mobile sounded, he jumped up and found himself standing in the nude wondering where he had left the dammed thing. He hoped he hadn't left it in his jacket pocket, which would mean he'd have to pass two windows with only a flimsy towel around him. He followed the sound, and bugger, that's exactly where it must be. He covered himself as best he could and ran to where his jacket lay.

"It takes you some time to answer your phone," Billy snarled. "This guy you dumped on us is gay, and if that's not bad enough, that copper was his lover. He was living with Amanda as a cover for his sexual tendencies. Didn't want his police mates to find out—or his wife."

"That would explain why he was so curious about me lugging Bank into the boot of my car and why he was so quick to call the law."

"Well, he'll not need any more lovers now," Billy sneered. "I'll dump him beside his boyfriend. You're doing well, Barton. We'll get the right guy one of these days.

Eddie was first in the office, an hour early, and he had to rouse the security guard to let him in. His excuse was that he had urgent work to do before traveling. He soon got his computer booted up and searched Google for information on pistols. When it finally came up, there were five pages to pick from. The model he finally decided on, if he could get one, was a SIG Sauer P230 blowback semi-automatic with an eight-round magazine. It was light and small but had power, easy to conceal and get rid of. His vision was to creep up behind the big stranger and empty the magazine into the back of his head. The biggest problem was where to get hold of such a weapon without leaving any trace. He would need to draw a considerable amount of cash from his account, and an unusual withdrawal would leave a paper trail. It was a chance he knew he would have to take. He could draw it out in small amounts until he had enough. That was it finalised. Now he'd get started. He'd pay Raymond Gibb a visit in prison; he may know where to get the gun.

The sound of other members of staff arriving gave him a bit of a start until he glanced at his watch and realised he had been at it for over an hour. He quickly closed his browser and set up his work program. Soon the sound of coffee cups rattling and kettles boiling filled the office. Everyone was greeting each other good morning, cracking a few jokes, and laughing. Nobody spared him a glance as he got up and walked out.

Eddie hadn't anticipated the rigmarole he had to go through to get a prison visit organised, but here he was, and Raymond Gibb was getting seated across the table from him. He gave a slight wave as Gibb got settled, shoulders hunched forward, body shaking. He was obviously suffering from drug or alcohol withdrawal. It took Eddie all his effort to avert his eyes from the scar on Gibb's cheek.

"Who the fuck are you, and what do you want?" Gibb grunted.

Eddie gave him his best smile. "Don't you remember me? I live next door to you."

Gibb nodded. "So what the fuck do you want, man?"

"I just came in to see if there was anything you need."

"Oh! You're one of those fucking do-gooder pests come here to patronize us inmates?"

"Far from it," Eddie said leaning in closer. "I really want your help."

"How am I supposed to do that?"

Eddie had a quick glance around the visiting centre and leaned closer still. "Do you know where I could get a gun?"

Gibb sprung up from his seat. "Come and see me tomorrow." He swung around and headed for the door.

Eddie's gaze followed the round-shouldered man, his frame twisted by drugs and booze, as he staggered towards the guard who let him through the door.

The woman at reception glanced up from her computer, the collar of her prison uniform digging into the flesh of her double chin. "What can I do for you?" she abruptly asked.

"I would like to arrange for a visit tomorrow," Eddie said, finding it difficult to take his eyes off her ample breast.

Following his gaze, she fluffed them up with her hands and then handed him a pen and a form to fill in.

"I want that pen back," she said, holding on to it tightly until he nodded.

He gave her his best smile as he handed her the form and pen. "See you tomorrow, sweetheart."

She grunted and grabbed the form, giving it a quick glance before grimacing back at him. "No, you won't. I'm not working."

CHAPTER 16

Barton wasn't completely satisfied that Marlin would give up trying to contact her estranged husband. Their separation must have left her with a lot of unanswered questions and problems; she would want answers, if his judgement of her was correct. While he still had his mobile in his hand, he gave her a call. The voice that replied was the auto answer saying that the person was unable to take your call. After four more attempts, he decided to take the chance and call round to her house.

He knocked on her door but got no response. He did the same at her front room window—still the same results. Her black Volvo estate was still parked in her driveway, so he reasoned that she couldn't be far away, maybe visiting that friend he'd seen her with that first day. He strolled back to his car and waited for her to return, listening to the radio. He sprang to life at the sound of his mobile and realised he must have dozed off again. Billy's name showed on the screen.

"What's wrong, Billy?"

"Where are you, Barton?" he bellowed.

"I'm trying to contact that copper's wife to make sure she doesn't start enquiring into the whereabouts of her ex."

"How do you hope to do that?"

"I'm thinking that if she learns he was gay, she might not want to have anything to do with him or care where he is."

"After you do that, carry on with that list, and for fuck's sake, make sure you get the right one next time, or I'll be asking for a discount on my money."

Barton could hear laughter in the background and wondered how many of Billy's goons knew what was going on.

Heavy rain started lashing at his windscreen, and Marlin was standing at the passenger's door about to knock before he noticed her. He jumped out. She was soaked; her long hair was stuck to her face and shoulders. The rain was running down her baby buggy's clear plastic covering.

"What are you doing here?" she asked.

Barton rushed around the car and took hold of the buggy. "We need to talk."

He rushed the buggy along the drive and could hear her chasing behind him. She opened the door and held it wide for him to get the child inside. After discarding their wet jackets and lifting the child out from beneath the plastic cover, they went into her living room. He had to grin at the effort it took her to get the baby into its walking pen. The little chap kept kicking and swinging his legs. Barton eased himself down onto the sofa and stretched out.

When Marlin had succeeded getting the baby in the pen, she sat beside him. "What makes you think we need to talk?"

"I contacted that friend," Barton said. He gave a deep sigh, looked into her eyes, and took her hand.

"Well?" she said impatiently and placed her other hand on top of his.

"I'm not sure how you are going to take this …" Another long sigh and a moment's silence. "My friend is gay."

She withdrew her hands. "What's that got to do with it?"

"He told me about the gay man who lived next door to the girl your ex was living with. She wasn't his lover; the neighbour was. Your husband was living with that woman only to disguise his sexuality from his colleagues."

Like a manakin, she sat there with her mouth wide open, eyes staring unblinkingly into his. She made to say something, but the words never came.

"I wish I could have found a better way of putting it." Barton reached out for her hands.

She suddenly jump to her feet and glared down at him. "You fuckin' liar. I would have detected it, would have sensed it."

He got up beside her and put his arms around her. "I'm sorry about all this. I spent all day trying to think of a better way to put it to you."

She stepped away out of his arms. "How long have you known this?"

"Since this morning."

She slumped back down onto the sofa, her head in her hands, and sobbed. "All these years and I never knew. No wonder he was so moody and unpredictable. Why couldn't I have seen it?"

He resisted getting down beside her and stood looking down at her head. "Another reason for him to disappear."

"It was bad enough thinking he'd left me for another woman. How do you think it feels now knowing he left me for a man?"

Barton had picked his words carefully and could feel himself begin to relax, but he knew that was a danger sign. He needed to stay sharp. He didn't want to make the mistake of saying the wrong words at the wrong time. On the other hand, he didn't want to leave her in this state. He put his hand on her shoulder.

"It's not your fault. It would have happened sooner or later. You're better off without him. Had he stayed, your life wouldn't have been worth living."

Carlisle. Eddie looked at the clock on the wall above the filing cabinet. He knew he wouldn't make it there in time for the appointment today. The instruction sheet had been left on his desk. He waved his assistant over.

"When did this arrive on my desk, Debra?" He liked Debra. It made him feel good when he called her by name. She was a feisty-looking girl an inch or so taller than himself with short hair and wide-set brown eyes, but she wore a wedding ring.

She smiled, picked up the sheet of paper, and glanced across it. "I've no idea, Mr Fisher. Must have been put on your desk when I was at lunch."

"Call them and tell them I won't be able to get there in time. Ask if they could postpone the meeting until tomorrow."

She nodded, grinned again, and returned to her desk. Eddie lusted over the sway of her shapely hips inside her tight, short skirt. He wondered what she would look like lying at his feet with blood oozing through that white blouse from her ample breast. He dragged his eyes away from her as she sat down, her skirt riding well up her thighs. *Control. That's what it's down to. Might meet a pretty girl in Carlisle. No, not a girl this time. It will have to be a young boy. Can't let the police make a connection.*

He sat facing his monitor, but his mind wasn't on the job. He'd just discovered he had a problem: the prison visit with Gibb had slipped his mind. This time he went to Debra's desk, and the sweet smell of her perfume accosted him as he approached. This caused a hitch in his breath, and he stuttered the words out. "What time did that company say the appointment was for?"

"They didn't say," she replied and turned to her monitor. "According to this email, it could be next week." She glanced up at him with concern; she knew what the boss's reaction would be.

Eddie cursed to himself. This could mean trouble with his boss; the policy was to always get to a meeting with the customers in plenty of time. He could feel Debra's sympathetic eyes on him as he got settled back behind his desk. To avoid eye contact with her, he stared at the screen with fake concentration.

She cleared her throat and disturbed his thoughts. Once again, she was at his desk looking down at him. He sat back on his seat and grinned at her.

"What is it, Debra?" It came out harsher than he intended.

Her eyes widened, and her head went back. "That memo isn't dated."

Eddie snatched it up and looked at it. "You're right, it isn't. So how was I to know when it arrived on my desk? Thank you for pointing that out." He gave her one of his warmest smiles, but in the depths of his mind, he could see her as a future victim.

Again, his eyes were on her as she returned to her desk. He wondered about her husband, what he was like. Was he a big man? Did he even stay with her? There was one stumbling block to making her a victim: she was too close. With them working together like this, he would be interrogated by the police. It had been hard seeing her every day, thinking the same thoughts. It came back to self-control; this was his secret in getting away with murder.

He knew she would be at the window. Nancy was good at guessing what time he would return from work. Quite often he would get in early to catch her out, but she managed to outwit him every time. Tonight, he was almost an hour late. She never changed, always watching for him. He parked his car in his usual spot and waved up at her as he headed for the door. She didn't return his gesture. She never did, just stepped away out of sight. He found her sitting at the kitchen table.

"Hi, honey. Had a good day?" He kissed her head and sat opposite her. "You're very quiet. Is something wrong?"

She hastily raised her head and gazed at him. "I had that witch from next door asking me why you'd visited that creep she was living with."

Eddie smiled and leaned in closer. "Just being neighbourly." He could feel the smile vanish as he thought of the consequences that that creep's phone call to that woman could have if he had mentioned anything about a gun.

Nancy got up and walked around the table. "What are you up to, Eddie?" she said from behind him.

He turned to face her. "I'm not up to anything." He reached out a hand. "Come and sit down and have a drink. Tell me what that witch said to upset you."

She slumped down onto her seat, leaned her elbows on the table, and put her head in her hands. "It's not so much what she said but what she implied and her attitude."

He placed his hands on her hands and carefully pulled them away from her face. "Tell me what you think she implied."

"It was as if you had no right visiting her man, that you must have had a damned good reason for it."

"I was in the area and had a few hours to spare. I arranged a visit. I was just being neighbourly. No reason involved."

"What did you and that creep have to talk about? Before he got locked up, you avoided contact. You said many times to make sure the doors were locked, that you didn't like the look of him. Said he was a danger to the public, would do anything to get money to buy drugs and booze. What reason did you have to go in and visit him?"

He withdrew his hands and slapped them on the table. "I told you I had no reason. You don't seem to want to believe me these days. Why?"

She sat up in her chair and pulled a cigarette from the packet she had left on the table. "You know damn well why I don't believe you." She sprung up from her seat and fled to the window.

Eddie knew what her next move was going to be; she'd open the kitchen window and light up. Nancy wasn't his main worry. He could see Gibb's scarred face. Whoever had cut him had made a good job of it. It started from his right eye down to the corner of his mouth so that when he grinned, the right side of his face seemed to drop and the eye closed. What had made him phone the witch? Had he asked her to check up on him, make sure he wasn't connected to the police in any way? Eddie knew it would be a waste of time asking Gibb about it. He'd just have to take a chance on him.

After deciding he had nothing more to say to Nancy, he went into the living room, slouched down on sofa, and turned on the television. He was still flicking from channel to channel when she came in and sat on her chair.

"Are you in a better mood now you've had a smoke?" he asked.

All he got in reply was a stern look from her. Eventually, when she got sick of him messing with the television, she shouted, "Will you pack in pissing about with that remote!"

He grinned and said, "Yes, mum," and put the remote down on a cushion.

Nancy got up and snatched the remote, switching the television off. She sat back down and pointed the remote at him.

"Are you going to tell me why you visited that creep?"

"I told you, I wanted to know when he was due out, because you and I discussed moving last week. I want to get out of this dump before he comes back. Now that's the truth. I was frightened to go to work and leave you here on your own."

She had learned a long time ago that he was a very convincing liar and for the moment pretended to swallow his story for the sake of keeping him calm.

Eddie was far from being calm and had a hard time hiding his rage. He dare not look at Nancy head on. He knew she would read his mood. Instead, he stared at his reflection in the blank television screen. He decided he was going to teach that witch a lesson, but not until Gibb could succeed in getting him a weapon. Maybe he'd save a bullet for her and Gibb. But that wouldn't happen until Nancy and he had moved.

CHAPTER 17

The rain had stopped, and it was well into the evening before Barton left Marlin bathing her child. As he closed the door, he could hear the child screaming. Obviously that was one little chap who didn't like the water. They had spent most of the afternoon talking, and like the previous visit, the sofa was put under pressure. He was confident she wasn't going to pursue any enquiries into her ex-husband's whereabouts. He was having trouble battling against his emotions. He was developing strong feelings for her, and the only way he had managed to control feelings like that in the past had been to go and find other women. He instantly thought of Nancy. He tried to compare his feeling for both women and failed to come to any kind of conclusion.

Hatchet Face was blowing smoke rings up in the air.

"Are you having fun?" Barton asked.

The man dropped his dogend on the floor and stepped on it. "Billy wants a progress report." He handed the mobile to Barton.

"Hi, Billy. Is something wrong? I just spoke to you this morning."

"I've had the police on the phone", Billy said, "wanting to know

about that John Bank. They discovered after many hours of interrogation, he was living with Amanda, and with me being suspected of vigilante activity in the past, they want me in for questioning."

"What do you want me to do about it?"

"I need you to go to his wife and persuade her to tell them that her husband was inclined to commit suicide, what with his girlfriend being murdered, losing his family, being in debt, and being gay."

"How the fuck am I supposed to do that? I've only just managed to persuade her not to make enquiries into his disappearance. He was one of them. They're not going to let it go on an ex-wife's word. Can it wait till tomorrow? Give me some time to think of a way."

"OK," Billy replied after a long pause. "Make it as early as possible; that way they might not need me to go in."

"I don't think it'll do any good. I'll do my best, but don't build your hopes up."

The signal got cut, and Barton handed the phone back to Hatchet Face, who was in the process of lighting up another smoke. Hatchet Face grinned, flashing a set of brown, tobacco-stained teeth.

"Trouble?" he asked and blew smoke into Barton's face.

"Not as much as you'll be in if you blow your smoke at me again." Barton slapped the cigarette out of his mouth.

Hatchet Face grinned and put his foot on his discarded smoke.

"Next time don't be smoking at my front door," Barton shouted at the tall bag of bones as he walked away.

He got a two-fingered gesture in response from over the man's shoulder.

"And the same to you," Barton called as he opened his door. But Hatchet Face was right; it was trouble with a capital *T*. He brewed himself a strong coffee to help him stay awake, giving him time to find a solution. He made a big mistake by getting stretched out on the sofa. The next thing he saw was the sun shining through his window onto his face.

After taking a quick shower and drinking the remainder of his strong coffee, warmed up in the microwave, he was on his way. The hoodie's car wasn't in its usual parking spot. Barton drove around the block to see if it had been left somewhere else but couldn't find it. When he got parked and got out his car, he glanced up at Nancy's window and noticed a slight movement. He wasted no time in getting into the building and running up the steps. As had happened the previous time, Nancy opened the door on the first knock. He was surprised when she threw her arms around him the moment she closed the door behind her.

He was guided into her bedroom, where she pushed him onto the bed and got on top of him, stripping her clothes off and kissing him at the same time. Barton eagerly assisted her, as she, in turn, helped him. It was well after noon when he kissed her and left, promising to return soon and saying, "A team of rugby players couldn't hold me back." And he meant it. Those last few hours with her had been paradise. He stopped on his way to Marlin's and phoned Billy to inform him that John Bank's wife hadn't been at home that morning and that he was on his way to try again.

"How early did you knock on her door?" Billy asked.

"It was about eight. Maybe she's staying with friends or something."

"See if you can locate her and get her to that police station before they come for me."

After the call, Barton turned his car around and headed to the outskirts of town, where he pulled into a small cul-de-sac. Barton had visited the house frequently in the past. He knew not to knock on Don Kilby's door, always to phone first. Don opened his door before Barton could approach it, and he got the usual greeting.

"What do you want, you big bastard?" Don grinned and had to make a grab for his false teeth.

Barton returned his grin. "I see you haven't gotten your dentures renewed yet." He pushed Don inside. "I need a cheap mobile, one that can't be traced and can be discarded after use."

Don disappeared into a room at the side of the short hallway, leaving Barton standing scratching his stubble. It reminded him he needed to get it trimmed soon. The room door opened, and the scruffy little leech appeared holding what looked like one of the first models invented.

Kilby grinned and again grabbed his dentures, trapping them with his hand against his chest. He replaced them in his mouth, and said, "Do you know how to operate one of these?"

"I'm not sure," Barton replied laughing. "I only need to send a text."

"Give me the number you want to send it to."

Barton watched his scrawny little fingers punch in the number. Then Kilby handed him the phone.

"Just type in your message and press that button."

Barton made a few mistakes, and Kilby had to correct them. In the end, the text got sent.

"How much do I owe you?" he asked.

"Give me a tenner," Kilby said, holding out his hand. After receiving his money, he snatched the phone out of Barton's hand, dropped it on the floor, and stamped his heel down on it.

"Well," Barton said, "that's the end of that."

"I was about to dump it, so no harm done."

"There could be people out there who collect old mobiles," Barton said as he walked out with Kilby edging him on his way.

"I've got plenty more," Kilby replied before slamming the door.

Barton drove his car out of the cul-de-sac and pulled into a side street, waiting a moment for the text to be delivered. After what he thought would be time enough, he called Marlin. It took her a while to respond, and he discovered she was out shopping.

"What time will you be home?" he asked.

She replied saying she was unsure, that when she finished shopping, she was going to the police station. Barton didn't quiz her any further.

"Give me a call when you get home, and I'll come over, if you want."

"Oh! Please, Richard. I think I need a shoulder to cry on."

"Why? What's wrong?" he could detect she was on the verge of crying.

"I'll tell you later."

Barton's next call was to Billy. He explained that he thought that John Bank's wife was on her way to the police station.

"That's good," Billy replied. "I'm on my way there now."

The call ended the way Billy always ended them: cut short just as Barton was about to add to the conversation.

Eddie sat for quite a while, listening to prisoners moaning to their visitors, before the guard escorted Gibb in. From that distance, Gibb looked different. It was only when he approached and sat down that Eddie could see his puffed-up eyes and the bruising around them.

"What happened to you?" Eddie asked.

"None of your fuckin business."

Eddie held up both his arms. "OK, sorry I asked. Did you manage to get info on that thing I wanted?"

Gibb nodded. "It'll cost you."

"How much?"

"Two big ones."

"How do I pick it up?"

"Knock on my door, and that woman will give you the details." He got up and staggered out.

It all happened so quick Eddie that could hardly believe how simple it was. Mind though, he had still to get the money and didn't want to withdraw it all at once. He knew Nancy had some cash from her husband's insurance. If he could borrow from her, he could pay it back to her over time. To do that, he would need to behave, control his passion. He got up and walked out and was surprised to see the same woman in reception. He couldn't resist asking about it.

"This is a surprise. I thought you wouldn't be here today."

She glared at him. "Somebody phoned in sick." She returned to her computer.

"I'm glad," he said with a smile, stepping over to the desk. "I get a chance to see you again."

She jerked her head back and stared at him. "You trying to get off with me?"

Eddie almost laughed but managed to calm it down to a smile. "Why not? I find you very attractive."

"Fuck off, you little tiddler. I could suck you in and blow you out in bubbles."

"That sounds kinky. When would you like to try?"

"Now!" she said, jumping up. She reached over the desk, grabbed him by the collar, and pulled him over. "That back office is empty."

Eddie hadn't the strength to fight her, and the next thing he knew, he was on the floor with her on top, her knees pinning him down by the biceps. She lifted her skirt, and he could see she had no pants on. He felt her grab his ears and pull his head towards her sexual organ.

"Let's see what you can do, you little tiddler," she cried.

Eddie always prided himself on the way he looked after his teeth, kept them strong and healthy, and he was glad of them now. She let out a deafening scream. He managed to push her off, and she lay there holding her crotch, doubled over on the floor, howling like a wounded animal. He wasted no time in getting out the building and into his car, all the way spitting out her blood and flesh mixed with pubic hairs. He drove out of the car park like a rally driver at the start of a race.

Nancy had a glint in her eyes that Eddie had never noticed before. He wasn't sure if it was of pleasure or anger. As she got off the sofa and went into the kitchen, there was a spring to her step. Eddie was confused. He didn't know how to react. But then it all changed, and she was back to her normal self as she stared at his shirt in awe. He followed her gaze and noticed the blood.

"I had a nosebleed," he cried after her as she ran to her bedroom with her hands on her face and slammed the door.

Eddie chased after her and knocked lightly. "Honestly, honey, it's the truth," he said softly, but he got no reply. He could hear her moving around the room and quickly opened the door to see her packing clothes into a suitcase she had placed open on the bed. "What are you doing?" he yelled, rushing over to grab her clothes out of the case and throw them on the bed.

"I'm getting out of here." She shouted, and she began repacking the clothes he had taken out.

"Why?" he cried. "This is our life. We belong together." He ran out the room and returned a few seconds later with one of the large kitchen knives held to his jugular vein. "If you leave me, I'll kill myself."

She had finished packing the first case and was busy opening the next. She let out a deep sigh and stopped. "I can't stand this life, not knowing what you are up to when you're not here. I can't sleep at night knowing you have killed people, wondering when the police will bang on our door and lift the both of us, you for murder and me as an accessory."

He lowered the knife and stepped closer. "I've told you that will never happen, and I promise never to do it again."

"You said that before, when that old couple was killed. I knew it was you. Then that woman in the park—if I hadn't noticed the blood on your coat, I would never have known. You promised then too. Shortly after, that girl was murdered in Bristol. Strange how you were there at the same time. I'm not stupid, Eddie. Whose blood is that on your shirt?"

He hurtled the knife against the wall and punched the suitcase. She screamed and ran out the room. This time he didn't follow. He ripped the suitcase lid open and tossed her clothes onto the floor. He picked up the knife and cut her clothing into ribbons. *You can't leave with nothing to wear,* he thought.

CHAPTER 18

In response to Marlin's call, Barton headed for her house and found her in a state of near hysteria.

"What's happened?" he asked. He put his arms around her and eased her onto the sofa.

She pulled her mobile from her pocket and held it up. "I got a text from John from a strange number and took it to the police station. It was a suicide note. I had to answer a lot of questions in a stuffy interview room, like I was somehow responsible."

Although he had steeled himself up for this, he could feel his blood run cold. "What did the text say?"

"He admitted he was gay, that he had a lot of debt to a loan shark, and he said that the woman he had living with was blackmailing him, threatening to tell his police colleagues. Both he and his lover decided to commit suicide together."

Barton could remember every single word of that text and knew she was deliberately missing out the part that involved her. He thought it better not to pursue it any further, however, and just let her pour her heart out about it.

He pulled her closer. "I know you're feeling responsible, and I would be wasting time telling you not to."

She raised her head and stared into his brown eyes for a long moment. "I'm glad you're here. I don't know if I could face it on my own." She wiped the tears from her eyes with her fingers and snuggled her head back into his shoulder.

"I'll always be here for you, sweetheart," he assured her.

"This thing between us has happened too quickly. Maybe we should slow down; it's only been a little over a week since we met."

"Whatever you're comfortable with will suit me."

"Can you stay with me tonight?" Again she looked into his eyes.

Considering what she had just said, Barton had just been about to suggest he leave. Now he was puzzled. What could she mean by slow down? He interpreted that to mean that they should not see each other so often.

"Of course. I'll stay with you for as long as you like."

"Just for tonight. Then we can decide what we want to happen."

"I understand you have been through a lot and maybe you're not thinking straight. As I have said, I have strong feelings for you, and I can't explain why it has happened so fast. Maybe after tonight I'll stay away for a few days and let you get your head sorted out. But I'll be phoning you, even if it's just to hear you voice."

She squeezed into him. "I'm frightened. I'm beginning to feel the same way about you. I just don't want to get hurt again."

After a simple meal, they sat on the sofa holding on to each other. Barton could feel the fear inside that he was beginning to believe his own words about how he felt about her, but this was different from how he felt for Nancy. She was an exciting challenge that appealed to his nature. He was drawn to her like a pin to a magnet, like a junkie to drugs. Marlin was a gentle, reliable, loving person he could easily spend the rest of his life with. The question was, could she cope with his ways? He was amused watching her bathe her baby, amused by the way the little chap screamed at first and then, when he got used to it, started kicking and splashing and laughing at his mother trying to dodge the water. It pained him to think that one day soon he would have to end this and not let her get too involved. She didn't need to get hurt again, but how could he live with her knowing that he had been involved in her estranged husband's demise. Eventually the truth would come out. Maybe it would be by a slip of the tongue or maybe by some other way, but one way or another, it would come out.

This time, her sofa got a reprieve, and they went to her bed. Barton lay awake listening to her soft breathing. He gently turned and admired her features as she lay facing him, her hair spread out over the pillow, one hand under her face and the other across his chest. She looked so vulnerable, so innocent. How could anybody hurt her? How could he even think about it? The way he felt at that moment, he just wanted to spend the rest of his life lying there, admiring her beauty. Her eyelids flickered open and she grinned.

"Good morning, angel," he said and kissed her softly on her lips.

Her eyes widened, and she jumped up. "What time is it?"

Barton glanced at his watch. "It's half past six."

She relaxed, smiled at him, and lay back down. "Young Daniel is about to let us know it's time he was fed."

Eddie jumped up and discovered he had slept on the sofa. He listened for Nancy, but the flat remained silent. Not up yet? The clock on the mantle read six thirty, too early for her. He got up and crept to her bedroom door. The room was silent until she shuffled in bed. He knew from experience when she was sound asleep; he had studied her many times as she slept and could tell when she was faking it. Back in the living room, he turned on the television with the volume down and sat on the sofa, wondering if the witch next door was up. It would be a good time to get that info from her while Nancy slept. The problem was that if the witch was still in bed sleeping off booze or drugs, he would wake up the whole building trying to get an answer. A slapping sound came from the passageway. His first thought was that Nancy was getting dressed or was returning from the toilet. He moved himself to the other side of the sofa and looked down the passageway, but he couldn't see or hear any sign of her. It happened again, and still nothing. This time he returned to her door and put his ear to it. It was not coming from there. It must be the witch next door. He decided to investigate and found a piece of folded paper lying behind the front door. When he unfolded it, he found that all that was written on it was a mobile number.

Without saying a word, Nancy had walked into the kitchen and was filling the kettle when Eddie discovered her there.

"Good morning, sweetheart," he said.

She swung round on him. "I'm not your sweetheart." She lifted a mug out of the sink, dried it, and banged it down on the table. "I'm your adoptive mother from now on."

"So, you're still angry with me?"

She prepared her drink, lit a cigarette, and opened the window, "Angry? Is that what you want to call it? I think it's more like terrified of you, of what you're going to do next."

He closed in on her, gripped her arm, and pulled her around to face him. "I told you I am not going to do it again. Why don't you believe me?"

She jerked her arm free. "I can't believe you. I've tried, but after that last girl and the way she was murdered, I found that cord in your pocket. If the police get hold of that, they'll find forensic evidence on it of both you and that poor girl.

"No, they won't. I'll get rid of it."

She froze and stared at him. She could feel her heart begin to race and pushed past him to the other side of the table. "It was you, then?"

He nodded and lowered his head. "I couldn't help it. She came on to me on the train and sat too close to me on the bus, breathing in my ear. When I got up to get off, she followed me."

Nancy knew he was lying. She could always tell when he was. But she knew not to question him further. She could tell when he was getting close to the edge.

The invoices and all the other paperwork were on his desk. He checked the time. It was about a four-hour drive to Carlisle. He collected up all the papers and packed them into his briefcase. Debra smiled and told him to have a safe journey. He returned her smile and gave her a slight wave, thinking, *I wish you were coming with me.* Before he started his car, he pulled the folded piece of paper from his wallet and called the mobile number. He connected the hands-free, got the vehicle in motion, and listened to the phone ring. It sounded a couple of times and then cut off. He made three more attempts on his way up the motorway, but they all failed. A time check informed him that he had made good time; he was almost an hour ahead. He pulled into Southwaite services, set his sat nav, and tried the number again. This time he got a man's voice. He mentioned Raymond Gibb's name, and the man asked if he had the money. Eddie confirmed that he could get it. He was then given another number to call at exactly 2 p.m. That could be a problem if this seminar hadn't finished by then. What excuse could he give to break it off if he happened to be the speaker at that time? What would he say to a room full of top company executives?

The nearest litter bin got his half-drunk plastic cup of coffee, and his chicken salad sandwich landed on top of it. Two girls strolled through the car park ahead of him, laughing and prancing on their way to their vehicle, which Eddie hoped wouldn't be too far from his. The girl on the right had long black hair, and her companion had hers almost cropped into her scalp. They both wore denim shorts and low- cut blouses, exposing tanned shoulders and legs. He felt sick at the way they flaunted themselves at the men who walked past. The sweetness of their perfume lingered in their wake. He couldn't resist tagging close behind them. He quickened his pace to get closer. They carried on past the last of the cars and stopped on the grass verge near the exit. *They don't have a car*, he realised. *They're after a lift.* He turned and rushed back to his vehicle, getting it moving in the hopes of getting to them before any other drivers. His heart skipped a few beats when he saw them, and it skipped a few more when they thumbed him. He stopped a few feet ahead of them.

The girl with the short hair stooped over. "Are you going to Glasgow?"

Eddie nodded and waved them in. They climbed into the back laughing and thanked him.

"Have you come far?" he asked.

The long-haired girl replied, "Just from Manchester."

Eddie caught her brown eyes in his rear-view mirror. They looked professionally made up, with false lashes and red shadow and thick, black eyebrows obviously painted. He caught a glimpse of her friend; she was made up the same. *A right pair of tarts* was his first thought. *Nobody's going to miss them.*

"I've got to call into Carlisle. It will only be a few minutes; hope you don't mind."

"That'll be OK," the short-haired girl replied. "We're not in any hurry." She nudged her friend, and they both burst out giggling.

"Do you both live in Manchester?" he asked as he pulled onto the slipway.

"Yes," the short-haired girl said. "Going to Glasgow for a concert."

"Whereabouts is the concert?"

"A place called Strathclyde Park," the long-haired girl interrupted. "Do you know it?"

"Yes!" Eddie cried. "That's where I'm going! I'm one of the organisers." He made a last-minute turn into an industrial estate. "Sorry about that. Almost missed my turn."

They both giggled again as he stopped at the nearest unit.

"Only be a minute," he said, and he trotted around the back, where he phoned the seminar saying he had broken down on the motorway. Then he called his office with the same excuse. When he got back into the car, he said, "I'm booked into a hotel not far from the concert. Where are you two staying?"

They looked at each other. The long-haired one shook her head, and her companion shrugged her shoulders.

"Don't know yet. Depends on how much it costs," she said.

He started up the car and got it on the move. "Don't take this the wrong way—I'm a happily married man with a lovely family that I adore—but if you're stuck for cash, you can share the room with me and sleep on the floor, if you like." He could sense them mulling his offer over. A secret glance in his mirror showed them staring at each other in doubt. "I had trouble booking a room a week ago. I doubt you'll find anywhere, considering the number of people heading there."

As the miles flew past his windscreen, the muffled debate between them continued. It seemed to him, from his occasional glances in the mirror, that the short-haired girl was all for it. He picked up on her saying, "He's only a little guy. If he tries anything, we should be able to handle him," and this convinced the long-haired girl, according to her nods.

"That will be OK," the short-haired girl said. "What's your name?"

"Just call me Eddie." He grinned through the mirror at them. "What do I call you two?"

"I am Cloe, and this is Dianne," the short-haired girl replied.

He flew past a services sign, glanced at his watch, and discovered that he had only fifteen minutes before he had to make that call.

"Would you both like to stop for a break—the toilet and a cuppa or something?"

"Oh, yes," they both sang out together.

"It's my treat," Dianne added.

Eddie shook his head. "No, I'll get it. It's not every day I get the pleasure of treating two lovely ladies."

He hardly had time to pull up the handbrake before they rushed out the car and headed for the toilets. They must have been bursting. He grinned at the thought of them rushing to the nearest vacant cubical. At two o'clock on the dot, he made the call.

All he got was another number to call when he was ready to pick up the goods.

Three calls later, he found a hotel with rooms available and booked up for one night for three—a family room with a single bed and a double bed. The girls appeared and walked towards him. He got out the car to meet them and waved them to the restaurant. Not only were they desperate for the toilet, but they were starving. Everything was working out well. To be that hungry, they must have left home days before and wouldn't be missed till well after the weekend when the concert wound up.

They ate their fill and downed three coffees each.

"I'm going out for a fag. Are you coming?" Cloe said to Dianne, and they both sprung to their feet.

They were well on their way out before Eddie had a chance to down the last of his drink. He was quick to follow but couldn't see them in the area that had been designated for smokers. *The toilet. Maybe they've gone there first to empty their bladders after all the coffee they had drank.* After pacing back and forth between the smoke area and the ladies' toilets for half an hour, he got the message. The bloody tarts had pissed off. He'd resigned himself to getting off back home when he noticed them climb into a truck. He darted through the vehicles, got into his car, and was on his way back onto the motorway. He soon caught up with the truck and stayed behind it at a safe distance. Ten miles later, the lorry pulled off onto a slip road. He watched it turn off onto a B class road from the roundabout and followed. The HGV driver pulled into a lay-by, and Eddie drove past. He saw the girls get down from the cabin. He turned at a farm road and headed back. They were standing, trying for another lift when he passed them. After a few hundred yards, he pulled onto a slip way and stopped, getting out and opening the boot. He grinned when he saw the crowbar lying in there. He threw it onto the front seat for easy grabbing.

They tried to run when they recognised him approaching. Cloe didn't get far. He drove onto the grass verge and rammed into her. She rolled over the bonnet and fell off to the side. He felt the car buck upwards and knew he had run over her. Dianne was now a hundred yards away, but in a matter of minutes, he had passed her and stopped. He jumped out, armed with the crowbar. She attempted to get over a fence but got her clothing caught on the barbed wire. The first blow landed on her shoulder. She screamed, but the second blow to the head shut her up. He pulled her from the fence, dumped her in the boot, and headed back for Cloe.

CHAPTER 19

The next name on Billy's list was a blind man, Barton discovered when he and his dog answered the door.

"Sorry to bother you," Barton said. "I'm here on behalf of Mr Billy Benson in regard to a gambling debt."

"There must be some mistake," he replied.

"You are Joe Crampton?" Barton asked.

The blind man shook his head. "I don't know anyone by that name."

Barton again apologised and was about to leave when a neighbour called over the fence, "Is everything alright, Mr Crampton?"

"I'm not giving that loan shark another penny," Crampton shouted and slammed the door.

Barton was still grinning when he got into his car. So, Cramton thought Billy was a loan shark. From what he knew about Billy's dealings, that blind guy might not have been far wrong. *Well,* he decided, *that's got nothing to do with me. Just get on with the job at hand.* The next address was at the top of a multistorey block of flats. He had to drive though city centre to get to it. There were three blocks standing side by side, all facing in different directions, which in Barton opinion was bad designing. He had to walk quit a distance from where the residents were supposed to park their cars. At that time of day, there were plenty of vacant spaces. He guessed most people would be at work and hoped that the person he was looking for was at home. He was relieved to discover that the lift worked and was clean. Still, when he selected the floor he wanted, he was hoping that it wouldn't break down. He didn't like lifts and avoided using them when possible. He felt claustrophobic in them.

He rang the bell and noticed that the light shining through the peep hole disappeared for a few seconds, but he got no response. He rang again. Still nothing. He tried the handle and found that the lock was engaged. In American films, the hero would bust the door in with his shoulder; that didn't work in real life unless you wanted to injure yourself. It could dislodge joints. Barton stepped back and attacked it with his foot. At the moment when his foot should have contacted with the door, it flew open. It was too late to stop himself, and he landed on top of an obese woman.

She screamed and punched at his face as he rolled off her and struggled to his feet. She continued to shout abuse at him.

"Who the fuck do you think you are?" she cried and scrambled over onto her front. "Help me up, you bastard, unless you're here to rape me."

She was one helluva heavy woman. He took hold of her arm and tried to lift, but he couldn't budge her. She offered no help, so he let her go.

"I'm looking for Tim Hamilton," he said.

"If you find him, let me know," she cried. "Now get me the fuck up."

"According to my information, he lives here."

"Not anymore," she gasped.

"Do you know where he is now?"

"No, I don't. Now get me up, you bastard. What are you, police or what?"

"Never mind what I am, and you're too heavy. If you don't try to help me, you'll have to lie there."

This time she helped. Not much, but he managed to get her onto her feet. He stepped back, breathing heavily.

"When was the last time you saw him?"

"A long time ago." She shook her head, and the flesh on her neck wobbled like jelly. "Why didn't you rape me when you had the chance?"

Not wanting to insult her, he said, "I just left the girlfriend a few minutes ago, and I've nothing left."

"Well, the next time you knock me down, make sure you've got plenty left, or don't bother coming."

When he eventually got into his car, he decided he'd had enough adventure for the day and decided to give Nancy a call. She was quick to answer.

"If it's OK, I'm on my way over."

She readily agreed and asked, "Where are you? How long will it take you?"

He told her it would be about half an hour, but it was almost an hour before he arrived and knocked on her door.

"Sorry, I got held up."

She lifted his arm and glanced at his watch. "We've not enough time. My son will be in soon."

The white, freckled face of the hoodie shot to mind, and Barton felt a chill through his senses. He reached for her hand.

"You seem frightened of him."

She smiled meekly. "Not frightened. Good heavens, no. Since my husband died, Eddie has become very protective of me." She pulled her hand away gently and walked into her living room. "I admit he is rather too protective at times." She sat on the sofa and invited him to sit beside her.

"It seems to me that it has become an obsession with your son," Barton replied and took her hand again.

She clasped her other hand over his. "I sometimes feel he is smothering me and want to get away from him, but other times he can be so sweet and considerate that it makes me feel guilty for thinking such thoughts. Not only that, but he is the sole bread winner. I don't know where I would go or how I could live."

"How long has it been since your husband passed away?"

"Almost fourteen years now."

"You must have been quite young when you were widowed. Has he been like this all that time?"

She nodded. "But mostly when he became old enough to realise he could dominate me."

"You said he was the sole bread winner. What kind of work does he do?"

"He works for a company of financial advisers, a kind of top sales representative. Not sure exactly."

The memory of the hoodie in dapper attire suddenly struck home, and Barton wondered why the man went about looking like a teenage lout when not at work if he was such a high-ranking member of a firm of financial advisers. Why were they living in a rundown block of flats? Surely his salary would allow them better living conditions. He moved his free hand

and combed his fingers through her long hair. He then pulled her head closer and kissed her softly.

"I wish there was something I could do to help."

"I know," she said and looked at his watch again. "I'm sorry, you have to leave now. He's due in."

The urge was strong for him to hang about the car park to see when her son arrived, but he knew she would be at the kitchen window watching. He got straight into his car and drove off without delay. Nancy's problem played on his mind. She seemed to be in a no-win situation, and he couldn't come up with a way out of it for her except to offer to let her move in with him. The big problem with that idea would be that if her son was as obsessed and dominant as she said, it would only be a matter of time before he discovered where she was living. He pulled up in front of his own flat and called Marlin to take his mind off Nancy for a while. She sounded like a child on Christmas day, wanting to know where he was and if he'd had a good day. He wondered if she had been drinking or something. Surely he didn't have all that effect on her. Still, it made him feel good.

Where is Hatchet Face? he wondered as he opened his door. He'd gotten so used to him standing there. He wondered what could be wrong with Billy. Were the police holding him? He decided the risk of phoning him would be too great, so he decided to go to Billy's office after a shower and a snack.

Billy's office was located on the second floor above his largest casino-cum-betting-shop. Barton had to wade through countless gamblers queuing to get onto slot machines and others putting bets on races at the reinforced-glass counters. Along one wall, men stood on platforms writing on white boards: the results and the odds of horseraces taking place that day.

The tall black man who'd helped Barton with Bank was standing guard at the door at the far side of the shop. He grinned when Barton approached and held out a long arm to stop him from going farther.

"The boss has just arrived. He doesn't look in a good mood; he's been down at the law shop all day," he said. Then he spoke into a speaker located at the side of the door. A loud buzzer sounded, and it slid open.

Barton walked into Billy's office, breathing heavily after bounding up the stairs. He received a nod to get himself seated and got a questioning glance.

"I wanted to know how you got on at the cop shop. Didn't want to call your mobile in case they were still questioning you."

"As it turned out, Bank's wife had been in with a text she had gotten from him saying he and his lover were about to top themselves, et cetera, et cetera." He sighed and leaned back on his seat. "I'm not sure if the coppers are convinced. The message came from him, but there was nothing else they could do for now."

He couldn't help grinning at Billy. "Did your little bird tell you about the text?"

Billy shot him a sharp glance. "Something like that. Now, what else have you learned from that list?"

"I had a word with a blind man called Joe Cramton. Accused you of being a loan shark. Said he's not going to give you another penny. He's definitely not on my list of suspects."

He keyed the name into his computer. "That guy hasn't paid his last bet. Hadn't enough funds in his bank account. He's down for a grand."

"I think Tim Hamilton is lying low. The woman at that address said he pissed off a while back."

He got onto his computer again. "You find him. He's into six big ones. I've had a run-in with that guy before about this. Used to work here. He was caught dipping into the till. Make him your priority. I wouldn't put it past him to take his revenge out on my daughter."

"Why didn't you mention this guy before? I could have gotten straight onto him. Might even have found him."

"I had a team looking for him. They couldn't find him. The last we heard of him, he was in Ireland. I put his name on the list. Didn't have much hope of you finding him, but with your bungling good luck, I thought what the Hell."

"If he's in Ireland, how could he have killed your daughter?"

"How long does it take to travel here, do the dirty work, and get back? It could be done in a day."

"He must be a very spiteful person to go to all that trouble to get back at you. What did you do to him when you had a run-in with him?"

Billy grinned. "Let's say he was in hospital for a while. When he got discharged, he got put into police protection. I think Ireland was where they sent the bastard."

Barton could have come up with a lot more questions, but he could see Billy was getting impatient, so he stood up. "I'll not waste any more of your time. The only thing I can do is go back to that woman and see if she has been in contact with him."

Billy leaned his elbows on his desk and smiled up at Barton. "A man of your reputation should have no problems getting what you want from a lady."

CHAPTER 20

Asking Nancy for a loan, Eddie decided, wasn't a good idea. She would want to know why, and he would need to come up with a good reason. OK, he could come up with one, but she would want to see the evidence. Best just to lift it out of his own account and be careful. That problem would come later. First he had to get rid of the two bodies, one in the boot and the other laid out on the back seat covered with a blanket. His plan was to drop them off miles apart, making the connection difficult to find for the police and for Nancy. He drove gently along the narrow country road, admiring the scenery of steep, sloping hills on both sides and a clear stream running adjacent to it. Few other vehicles drove towards him, and none were behind him. He pulled into a small parking place and sat listening to the radio for a while. When no other cars could be seen or heard, he got out and dragged Cloe's body from the rear seat, pulling her into the long heather still covered in the blanket. Then he drove back the way he had come. Before he booked into the hotel, he called Nancy to say he would have to stay overnight. He didn't get the reaction he was expecting. She fired no questions at him and actually sounded relieved. He had a good mind to drive straight home and catch her at whatever she was up to, but he was tired and hungry, and the place looked tempting and homely. The girl behind the reception desk reminded him of Debra, the girl at work, and he almost called her that. She smiled warmly as he handed her his debit card and asked if he had any luggage.

"No this is a last-minute decision."

She guided him to the restaurant, told him where the bar was, and handed him the key to his room.

"What time do you finish?" he asked. "Would you be so kind as to have a drink with me?"

She flicked her blonde hair back with her fingers. "Another half hour to go yet." She was about half a head taller than him. She nodded and said, "Just one drink. Then I have to go home and let my babysitter go."

"Good," Eddie said with a smile, "see you then." He admired the sway of her hips as she walked back to her desk. When she sat down and gave him a wave, he returned the gesture before heading into the restaurant.

The instant Eddie's call finished, Barton's mobile sounded. He saw Nancy's name on the small screen.

"HI, Nancy, how are you?" He listened to her and smiled. "Yes I can come over," he replied. "Be with you soon."

He had been heading back to that high-rise flat and the obese woman. He wasn't looking forward to another encounter with her, and Nancy's call was the excuse he needed to postpone it. He turned his car around and headed to her. When he arrived, he was about to ask Nancy if her son had arrived but didn't get the chance. The moment he stepped inside the door, she threw her arms around him and, like the last time, steered him into her bedroom. Barton had no resistance from this woman and let himself be seduced.

After an exhausting hour, they got up and went into her living room. He sat on the sofa while she was in the kitchen making drinks. She brought the mugs of tea in and sat beside him.

"We need to talk," she said and shook her blonde hair back.

He put his arms around her shoulder. "What would you like to talk about?"

She placed her mug on the small table at her side of the sofa. "I told you about my son, Eddie, and his overpowering nature."

Barton gazed into her blue eyes and nodded.

"I think he suspects I'm seeing someone. He doesn't know who, and I hope he never will. What I'm trying to say, Richard, is that I'm falling for you, as I hope you are for me. We have to be careful. I've no idea how he will react if he finds out for sure."

The fear Barton felt was for her. He knew that face to face, he could blow the little shit away. "Are you sure you're not scared of him? You don't seem to be too secure living with him."

"He's never threatened me or showed any violence towards me. I just don't know how he would react if he discovered about us."

He knew he may regret it later, but nevertheless, it came out: "I've got a big flat, if you want to move away from him."

"I would love that," she replied, snuggling into him, "but that wouldn't work. He would hunt me down."

"What do you propose we do, then?"

"We have to be careful. We can go on seeing each other till we think of something."

"When do you expect him home?"

"He won't be home tonight. He called to say he was staying over."

"Where is he?"

"Carlisle, as far as I know. The meeting he was at must be carrying on through tomorrow."

"Does that happen often?"

She shook her head, lifted her cup, and drank the last of what was in the mug. "It hasn't happened before."

"Are you sure that is where he is? He may be trying to catch you out."

"I've thought about that. He's more than capable of a trick like that."

"Do you want me to leave? Not that I'm frightened of him. It's your safety I'm concerned about."

She pulled away from him and lifted the empty mugs. "I don't want you to leave"—she stood up and looked down at him—"but we must be careful until we can think of something." She carried the mugs into the kitchen and was there for a few minutes before she returned and stood at the door. "I don't see his car."

Barton got up, and they came together. She pulled his hand towards the bedroom.

"Let's make love again before you leave."

Barton, being the gentleman, obliged readily. The session lasted longer than they both had intended it to. The digital numbers 22.00 glowed on her bedside alarm clock. He felt her jump up and run to the toilet. The silhouette of her nude figure against the background light from the street sparked up his carnal needs again. He rolled out of bed, intending to get hold of her, but was too late. She had managed to get into the toilet and lock the door.

"Calm yourself down," she cried through the door. "You'll need to get moving in case he decides to drive straight home. Judging by the time he called me, he won't be far away by now."

The thought of the squirming little hoodie magot bursting in the door soon dampened his desires. He was dressed when she entered the living room wearing a bathrobe. She walked over to him and put her arms around his neck. He held her by her waist, and after a session of wet kisses, they tore themselves apart. They kissed again at the door, and then he reluctantly left.

He waved at her at the window as he drove out of the car park. His dashboard clock showed 22.30. He wondered if Marlin would still be up. He knew she was an early bedder because of the child but pulled over anyway. Like the last time, she answered instantly.

"I thought I'd call to see how you are and to tell you I'm missing you like hell."

"I'm missing you too," she replied in a sleepy voice," but remember our agreement."

Back-to-back days with no Hatchet Face at the door. May be getting too late for him. He's missing his bedtime story, Barton ruminated as he took a cool shower, grinning to himself. Now that he had Marlin on his mind, Nancy's problem had diminished. Maybe a night in his own bed without a female could clear his mind so he could work out how he was going to contact Tim Hamilton without having to go back to that multistorey block of flats and that obese woman.

The shrill of his mobile roused him from a wonderful dream. With half open eyes and long hair hanging over his face, he fumbled about on his bedside cabinet, found the mobile, dropped it, and had to get out of bed to retrieve it from the floor. By the time he got his finger to the receive button, the caller had rung off. If he'd had an audio recorder and had recorded the language he let rip at that moment and then played it back to himself, he would have denied saying it. Naked, he stepped into the shower. He got out only to discovered he had no dry towels. More disgusting words flew from his mouth. *I need a woman in this place*, he thought. *I'm too busy to remember all this domestic shit.*

After breakfasting on baked beans and a Mars bar washed down with a half glass of stale beer he hadn't finished three days previously, he got up and left with a foul taste in his mouth. He had run out toothpaste. This didn't deter him from going to the high-rise flats, however. The obese woman wouldn't notice. Nevertheless, he stopped at a sweet shop and bought a packet of mints, just in case Marlin called.

He rang the bell and noticed the shadow cross the peep hole, and the door flew open again. The woman grinned and held blubbery, naked arms out, her brown eyes bulging in pleasure.

"Come to mama," she cried. "I knew you would be back. You just can't resist me." She grabbed his arm and pulled him inside. Then she slammed the door shut and charged at him.

Barton managed to hold her back, but he had been forced against the wall. "Before we start," he said, "I want to know what you know about Tim Hamilton."

It seemed she hadn't heard, for she steered him into her bedroom and started to strip her clothes off.

"If you want to know about that good-for-nothing shitbag, you have to work for it."

Now stripped naked, she charged at him again, knocking him onto her unmade bad.

Barton prided himself on his libido, but with this large woman, there was just no pleasing her. When he managed to break away from her, he managed to say between gasps of air, "Now, tell me what you know about Tim Hamilton?"

"One more time," she cried and pulled him back in beside her on the bed.

He managed to force her hand away and rolled off the bed onto his feet. "First tell me what I want to know, and then you can have it as many times as you want."

She giggled. The rolls of fat and flesh of her body wobbled. "One piece of information at a time."

"No way," Barton said. "You tell me all you know, or I'll slit you throat." He bent down, lifted his jacket off the floor, and pulled out a flick knife. He held it close to her face as he operated the blade, which shot out, causing a gash below her eye. In a heartbeat, blood flowed down her ample cheeks.

"You bastard," she cried, wiping the blood with her fingers and gazing at it in horror. "You didn't need to do that." She rolled off the bed, pulling the duvet with her and wrapping it around her massive shoulders.

Barton jumped over the bed and grabbed her by her dyed-blonde hair with one hand while the other held the knife at her throat. "Tell me what I want to know, or I'll leave you here to bleed out with your throat cut."

He forced her head farther back to the point that she almost fell. Her arms were swinging wildly, trying to land a blow, but it was all a waste of energy. Nothing hit the mark. Finally, when she had spent all her energy, she flopped to the floor.

"He phoned me a few days ago."

"Where from?"

"He never said."

Barton jerked her head back, and she fell onto her back. He got down on his knees and held the knife at her neck.

"What did he have to say?"

She tried to wriggle away, but he grabbed her hair again and held her fast.

"He's coming to collect his cocaine."

"Is he a dealer?"

She tried to shake her head, but he held her so tight that she couldn't move it. "He hasn't the brains to be a dealer. It was stuff he managed to steal from a guy he used to work for."

Barton's ears suddenly pricked up. "What guy did he work for?" He pressed the knife in closer.

She felt the blade pierce her skin and guessed it would start to bleed. "I don't know who the guy was. All I managed to learn was that he's the owner of a big gambling syndicate."

CHAPTER 21

After an early breakfast, Eddie got on his way and soon got onto the M74 heading south. He still hadn't decided where to dump Dianne's body. As far away as possible from Cloe, for sure. Maybe down in the West Counties. That would take quite a bit of time and driving but would be worth it. He had enjoyed the company of the young receptionist, but she'd had to rush out. The one drink she'd promised to have with him had turned into three, and he had tried to persuade her to have another, but she'd refused. *You're one lucky girl,* he'd mused as he had watched her rush out the door.

As the M74 became the M6 and the scenery flew past, his mind drifted into tranquillity at the thought of his achievements over the past day. Dianne was his sixteenth with many more to come. It hadn't been his intent to kill another female so quickly after the girl in Bristol, but hell, the opportunity had been there, and she'd been begging for it. The huge blue sign informed him that he had only twenty miles before his turn off. He decided to pull into the next services and call the number he had been given before collecting the gun. Another problem arose: when he made the call, the guy at the other end informed him that the £2,500 must not be drawn from the bank, as they normally paid in new notes with corresponding numbers that could be traced easily.

"What am I supposed to do? I don't have that kind of cash in used notes," he shouted at the caller, but he discovered he was shouting into a dead mike. With reluctance, he made his next call to Nancy. Her phone rang for quite a while before she answered. *Fucking lazy cow still in bed at this time.*

"You just up?" he shouted.

"I've been up for a while," she shouted back at him.

"I need a favour."

"What kind of favour?"

"Do you have any cash in the house?"

"How much cash are you talking about?"

"I need two thousand five hundred. Don't ask what for. I need it. You'll get it back soon."

"Why can't you go to a bank and withdraw it?"

"Do you have it?" he roared, starting to lose his patience.

"No, I don't have it. What would I be doing with all that money in the house in an area like this?"

"OK, this is what we'll have to do. You go and draw money out of your account from an ATM. Draw out your limit and then try another and do the same. Keep doing this if you can. I'll do the same until we get that amount."

He noticed a cash dispenser inside the door of the restaurant on his way to the toilet. The limit was £50. He cursed at it and tried again but drew a blank. *Can't even get control of my own cash*, he thought. He tucked the notes into his wallet and carried on into the gents. Another attempt on his way back out failed. Cursing and swearing to himself sitting in his car, he called his workmate Debra.

"What's been happening?" he asked.

"Where are you, Mr Fisher?" she asked. "The bosses are going mad because you never turned up at that seminar yesterday." Her voice shrilled in his ear.

"I phoned in and reported I had broken down on the motorway. I got towed to a garage and was told that the spares required would take a day to arrive. I had to book into a hotel and stay over."

The voice that replied gave him a start, as he recognised it as the head of his department telling him to get back to Carlisle. Another meeting had been arranged.

"I'm sorry, Mr Chambers. There was nothing I could do, and I did phone them and explain."

Chambers growled, "This is not good enough, Fisher. You could have hired another car. Where are you now?"

"A few miles north of Preston."

"If you get moving now, you should get there. The meeting is at 12.30 p.m."

"Ah! Here he comes now," the tall figure standing behind the podium shouted.

Eddie walked down the aisle between the seats. All heads turned and stared at him. He guessed there must have been about a hundred pairs of eyes on him, following him all the way to the podium. He took his speech from his briefcase and began. He could feel hostility from his audience, and waves of nervousness rushed through him. When he finished, he got bombarded with questions, most of which were, to his mind, stupid and irrelevant. His eyes fell on a lovely blonde girl at the front. She smiled and waved her fingers at him. He was unsure what he read from her demeanour. Was she flirting or maybe just feeling sorry for him? Her eyes followed him as he headed up the aisle towards the door. Time was running short, and he had to make excuses to get off on his way.

"My wife is expecting a baby at any time now," he lied to the tall man who appeared to be the organiser.

"You could stay for a few minutes and have a cup of tea and a bun," said the blonde girl, who appeared from behind the organiser.

The tall man ruined Eddie's chances by informing her that Eddie's wife was expecting her baby any moment. The warmth left her smile, and her shoulders dropped. She excused herself and joined the group mingling nearest them.

She will never know that that tall, skinny piece of shit just saved her life. He grinned as he stepped out the door and got into his car, thinking, *If she only knew about the girl in the boot of my car.* He started up, and his smile developed into laughter as he drove away, wondering if her thoughts were still on him. He took the road leading to the city centre and found another ATM. This time, the limit was £200, still a long way off the target. Nancy wasn't having much success either, he found when he called her.

"Why didn't you go to the bank?"

"I don't have that kind of cash in my account," she snapped back at him.

He cut the connection and drove along the street, soon finding another cash dispenser. He got another £200 and then headed for the motorway. Time was wearing on. He decided to dump the girl's body at the next slip way. He'd make it look as if she'd been hit by a vehicle and left there. To his misfortune, the junction was much too busy, and he had to continue through several villages before finding a deserted lay-by. On the opposite side of the road, he noticed a thick coppice and decided it was ideal. This proved to be a lot more difficult than he had thought, as he found it had been easier to dump her body in the boot than it was to lift it out. At one point, he heard a car coming and had to push the corpse back in and duck behind the car out of sight. He found her too heavy to carry, so he dragged her across the road into long grass. He was walking backwards and didn't see the deep ditch. Before he realised what had happened, he found himself lying in running water with her body on top of him.

Mud and water were clinging to his clothing. He hoped that the car heater turned on full blast would dry them out before he got home. The last thing he needed was Nancy quizzing him about the state of his suit. At least the place where he had left the body should take a while to discover, and the distance from Cloe's body should be enough that the police wouldn't be able to make a connection.

The obese woman was wiping her wounds with tissues and swearing at Barton when he darted out the door. As the lift descended, he gave Billy a call.

"That guy Hamilton," he said before Billy had a chance to speak, "You said he was caught with his hands in the till. Did he also nick cocaine from you?"

"Where did you get that information?" Billy quickly responded.

Barton laughed. "A little bird."

A long silence passed before Billy said, "OK, I do a little trading in dust, but only at the request of a few customers. It's nothing big, just a few grams now and then."

"Well, it seems that Hamilton has got some stashed in his home, and the woman he lives with says he coming to collect it."

"Did she say when?"

"No, she didn't know."

"Where are you now?"

"I'm just leaving his home."

"Get back there and wait for him. I don't care if you have to sleep with that woman. Just be there when he comes. And see if you can do some snooping about the house; you might just find the stuff."

"She's not going to let me in, I threatened to cut her throat and drew blood in the process."

"Well, just get back there and apologise or kick the fucking door in, anything. Just get that bastard and that cocaine."

The lift came to a sudden stop, almost making his knees buckle. The sliding doors opened, making a scraping sound like a tin sheet on gravel. Barton had no idea what Tim Hamilton looked like, but the scruffy figure waiting to get in the lift sent a shiver through him.

"Hi! Tim?" he said, searching the man's small, sunken, dark eyes for a response.

"Who the fuck are you?" the man replied, swiping his long, greasy black hair from his face.

Barton launched himself at him, grabbing his hair and pulling him into the lift. He landed a few sharp punches to Hamilton's jaw. The scruff buckled and slid down the wall of the lift to the floor.

"I'm your biggest nightmare."

"What do you want?" Hamilton howled up at him.

"It's not what I want, it's what Billy Benson wants." Barton landed a kick to his thighs.

Hamilton's eyes widened, and he curled into a ball. "What does Benson want from me this time?" He squirmed.

"He wants you for killing his daughter, wants the money you owe him, and wants the cocaine you nicked." Barton pressed the button on the operating panel, and the doors closed. He felt the lift move. "Now you know what he wants, and I'm here to collect."

He grabbed a handful of greasy hair and pulled Hamilton to his feet. The lift stopped and the door opened. He dragged the scruff out and forced Hamilton's face in front of the peephole, and the door soon opened. Barton pushed him in on top of the obese woman.

"He's here for the cocaine," he shouted before she had a chance to scream. He stood over them as they struggled to their feet, listening to them howling and swearing at each other. He pulled out the knife and stuck it under Hamilton's nose. "Get the fucking cocaine."

"Better do what he says," the woman shouted. "He's a nutter. Threatened to cut my throat and raped me."

"He must be a nutter if he raped you," Hamilton mumbled.

Barton pushed the point of his knife against Hamilton's upper lip. "Get the drugs before I hack your face off."

"I don't have any drugs," he yelled. "I don't have any money. And I didn't even know Benson had a daughter."

"You can tell that to Billy Benson yourself." Barton brought the handle of the knife down on the back of Hamilton's head, and he fell to the floor, out cold.

"You've killed him," the woman screamed. "You've killed my man, you bastard."

Barton punched her, knocking her back against the wall, where she slid down onto her fat buttocks. "I'll be back for you."

He dragged Hamilton out the door and along into the lift. He carried Hamilton like a drunk out of his mind, jammed him into the boot of his car, and phoned Billy. He got the same instructions as before. When he arrived at the old warehouse, Billy and his goons hadn't turned up. He jumped out and dragged Hamilton out, finding he had regained consciousness. "Billy's on his way here with some muscle, so I hope you've got your answers sorted out."

Hamilton gazed around. "I know this place. This is where Benson stashes all his drugs. There's a shooter in there, and he'll have a bead on us."

"You've been here before?" Barton grabbed the collar of Hamilton's jacket and pushed him against the car. "Is this where you nicked the drugs from?"

"I never nicked any drugs from here. It's too risky with that shooter hiding somewhere."

"How about Billy's daughter? He thinks you killed her to get back at him for the last beating you got."

Hamilton shook his head. "I didn't know he had a daughter."

This time Billy was being driven in a four-by-four that crunched its way towards them. Billy was first out, and he rushed towards Hamilton wielding a large chromium spanner, smacking him on the nose with it. The scruff fell to his knees, both hands holding his face and blood oozing between his fingers.

"Get the bastard inside," Billy told the two men that had rushed up behind him. He turned to Barton. "Did he say where the drugs were?"

Barton shook his head. "I think he needs more persuading."

"You get back to that house and search the fucking place. He must have them stashed somewhere."

"How much of the stuff am I looking for?"

Billy walked towards the building. "You'll know when you find it," he said over his shoulder.

"Can I have somebody to help me search that house?" Barton shouted, but he got no reply.

"Hi, Marlin," he said when her name came on the screen of his mobile, "is something wrong?"

"Nothing's wrong," she informed him.

Just the sound of her voice made his heart skip a beat. She was going to visit her parents for a few days in London. Barton couldn't understand why he felt so disappointed.

"When are you leaving? Give me a call to let me know you arrived safely."

She agreed, apologised, and cut the connection. He was worried, though he couldn't understand why. Was this her giving him the brush off? As he headed for the high-rise block of flats again, he couldn't get her out of his mind. She had sounded distant, unlike when she'd responded to his last call. He had the sudden urge to call her back and ask what was troubling her but decided against it. She might be driving.

He found it difficult to get a parking place and realised people would be home from work at this time. He cursed at the thoughtless way the vehicles had been abandoned. There were plenty of spaces, but none of them were wide enough. He abandoned his likewise and hoped nobody would need to get out.

He had every intention of kicking the door in again, but for some reason, he decided first to try the handle. It came as a bit of a shock, but it turned, and the door opened. With a cigarette hanging from her mouth, the woman rushed into the passageway and screamed. Barton lunged at her, gagging her with his hand and tripping her backwards onto the floor.

"I want the cocaine," he shouted into her ear. He loosened his hold on her to let her reply.

She shook her head, the flesh on her neck wobbling against his hand. "I don't know where it is."

"Now's your chance to help me find it. If we don't find it, you know what will happen."

"I'll scream the place down," she threatened.

"Do that, and I'll cut you throat and find it myself."

"Help me up, you bastard. I should have called the police the last time you came here."

"And let them find the drugs? Spend the most of your life in the nick? Best just to let me cut your throat."

With his help, she breathlessly got to her feet, dragged herself from of him, and said, "Of all the bastards I've met in my life, you take the biscuit."

Barton laughed and pushed her through the door into the living room. "Glad to have you as a number one fan."

"Just fuck off, will you," she shouted and almost fell over the back of her sofa.

Barton caught her arm and steadied her. She chanced a swing at him but was too slow. He hefted her over onto the sofa, and she landed on her back, her blubbery legs high and wide, exposing her naked sexual organ. His libido kicked in, and he guessed that maybe a little passion might make her more cooperative. Five seconds later, she stopped struggling and threw her arms around him.

"I knew this was what you wanted," she gasped. "Playing the tough guy always works with me."

Half an hour later, when they had spent their emotions, she willingly took him to where the cocaine was hidden.

"Remember what you promised," she said as she handed him about a kilo in a polythene bag.

"I never break a promise to a lover," he said, looking at the bag. "I'll come back to you as soon as I return this."

"Do that, darling," she said, grinning widely, "and I'll tell you to where another five bags are stashed. Tim told me that his exboss boss has a lot more hidden somewhere."

Barton was stunned at this piece of information. "What boss are you talking about?" he asked, tucking the bag inside his leather jacket and zipping it up.

"The one he nicked that one from," she said, pointing at the bag bulging inside his jacket.

Barton took hold of her hand. "Promise you won't say a word to anyone about this." He followed her to the door, and she kissed him and opened it. He slipped past her.

She puckered her lips and said, "Don't take too long." She put her hand on her crotch. "This is waiting for you."

He waved back at her as he entered the dreaded lift, thankful that he hadn't passed any of the residents, and sighed when the doors shut. That wasn't normal for him; he hated lifts. He'd gotten stuck in one once and was in there for two hours before getting recued. When the lift doors opened, he stepped out and had to smile to himself at the number of times he had had sex with her and never asked her name. Although she was overweight, she had nice features. He estimated her age to be about thirty-five.

He took the bag from his pocket, pushed it under the passenger's seat of his car, and called Billy to tell him about retrieving the cocaine.

"How much of it did you get?" he asked.

"About a kilo."

"That's not even half of what that bastard nicked from me."

"Is he still alive?"

"For now," he said. "I was waiting to see how much cocaine you could get before we got started on him."

"Do you want me to bring this lot to that old building?"

"No, I'll send somebody to pick it up at you house."

CHAPTER 22

The mud was still clinging to Eddie's jacket and trousers, but at least they had dried out. This, however, was the reason he had forgotten about it.

"Hi!" he greeted Nancy when he walked into the living room. "Did you manage to withdraw some cash from your account for me?"

She got up out of her chair and gazed at him in horror. "What have you been doing? Your clothes are thick with mud."

"I got a puncture on my way home and slipped when I was changing the tyre."

Maybe she was being paranoid, but she couldn't bring herself the believe a word he said. Still, what could she do but listen?

"Get those dirty clothes off and take a shower."

"Did you get some cash for me?"

"I could only get a thousand. That's all that's left in my account."

"Did you withdraw it at different times?" he asked, taking his jacket off.

"Why? What's the difference? It's all money."

"Let me see it," he insisted, and he gazed intently as she pulled the notes out of her handbag and handed them to him. He stared at the notes in horror. "Fuck! It's all in new fifty-pound notes."

"So, what's the difference?" she asked. "What were you expecting?"

"I told you to go to different cash machines and withdraw it."

"That was going to take too long. What's this all about it? What do you want it for?"

"Never you mind," he snapped back at her. He threw the cash down on the sofa and stormed out to his room.

"You should think yourself lucky I withdrew the last of my money for you," she shouted after him. All she got in reply was the slamming of his bedroom door.

There was a hell of a lot of mud on his suit, mostly all at the rear. No wonder she'd gotten upset. He was quite shocked by it himself. He hadn't realised it was so bad. The seat in his car must be caked with it. He must get that cleaned before sitting on it again. Another thing he noticed with horror was specks of blood on the cuffs of his shirt. He must have got them when he lifted that girl into the boot. Shit, Nancy was going to see that. After a quick change of clothing, he slipped into the toilet and washed the cuffs with shampoo, scrubbing them with a nail brush. Whilst he was cleaning the sink, the door opened. Nancy was standing there with her hands on her head as if ready to scream.

"Cleaning the mud off my shirt," he explained.

She snatched the shirt out of his hands, examined it, and pointed to the seam. "That doesn't look like mud, more like blood."

"I cut myself shaving this morning." He pushed past her into his room and once again slammed the door.

She sighed, took the shirt into the kitchen, and lobbed it into the washing basket. She stood at the window, hoping Richard would turn up, but she knew that must never happen, not while Eddie was alive. She hated herself for thinking this way, but how else was she going to get free of him. The headlights of a car flashed across the car park. Her heart raced for a moment, and then just as quickly, it calmed down when she noticed the vehicle belonged to a neighbour. She turned, and there Eddie stood, only a few inches from her. The jolt to her nerves made her scream and swipe out at him. She felt her hand impact his face, and he fell backwards, toppling over a chair. She couldn't believe what she had just done. Never in her life had she struck another person. She rushed over to him.

"I'm so sorry! I didn't mean that. You gave me such a fright," she cried trying to help him up.

Eddie jumped to his feet, threw the chair against the wall, and lunged at her in a rage. He grabbed her arm and threw her to the floor, landing hard kicks to her ribs. He leaned over her and jabbed a finger at her.

"Do that again, and I'll fucking kill you."

She heard him storm out and tried to get up, but she felt the first stabbing pain on her side. She slumped back down, trying to find a position that was pain free. The slightest movement of her left arm sent an excruciating stab of pain through her, taking her breath away. He must have broken some ribs and maybe caused some internal damage. An attempt to shout for him to help caused more agony. Panic was rising within her. What could she do? She was at his mercy.

His room door opened, and she heard him stomp his way up the hallway and into the living room. The next thing she heard was the outside door slamming. Her feelings were mixed. She was glad he was away, but on the other hand, she had no one to help her. Her first thought was to phone Richard, but how to get to her mobile. She had left it on the table. She lay curled up on her right side, unable to use her left arm for the pain. Her attempt to roll over onto her front hurt so bad that she could feel herself almost pass out and gave up. That was the last thing she wanted. After waiting a time to get her breath back, she attempted to roll onto her back. This proved to be less painful, and she gradually succeeded in moving by pulling herself along using her legs. She reached the nearest wall, pressed her back against it, and eased herself up it onto her feet. She cringed in pain as she reached for her mobile, but with one hand, she had to make a few attmpts before she managed to get his number. He answered on the third ring.

"Richard, I need your help." She explained what had happened, missing out the part where she'd discovered blood on Eddie's shirt and mud on his suit. She went on to tell him she was frightened to stay there and had to get out. "I think I need to go to hospital."

He assured her he was on his way, and she cut the connection and sat on the nearest chair, fearful of what would happen if Eddie turned up while Richard was still there. The thought of the two of them in the same room under these circumstances was a nightmare. She guessed that Richard was no gentle giant. Eddie, on the other hand, was a cunning psychopath and was very manipulative.

Eddie had scooped up the crisp fifty pond notes from the sofa before he'd charged out the door. He sat in his car, counted out the money, and found he was short. Soon he was driving into town centre. He stopped at the first ATM, withdrew what he was short, and phoned the gun dealer, informing him he was on his way. He recognised the voice on the phone as the same one as before. He was instructed to drive to Sandbach services on the M6. He had to give this man his registration and was told to sit in his car.

Eddie had checked the time of his arrival and saw that he'd been sitting there for over half an hour before his phone sounded. The same voice asked him where he was parked. Eddie gave a brief description of his surroundings, and the phone went dead. After another long wait, he was about to give up, but a knock came to the passenger's window. A black, hooded face glared in. The man opened the door and got in.

"Give me the money," the black man said and held out a huge hand.

Eddie shook his head. "Not before I see the gun and have tested it."

"If you want the fucking weapon, man, give me the money," the black man snarled.

"Let me see it."

The black man dug into his jacket pocket and pulled out the item wrapped in a rag. He unfolded the rag and held it towards Eddie.

"How do I know it's in working order?"

"You'll just have to take my word for it, man. I'm only the delivery driver."

"You're the guy I spoke to on the phone. I recognise you voice."

The black man sighed. "Look, man, do you want the fucking thing? I've not got the time to fuck about here all night."

Eddie grabbed the weapon. "Where's the ammo?"

The black man held out his hand. "Where's the cash?"

They swapped packages and each checked the contents. Then the black man jumped out and was soon lost amongst the crowded parked cars.

Richard was faced with a conundrum. Nancy was in too much pain for him to assist her to his car. That meant he'd have to put his arm around her, causing her to scream in agony. The last thing Barton wanted was to call an ambulance. There would be too many questions that he couldn't answer when they arrived.

"I'm sorry, honey," he said. "We're going to have to find a way to get you to my car without causing you too much pain, and we're going to have to do it before your son comes back."

He could feel her agony as he gently walked her to the stairs. He held her right arm over his shoulder, lowering himself to her level, and they took one painful step at a time. Manoeuvring her into his car proved to be the worst and most painful part for her. She whimpered all the way to the A & E, where he rushed to the reception desk and asked for assistance to get her in.

She was put into a wheelchair, and the warder pushed her along a corridor and into a treatment room. Barton sat by her side until a doctor arrived and advised him to wait at reception. Luckily, she was able to answer all their questions, and all he had to do was wait. He picked up a magazine but failed to concentrate on it, so he got up and sauntered out the building to phone Billy.

"I've not been able to get back to that house," Barton informed him. "A friend has had an accident, and I had to take her to hospital. Your man hadn't turned up for the bag, and I couldn't wait. I'll get back as soon as I can."

"I've had a word with Hamilton," he replied, "and he tells me all the drugs are still in his house. Told me he had a customer and gave me the details. I want you to deliver."

"I'm not too keen on that idea. Far too risky. Where do I have to deliver it to?"

"Just pick up the stuff and give me a call when you have it. I'll give you all the details then."

"What's in it for me?"

"You'll get your share." With that, Billy cut the connection.

Barton walked into the reception area and met Nancy, who was being pushed towards the waiting room in the wheelchair by a nurse.

"How is she?" he asked.

The nurse smiled. "And you are?"

"That's my partner," Nancy interrupted.

"We've X-rayed her. She has no broken bones but does have some badly bruised ribs. No internal injuries that we can see. I'll go and get her prescription."

Barton thanked the nurse and sat next to Nancy. "How are you feeling?"

"Sore," she promptly replied. She smiled weakly. "I think I'll live."

"You can't go back to that flat. You won't be safe. If he can beat his mother up, hell knows what he's capable of."

I know what he's capable of, Nancy thought. "Where else can I go?"

"You can stay at my place. I've been wanting to ask you that for the past few days."

"Are you sure that's what you want? It's a bit sudden. We hardly know each other."

"That first day I saw you in the park, something clicked, and I knew I had to get to know you."

She tried to reach for his hand, but the pain shot thought her side, and she withdrew. "I don't know if I'll be able to get to sleep with this."

"Don't worry. You can have the bed to yourself. I'll use the sofa."

With only enough time to slip three rounds into the magazine and cock the weapon, Eddie got out his car and went searching for the tall black man. It didn't take him long before he saw him standing, talking to a plump woman sitting on a bench a bit too close to a restaurant door with customers entering and leaving. He decided to be patient. The time would come soon enough when the black man would head for his car, hopefully alone. If that woman was with him, that would be her misfortune. He noticed that the corner of the building offered good cover and was in the shadows. It would give him a good vantage point from which to observe the couple. He'd only managed to reach the corner when the woman got to her feet and they both walked away, arm in arm. Eddie knew he would have to be careful. This man was a crook. He might even be wanted, so he'd be looking over his shoulders constantly. Eddie cursed himself for not taking the time to put more rounds into the magazine as he followed them at a distance. They were quite distinctive, difficult to lose in a crowd with him being tall and thin and her, in contrast, short and dumpy. They looked comical as they strode through the parked cars. Finally, they approached their vehicle. He got in the driver's side and she the opposite. Eddie took a quick glance around him, could see no other pedestrians, and rushed over. His first shot went through the driver's side window. He saw the big man's head jerk sideways onto the woman's shoulder. This gave him a clear shot at the woman, and the bullet hit her square in the face. He casually extracted his cash from the big man's jacket pocket, got into his own car, counted his cash, and drove off.

Nancy's clothes were in the wardrobe—the ones he hadn't cut up—and her jewellery was still in the box on her dressing table. Her dirty linen was still in the wash basket. So, where was she? Her mobile was on the kitchen table; he had no way of contacting her. Eddie had been in an elated frame of mind when he'd gotten home, satisfied with the way the deal with the gun had gone. The weapon was in the car and the money in his pocket. Most importantly, he had added two more victims to his collection, making his total eighteen. His exultant mood was gradually diminishing as he realised he may have gone too far with Nancy. He remembered losing his temper with her and rushing out. Surely that was not a reason for her to just disappear like this. She'd never done it before when he had gotten angry with her. Then like a flash, it struck him. How could he have forgotten the kicks to her body? Had he hit her harder than intended? She could be in hospital. He darted to the kitchen window; her car was still in the same spot. Where could she be? He got little information from the hospital receptionist, only that the lady in question had been admitted at 8 p.m. and discharged at 10 p.m. When he asked how she had been brought in, he got no information. He began pacing the living room and thinking, trying to work out how she could have gotten into hospital. It was then that a vision of the big stranger came to the fore. He concluded that his suspicions had been correct all along and that he and Nancy were having an affair. It must have been that gorilla who'd given her a lift to the hospital. He grinned as he thought of the gun and all the ammunition in the glove compartment of his car. He checked the time on the mantle clock. They'd be on their way back now. He dashed out and down to his vehicle, got the weapon and the ammunition, and drove his car to a side street, where he parked it up.

Breathless after his run up the stairs, he planted the now reloaded pistol between the cushions of the sofa, turned on the television, and sat down to wait for their arrival. He was back in his element again, ready for the kill.

He wasn't paying much attention to the television until a news flash came up reporting that gun shots had been reported in Sandbach services and that police had later discovered the bodies of a man and woman, who had been shot in their car. This added to the thrill, and he couldn't wait for Nancy and her lover to arrive.

The three steps to Barton's front door must have felt like the face of mountain for Nancy. He carried her as best he could, but every time he tried to support her, she gasped with the pain. He managed to get her seated on his sofa and could see she was in agony just sitting there.

"I'll get you a drink and get these pills down you."

He opened the bottle and handed her a few. Then he got her a glass of water. She popped them into her mouth one handed, and even this slight movement caused her pain.

"Maybe by the time those pain killers kick in, you'll be able to go to bed and get some rest."

She nodded but didn't look convinced. "I'm sorry for lumbering you with this."

"You don't need to apologise. I'm glad you're here. It's just a pity it wasn't under better conditions."

"As soon as I'm well enough, I'll get out of your hair."

"You can stay here for as long as you like. If it were up to me, you'd stay for good."

She moved uncomfortably and moaned. "I need to get back and collect my things. I'll need a change of clothes soon."

"I'll do that for you. Will you be alright till tomorrow?"

She grinned. "That'll do fine. Eddie should be at work then, but just check his car's not there before you go in.

"After what he has done to you, he better not be there, or it'll be him that's going to hospital next."

Nancy's reaction to that surprised her. Maybe she was still in shock, because it just came out. "What he's done to me is nothing in comparison to what he's done to others."

She wanted to eat her words, but it was out now. She gazed into Barton's brown eyes for a reaction, but his phone sounded. The distraction was a relief, and the tensions drained from her as he turned away to answer it.

Barton soon dismissed what she had said, thinking it couldn't be anything physical for a small guy who spent most of his days sitting in an office. Billy's voice rang in his ear, asking where he was.

"I'm still looking after my injured friend."

"Well get over to that place Hamilton lives in and get that cocaine."

"I'll be on my way soon."

Again the phone went dead on him.

Ignorant bastard, Barton thought, and he turned to Nancy.

"Will you be OK? I've an urgent job to do. I'll get back as soon as I can."

She attempted to get up, screamed, and fell back down. "Just take me home," she moaned. "I'm getting in the way."

Barton kneeled beside her and gently took her hand. "You are not getting in the way, sweetheart, and I'm highly delighted to have you here. This is your home now, if you want."

"You're only being kind to me because of my injury."

"That's not the case. I feel very strongly about you and want you to stay."

She forced a smile through the pain. "Will you help me into bed?"

Slowly and with care, he managed to lay her on his bed and covered her with the duvet.

"I'll be as quick as I can." He kissed her soft lips and left.

The obese woman was in her night attire and looked as though she had just gotten out of bed. Her eyes lit up when she saw him standing there. He pushed his way passed her into her living room.

"I would have phoned you, but I don't have your number. I don't even know your name."

Barton didn't get her name or her number. They were interrupted by a loud thump from her bedroom and the sound of bare feet padding on the laminate flooring in the passageway. A bald- headed man appeared at the door, naked. His physique resembled that of a panda bear, with short bow legs.

"Who's this?" Barton shouted. "Have you been two-timing me?"

"No, no," she cried. "This is just a friend. He stays next door. His water has been cut off, and he asked if he could have a shower."

Despite what he had gone through earlier, Barton couldn't help but burst into a fit of laughter. He almost buckled over. To think that this stupid woman would think for a moment that he would swallow this barefaced, childish lie.

He turned to the man. "Get your clothes on, mate, and get the fuck out of here. If I catch you near my girlfriend again, I'll slit you throat."

The bald fat man turned and ran up the passageway. A few moments later, the door slammed. *He didn't have time to put his clothes on,* Barton mused, *or he didn't bring any in from next door.*

"So, this is how you treat me the minute my back's turned? You fuck another man?"

"I didn't fuck him. He was in the shower," she explained with open arms.

"He didn't look very wet for someone who'd just come out of the shower."

"He must have dried himself before he came in here."

He took hold of her shoulders and pulled her closer. "I come here to make love, and I find you with another man. What am I supposed to think?"

"I'm sorry," she whimpered, her lips quivering and a trace of tears in her blue eyes. "I'll not let him use my shower again."

He steered her over to the sofa and pushed her down onto it. She lifted her nightdress and spread her legs. What more could he do but accommodate her? The sofa was the type that had wheels, and when they had spent their emotions, they found themselves almost in the kitchen. They laughed together as they put it back in its original place. She reached for her cigarettes, lit one, and blew a cloud of smoke up at the ceiling.

"Did you really come here to make love to me?" she asked without looking at him.

"Why else would I have come?" he asked, taking hold of her chin and turning her around to face him.

"I thought maybe you had come for the rest of the cocaine."

He let her chin go, stood up, and stared down at her. "Why? Is there more of that stuff in here?"

She stood up beside him and nodded. "I got the fright of my life earlier today. A police car pulled into the car park, and three constables ran into the building. I thought they had come for those drugs."

Wow! Barton marvelled to himself. *Things are getting easier.* He had steeled himself for a fight with her.

"I think we had better get rid of them," he said. "It's only a matter of time before they get hold of your ex-boyfriend and make him talk."

"Could you take them to that guy you took the last lot to?"

"It's a big risk. If I get stopped by the law with that lot, I'm right in it. But to prove how much I think of you, I'll do it."

They kissed at the door, and he left with the cocaine in two plastic shopping bags. He hid them under the passenger's seat of his car and drove off with a wide grin on his face. There must have been about fifty thousand quid's worth. It'd go a long way in helping him get settled down with … whom? The question now was what kind of story he'd be able to come up with to convince Billy that the drugs hadn't been there. He turned into a side street, stopped, and phoned Billy. The sooner he knew that Hamilton had been lying to him and had sold the cocaine, the sooner the scruff would be dealt with, and the easier it would be for Barton to deny finding them.

"What's wrong now, Barton?" Billy bellowed at him.

"Have you still got Hamilton in that warehouse?" Barton asked, nervously drumming his fingers on the steering wheel.

"Why do you ask?"

"I think he's been lying to you about those drugs."

"What about the drugs?"

"They're not in that house. I went through it from top to bottom. The woman helped me. We couldn't find them. She said he was spending money rapidly before he left her. She thinks he went abroad somewhere."

"He doesn't look like somebody who's been spending money."

"Maybe she's been dipping into the cocaine and has it hidden somewhere else," Barton replied, trying to sound convincing. He was glad this conversation wasn't face to face.

"One of my boys hit him a bit too hard. He's been out cold for the past ten hours. I haven't been able to talk to him since. He swore he had left them in that house with his girlfriend before he got hit."

"Do you want me to go back and get her and bring her to you?"

"No, you continue hunting for the guy who killed my daughter. We finally got to bury her today."

"I'm sorry. Had I known, I would have attended."

"By the way," Billy started, delaying a moment before continuing, "one of the names on that list you can forget about. Hemmings. He and his partner were shot in Sandbach services tonight. Police said it could have been gang related."

Barton pulled the list from his glove compartment and saw Hemmings was last. "That's fine. I see it, and I'll scrub it out."

"Make sure that list is well hidden in case the police stop you and find it."

"How are you?" Barton asked. Nancy was lying in the same position he had left her in. He could see she was in pain and felt so helpless. "Did those pills help in any way?"

She cautiously turned her head to face him and smiled weakly. "A little bit."

"I'll get you another couple," he said. He left and returned with the bottle and some water. He held her head up, put two pills in her mouth, and held the glass for her to drink from.

Nancy lay back on the pillow and cringed at the movement. "Why are you being so kind to me? You hardly know me."

"I've explained that to you. The moment I first saw you, something inside me clicked. I had to investigate what it was all about."

She smiled, and it ignited hidden emotions he had long ago forgotten existed. He kissed her forehead and watched her eyes close before softly retreating from room.

Stretched out on the sofa with the television on and the volume low, he flicked through the channels until he found the news. He caught the tail end of a story about the murder in the services that Billy mentioned. The wording about it being gang related puzzled him, and he wondered how deep Billy was involved. It must have been drug related, if Hamilton's woman was telling the truth about knowing that another five bags of cocaine were hidden somewhere. If Hamilton had told her about it, who else could he have told? One thing Barton was certain of was that the somewhere she talked about must be that old building he'd taken those men to. He remembered Hamilton talking about a shooter being there. Why have a shooter to protect an old building?

CHAPTER 24

Eddie woke abruptly and found himself lying on the floor with the sofa cushions on top of him. He realised he must have dozed off and rolled onto the floor. He jumped up, gazed at the mantlepiece clock, and panicked when he discovered he had overslept for work. Within ten minutes, Eddie was in his car and driving like a boy racer. He was neither washed nor shaved. He had merely jumped into his one remaining suit and wore yellow and blue trainers on his feet. His leather shoes were caked in mud, and he hadn't the time to clean them. When he got out his car at work, he was struck by the memory of the gun. It must still have been lying on the sofa. Panic again stampeded through his mind. He feared that Nancy would return and find it. That brought on another concern: Where was she? Why hadn't she come home from hospital? Was she with that big stranger, and had she spent the night at his place?

Debra looked at him in a manner he had become accustomed to when there was trouble. She was on her feet the moment he sat behind his desk.

"The boss want's a word. Said to tell you the moment you came in." She slapped some papers on his desk and strutted back to her own.

"Any idea what it's about?" he asked as he passed on his way to the boss's office.

"I'll give you two guesses," she said, glaring up at him.

"That bad?" He walked on, shaking his head. When he got to his boss's office, he knocked on the door and stuck his head in. "You wanted a word?" he asked the white-haired, ashen-faced man sitting behind a desk so big it could have been converted into a snooker table.

Chambers stood up. "Have a seat, Eddie." He reseated himself, pulled a tissue out of a box on his desk, and wiped the remains of a snack he had been eating from his mouth. "I've had some troubling reports from Carlisle about the way you handled things up there."

"I don't see why. I apologised for braking down on the motorway. These things happen, Mr Chambers."

"Yes, I understand, Eddie, but head office won't accept that as an excuse. They say you should have travelled up there by train and, if necessary, stayed over."

"But it's only a four-hour drive."

"Yes, yes, I know that, but with such an important seminar, you must be a hundred per cent sure of getting there on time." He sat in silence, staring into Eddie's eyes for a long period, as if deciding what to say next. Finally, he cleared his throat and said, "You've left us with no other choice than to sack you instantly."

Eddie stormed out, slamming Chambers's door. *You'll be my next victim before too long*, he thought. He then glared at Debra as he rushed past her desk. *And you soon after.*

He raced home once again and once again breathed a sigh of relief when he found that everything in the house was as he'd left it. The gun was lying exposed on the sofa cushions where he had placed it. The relief was short lived, however, and he soon felt the loneliness of the empty flat. Everything he looked at and the lingering odour of her perfume brought it all crashing down on him. Where could she be? Was she with that big stranger, living in his house? A part of him was saying, *Yes, she's pissed off.* The other part was telling him, *Not my Nancy. She would never leave.* After rummaging through all her clothes and personal things, he decided he had two options: hunt her down or wait for her to come and collect her belongings. The latter seemed the best and the quickest. She didn't know he was not working, and that would be the likely time when she would come—during the day.

How stupid could he have been? How could he have missed it? Lying on the kitchen table was her mobile. Why hadn't he thought about this sooner? He scrolled through her contacts. Most of the numbers in her call log were his except for two made to a strange number. She had been clever not to enter a name with it, but the number was all he needed. He calculated that it would be unwise to call it too soon; they'd be expecting it. He needed a distraction and instantly thought of Chambers. It would be worth the effort to see him squirm. The problem there was that the police would start searching for someone with a grudge against him. No, he thought, Debra would suffice. He'd always had that feeling she was after his job. Now that he'd been sacked, she'd be grovelling before the bosses. *Don't rush*, he told himself. *It's too soon after the Sandbach murders. Relish stalking her first.*

He knew she was a creature of habit, always lunched at the same cafe, walked there at the same time. He could almost bet she ate the same meal, after which she always had her cigarette on the walk back. He didn't want to shoot her—too quick. He wanted to see her bleed and wondered what her blood would taste like.

True to form, she entered the cafe—he glanced at the time— exactly when he'd expected. He got out his car and followed her in, almost colliding with her as she carried her food.

"Hi!" she said. "Never seen you in here before." She smiled and steered past him.

He ordered a tea and sat across from her at the same table. "I was passing and noticed you come in here. I thought I'd say hi."

"I was sorry to hear you got sacked," she said before taking a bite from her burger.

"No need to be sorry; it was my own fault."

"It wasn't your fault you broke down on the way up, and you did phone in to report it."

"They said I should have gone up by train and stayed in a hotel."

She swallowed her bite and took a drink from her juice. "And have them complain about the expenses."

The place was beginning to fill up with patrons. Eddie was beginning to feel crowded with people crushing him with trays of food in their hands to get seated behind him. He drank the last of his tea and stood up.

"I'll leave you to it," he said. "Have a nice day." And without a backward glance, he walked out.

A minute late, she came scrambling out, edging herself past the customers queuing to get in. He grinned when the cigarette packet came out and she lit up. How predictable some people were. He drove slowly, following her. She turned the corner and walked across the car park, tossing her spent cigarette butt away before entering through the main doors of the office.

He knew where her car would be parked, knew the make, colour, and registration, as he did with all the employees in the company. He kept a notebook in his glove compartment with all their vehicle details. To his advantage, the company car park was on the blind side of the building. He parked where he normally would and strolled over to Debra's vehicle. He thought back to how he'd cut the brake- pipe on his adoptive father's car all those years ago—not too much, just enough to let the fluid trickle out under pressure—in such a way as to make it look like wear and tear. Her car was quite old, so that wouldn't be a problem. With his hood pulled down almost covering his eyes, he checked that nobody was close enough to see what he was doing. Then he got down and reached under the car to locate the nearside brake line. He knew the best place to cut was at a bracket that held it to the chassis. Using a set of needle-point wire cutters, he snipped a small incision into the line. He then wet a finger and drew it across the under body to collect a small amount of road dirt, which he rubbed over the cut. In four hours, she would be finished with work, and he would return to follow her on her way home.

Damn and blast it! Barton cursed himself. He had just rolled off the sofa and gone into the kitchen to make cups of tea for Nancy and himself and found that he had no milk or tea bags. *I'm about as organised as a sheep.* He abandoned the idea and went into the bedroom. He found her struggling to sit up.

"Lie where you are," he said, easing her back down. "Do you drink tea or coffee?"

She smiled. "I'd love a cup of tea."

"I'm sorry for being a typical man, but I'll have to go out and get some milk and tea bags."

She laughed but at the cost of pains shooting down her injured side. She yelped softly.

"I'll call round to your flat and pick up your clothes while I'm out, if you want."

"I don't think I've brought the keys with me. I've left my phone as well." She whimpered in pain as she tried to move. "I hate to ask you this …" A few moments passed before she finally said, "I desperately need the toilet. Could you help me?"

"As much as is possible." He returned to the bed and eased her legs out. She gasped in agony with every movement. In the toilet, he pulled her trousers and underwear down over her hips and lowered her onto the bowl. He quickly walked out, closing the door and saying, "Shout when you're finished."

What have I gotten myself into? he mused as he sat on the sofa listening for her call. It came, and so did the thing he dreaded. He guessed it had to come. It would have been quite normal had they been kinky lovers. She couldn't wipe herself. She was so embarrassed, and so was he. But in the end, they accomplished it, and he got her back into bed. In all that time, they'd been frightened to look at each other.

"I'll go and get some milk and tea bags," he said softly. And he left her still whining in pain.

The painkillers the hospital had given her weren't doing much good, so while out, he bought the strongest he could purchase from a deregistered doctor the mob used. When he got back, she was asleep, so he left her and made himself a brew. Afterwards, he crept out and gently locked the door.

In his car, he thought of a problem that he hadn't considered when he'd decided to keep the cocaine. Billy, he decided must be one of the big dealers in this area, so there was no way he could sell these drugs here without him getting word of it. As he sat there wiping the condensation off the windscreen, a familiar figure appeared, walking along the street towards him. He stepped out and gave Hatchet Face a fright.

"You're a busy man," Barton said.

"You bastard," Hatchet Face cried. "You might have flashed me to let me know you were there."

"Why are you here?"

"A message from Billy. You're not to phone; he thinks the police are wired into his communications."

"Do you have a phone with you?"

"No, it's got to be word of mouth. I think he may be getting paranoid."

"So now you're the carrier pigeon?"

"If that's what you like to call it, yes."

"That's all very well until you misquote me."

"If it's a long, complicated message, you're to write it out and put it in an envelope."

"If that's the case, I'll arrange a meet through you."

"I'll inform the boss of that," he replied, in the process of lighting up a cigarette.

Barton took a quick glance around. "Where's your car?"

Hatchet Face, about to walk away, said, "Parked a couple of streets away. I was instructed not to drive to your house. If you're heading that way, you can give me a lift."

"You're a pigeon. You can fly," Barton replied with a grin.

"Ha ha! Very witty this morning. Have you been having fun with that drunk woman I saw you carry into your house last night?"

"If you want a lift, you can put that out," Barton said and pointed to the cigarette.

Hatchet Face took a long look at his cigarette, took a last drag, and tossed it into a neighbour's garden.

Barton had hardly gotten his car rolling when Hatchet Face said, "Stop, this'll do. I'm just over there." He pointed to a white Range Rover parked off the main drag in a side street.

A bit too close to the junction, Barton noticed; a young constable would jump at charging him for that. "You shouldn't park so near a junction like that.

You'll attract the attention of a police patrol, and they'll do a search of your vehicle. If they find any of the messages I give you for Billy, we're all in the shit."

Hatchet Face grinned widely, exposing a set of twisted, brown, stumpy teeth, which reminded Barton of a row of condemned houses. The stench from his breath was like that of a septic tank. When he got out, the smell remained, forcing Barton to open all his windows.

Barton lingered to watch the man's skeletal physique cross the road in a jacket that looked three sizes too big. He had an exaggerated spring to his step that appealed to Barton's sense of humour. He drove off laughing to himself and wondering where Billy recruited his thugs from. He must have picked Hatchet Face off the street living rough.

There weren't many names left on Billy's list that he hadn't yet visited, but there were still a few that he'd never got a response from when he'd called. His priority was to find a place to stash the cocaine— not so easy when considering the amount of cash involved. He couldn't think of anyone he could trust with it. He pondered taking it back to Hamilton's flat and persuading the obese woman to hide it again, making the excuse that he couldn't find that place she'd talked about. He thought about promising her the good life with him when he sold it. He doubted she would do it after his warning of a possible police raid, though.

The cocaine bags were still under the seat in his car. He didn't want to be seen carrying the same bags in that he had previously taken out, never know who was watching from all those windows. Every time he walked towards that block of flats, he could sense eyes on his every move. It was a fair walk from the car park, giving observers time to assess who he was. Carrying the same bags in and out would surely arouse suspicions from some of the tenants. Like his previous visit to her flat, he tried the handle, found it locked, tried the bell, knocked, and got no response. He kept his eye on the peephole, but nothing moved. Rather than drawing attention to himself, he about-turned and quickly slipped out.

He sat in his car, puzzled, thinking that she didn't strike him as being the type of woman who went out very often. Her living room window was at the rear, so there was no chance of seeing any movement from where his car was parked, and her front bedroom always seemed to have the curtains closed. He cursed himself for not having had the foresight to get her mobile number and even her name. Then it came to him like a flash—the part in his conversation with Hatchet Face when the man had mentioned him carrying "that drunken woman" into his house. Barton couldn't believe how slow he had been to catch on at the time. How in the hell could he have known about that unless he had been snooping about the area? Had Billy given Hatchet Face the job of tailing him? On thinking about it, that white Range Rover did look familiar. Constantly glancing in his rear-view mirror and seeing no trace of the Range Rover following him, he wondered if he was being paranoid. He drew into a bus stop lay-by and waited for about ten minutes, all the while looking around. In the end, he had to pull away when a bus wanted to get in.

He was delighted to discover that Nancy had managed to pull herself up against the headboard so that she was partially seated.

"How are you?" he asked as he sat on the side of the bed. "Sore, but I can just about move my left arm."

He pointed to the bedside cabinet. "I got you some stronger medication. I'll get you some water, and you can try it."

He drew a chair up to the bed, and together they ate a delivered meal.

"Are those pills doing any good?" he asked.

"May be too soon for them to kick in."

CHAPTER 25

Giving himself ample time, Eddie drove to the car park and parked where he could see Debra's vehicle. When she walked out, she was accompanied by one of the other office girls Eddie didn't recognise. They both got into Debra's car. "Ha!" he gasped in delight. Two for the price of one. He started up his car and drove out behind them, guessing they wouldn't be paying much attention to traffic following them. They would be yapping all the way, so keeping a safe distance wouldn't be worth bothering about.

He almost blew it. Debra made a last-minute left turn, and he couldn't follow. There were too many vehicles too close behind him. He had no other option but to carry on until he could get turned. When he eventually drove into the street she'd turned down, he found it was a dead end, full of parked cars. But there was no sign of Debra's. He snapped into one of his tempers and slapped his hands on the steering wheel, cursing and swearing. He swung his car around,

"I'm on my way to visit some relatives. This is a shortcut I use when I go there. Can I drop you off anywhere? I pass through the village you live in."

"That's a good idea," Franky said. "I'll get your car pulled out of there and get it to you. It'll be a write-off."

Eddie stepped over to the edge of the road but dared not to go too near, as his vertigo would make him dizzy. Standing on the safe side of the broken wooden fence, he noticed her vehicle hadn't landed at the bottom of the ravine, where a small stream ran, but crashed into a tree about halfway down.

He nodded at Franky. "Definitely a write-off."

He helped Debra into the passenger's seat while Franky moved his tractor off the road to let them pass. It was a tight squeeze, but in the end, with the young farmer marshalling, he was soon on his way. He tried to make light of the situation, complimenting her on her calmness and telling her the insurance would soon get her another car. He smiled at her and told her that before she knew it, things would be back to normal.

"I think I should take you to a hospital to get you checked out, just to be on the safe side."

"I'll be fine, Mr Fisher. Just drop me off at home."

In a matter of minutes, they were driving though the village. She directed him to her house.

"Are you sure you don't want to go to hospital?" he asked, helping her out of the car door.

"Honestly, I'm OK." A youth with long hair and a beard came running out the door of her house and took hold of her by the elbows, helping her along the path.

Eddie smiled and waved as he drove away, but the smile was false. Inside he was seething. He needed to take his frustration out on something or someone. He would have done so if it hadn't been for that farmer. She was a lucky girl to survive the crash and even luckier to have survived him. The solution to his anger came as a cat appeared crossing the road. He swerved and felt the bump when his car ran over the small body. His fulfilment at killing the cat only lasted a moment, though, and soon he was back to feeling cheated and angry. He needed a human victim to replace Debra; she was out of the equation, for the time being.

The countryside rolled past. It felt as though he had been driving for hours. The roads were narrow and winding, and he'd met few oncoming cars and could see none following. He had passed through a few hamlets but could see no signs of life. He drove into a forested area where tall overhanging trees formed an arch. It seemed like he was driving through a tunnel, and he had to put his headlights on. At first, he thought his eyes were deceiving him, but as he drew closer, the reality struck him. A woman stood in the middle of the road waving him down. He instantly jumped on the brakes. He opened his window as she approached.

"What's the matter?" he asked.

"Please help me," she pleaded, her eyes brimming with tears. "I've been abducted and assaulted by three men with a van and dumped in that wood."

"You better get in, then." He reached over and opened the passenger's door. He admired her as she skipped around the bonnet and got in. "What do you want to do, go to the police? Or shall I take you to a hospital?"

She was a beautiful girl with wide, blue eyes and long, flowing blonde hair. Her clothing had been ripped, and she held her blouse closed at her breast. Eddie estimated her age to be about sixteen or younger.

"Could you take me to the nearest police station, please?"

"I'm not familiar with this area. I don't know where the nearest one will be. I've got a map in the boot, though. I'll get it."

He did have a map in the boot, but he didn't grab only that. He also grabbed the crowbar. He opened the passenger's door.

"Are you any good at map reading?" he asked, unfolding the map and holding it so she could look at it. At the exact moment when she eased herself closer, he grabbed her blonde hair and pulled her out, striking her four or five times on the back of her neck with the crowbar. She slumped down by the side of the car. Again he hit her to make sure she was dead. He dragged her body in amongst the trees out of sight from the road.

With a wide, satisfied grin and the car radio on, he drove on, admiring the scenery. He loved the countryside when the sun was shining. The day had turned out nicely.

Barton crumpled up the containers from the food they had just eaten and got up off the chair.

"How are we going to get your things from your flat?" he asked Nancy.

"The only thing I can think of is to wait until I'm able to get about. I can phone Eddie and make arrangements and hope he's going to be sensible about it."

"Your car is still parked there. I could get a taxi and bring it back here, if you want."

She shook her head. "I don't have the keys."

"That's not a problem," Barton said with a grin. "I'll soon get it started."

Again, she shook her head. "No, just wait till I'm able, and we'll both go and get it at the same time as we pick up my things."

"I'm going out for a while. Do you need the toilet?"

"Not at the moment. How long will you be? I might need it later if you are going to be a while."

"I'll get back as soon as I can," he said, heading for the door.

The white Range Rover was parked a short way down the street. It not for the large van that it had been parked in front of it pulling away, Barton would never have seen it. When he got in and started his car, he glanced in his mirror, recognising Hatchet Face in the driver's seat and another man beside him. He grinned. *Let's have some fun.* He took the first right turn and a few yards farther along made another right. Then he did the same again and found himself behind the Range Rover. When Hatchet Face made the first turn, Barton drove straight on and blew his horn.

Hatchet Face slammed on his brakes; Barton couldn't miss seeing those large red lights. Then in a heartbeat, the white reversing lights came on.

Barton pulled between parked cars, got out, and strolled through the gate of the house opposite his car. He stood at the door as if waiting for a reply, which he knew wouldn't come, for he hadn't knocked, and Hatchet Face drove past without realising he had been duped.

Barton stepped out of the lift and was about to head for the obese woman's flat but stopped in his tracks. Two uniformed constables were standing at her door, which was open. He hastily stepped back into the lift. That's when he heard the sirens. He was almost knocked over by rushing police and ambulance crews when the lift doors opened. The car park was ablaze with flashing blue lights and full of people rubbernecking, wanting to know what was going on, as he did himself. He decided to hang about to satisfy his suspicions, and he didn't have to wait long. Four paramedics carrying a stretcher between them answered his question. It would have taken four men to carry her obese body.

When the medics passed, he noticed one was carrying a drip, holding it above her head. He sighed. *At least she's still alive.* Panic set in when he noticed residents from the flat standing at the door. All it would take was for one to recognise him. He pulled up his collar and stole away to his car, feeling fortunate when he reached it that nobody had paid any attention to him. They were probably too busy watching the action. On his drive back, his mind was full of questions. Had she fallen ill, or had she been beaten up over the drugs he had stashed under his passenger's seat? If that were the case, it would have to have been Billy's thugs who had paid her a visit, which answered his question about why Hatchet Face had been tailing him.

Hatchet Face had his outstretched hand on the handle of the door when Barton threw a kick to the back of his knees. The man fell backwards, and Barton gripped his neck and dragged him to the ground.

"What the fuck do you think you're doing?"

"You sneaky bastard, always coming up behind people," Hatchet Face croaked.

Barton gave his neck another wrench. "Was that you trying to get in my house?"

"Just doing what I'm told."

Barton roughly released his neck and landed a kick to his head. Hatchet Face lay still. Barton dragged him up against that wall, sitting him upright and slapping him a few times until he came to.

"Were you doing what you were told when you beat up that woman?"

"What woman are you talking about?" Hatchet Face replied groggily.

Barton made a fist and drew it back, ready to let it fly. "You know what woman I'm talking about." He didn't throw the punch but instead grabbed the man's collar. "Where's your mate?"

"I'm here, right behind you," a gruff voice said.

Barton turned and found himself looking down the barrel of a pistol. Behind it stood a stocky guy with a tammy pulled level with his eyebrows, his brown eyes lined up with the sight of his weapon.

"Get your hands behind your back," he commanded.

Barton complied, and the gunman drew a cable tie from his pocket and tossed it to Hatchet Face. Barton felt his wrists being wrenched together. Next came a blow to the head from behind. It wasn't enough to knock him out, but it shook him and almost made him lose his balance. Hatchet Face went through Barton's pocket and stripped him of his wallet and the keys to his door, the keys being the main object of his search. He unlocked and opened the door, and the gunman pushed Barton inside. He was pushed into his living room and forced onto the sofa.

"What the fuck do you want?" he shouted.

"The two bags of cocaine," the gun man snarled.

"I don't know what you are talking about."

Hatchet Face stepped closer. "That woman told us she gave them to you."

"Well, she's lying."

"After the thumping we gave her, I don't think so. And we wrecked her house looking for it, so you must have it," the gunman said, waving his pistol in front of Barton's face while Hatchet Face started searching in the kitchen.

Barton could hear dishes being smashed, cutlery being tossed to the floor, cupboards being pulled open, and their contents being tossed out. Hatchet Face returned to the living room, shook his head, and started searching in there. Barton was dragged off the sofa, and Hatchet Face set about it with a knife. The next was the television, which he put his foot through. When they had finished in the living room, Barton was dragged into the bedroom. Nancy had somehow rolled off the bed and was lying at the far side of it. Hatchet Face saw her and pulled her by her ankles to the middle of the room. Barton thought her screams must be heard by pedestrians walking past the house.

"You'll regret you did that," Barton shouted at him.

Hatchet Face ignored him and started slicing the bedding, finishing up by tipping the bed over. Next he started inside the wardrobe, hauling all the clothing out and tipping over shoe boxes. Then he started ripping up the carpet. Gasping for breath, he turned to the gunman.

"Nothing here."

The gunman jabbed his weapon into Barton's back. "Where did you park your car?"

"It's in the garage getting fixed. It wasn't starting. I walked here."

"It started easy enough earlier today," Hatchet Face said.

"Don't give me your crap. You think we're stupid? Where is it parked?" the gunman said and slapped Barton on the ear with the barrel.

Within a few seconds, Barton's ear was burning, and he could feel warm blood running down his cheek.

"You'll regret that, fuckface," he shouted, struggling against the retainers.

The gun got pushed into his spine. "Take us to your car now, or I'll put a slug through your girlfriend's face."

Nancy lay on the floor where Hatchet Face had left her, whimpering both with pain and fear.

"OK," Barton said, "I'll take you to it." He felt himself being pushed towards the door and thought this was it his last chance. But how to take the two of them with his hands tied behind his back. Then, as if by magic, the gunman told Hatchet Face to stay with the woman to make sure she didn't get to a phone.

A golden rule Barton had learned in his army days was to keep at least an arm's length away when walking behind someone holding a gun at their back. The gunman had never been taught this and was much too close. Barton pivoted around on one foot, bringing his other one around with such speed and ferocity that he knocked the gunman off balance. He followed through with a headbutt to his nose, finally managing to land a good, hard kick into his groin. The gunman went down and received another kick to the head. This one put him out cold. Using the corner of the brick wall of his house, he rubbed the cable ties until they snapped. He sprinted over to the gunman and soon retrieved his car keys from the man's hand.

Hatchet Face had his back to him, lighting a cigarette, when Barton entered the bedroom. His small, deep-set eyes flared up at the sight of Barton charging at him, and the lighter slipped from his hand. He was far too slow to react and never saw the gnome Barton had picked up from a neighbour's garden in

Barton's raised hand. It crashed down on Hatchet Face's narrow skull and smashed into numerous pieces. A kick to Hatchet Face's leg confirmed he was out cold or dead. Barton didn't stay to make sure. His priority was Nancy. He lifted her up the same way he had done previously and carried her out to his car. He passed two pedestrians standing over the gunman and carried on past them. By the time he got Nancy into his vehicle, the police had arrived. He normally cursed the overgrown laurel bushes in the neighbour's garden for making it difficult to see the traffic coming down the street, but at this moment, he was grateful they blocked the view of the police officers, who were attending the scene where the gunman lay. They would have found the gun and put the assault down to gang warfare. Nancy whimpered as he pulled away, as careful as he was. She cried out with every bump or turn he had to make.

The first bus stop lay-by was available, and he pulled into it.

"I have to make a call," he told Nancy, and he could tell she wasn't paying much attention to him. He got out, and a few paces away, he called Marlin. "When are you due home?"

She replied saying she was staying with her parents for another week. He checked his pockets for the key she had given him and cursed at himself for leaving it at his house. He stood there for a while, searching his memory, trying to visualize her hallway and figure out if she had an alarm fixed there. He couldn't even guess the answer and wished he had paid more attention. He decided to take a chance. He parked a few houses away from Marlin's, and leaving Nancy again, he strolled to the front door with a few tools he'd had in the boot. He had the door open within a few minutes.

"Whose house is this?" Nancy asked through the pain of getting carried in the door.

"Belongs to a friend who's on holiday. That call I made back there was to ask if we could use it for a few days."

Unlike in his own house, Marlin's bedroom was upstairs, and her toilet was downstairs.

"Do you need the toilet before I take you up to the bed?"

"Oh! Yes, please. I'm desperate."

They went through the same embarrassing routine as before, and then he manoeuvred her up the stairs. He wondered how the neighbours didn't hear her screams. When she was settled on the bed, he sat on the edge and placed his hand on her forehead.

"How are you?"

"In pain and very frightened," she replied. She sniffed the pillow. "I can smell a woman's perfume in this bed."

"That'll be from my friend's wife. What are you frightened of?"

"What am I frightened of!" She rolled her eyes and winced with pain. "I thought living with Eddie was dangerous enough. Now I've gotten myself involved with a gangster."

"No, you haven't. I'm no gangster. That was a misunderstanding."

"That must have been some misunderstanding, being pushed into the bedroom with your hands tied behind your back by two men with a gun."

"Sorry about that. It won't happen again."

"I know it won't happen again, not to me."

"Is this you giving me the push?" He blurted out the first lie that came into his head. "Those two men were dealing drugs to young students. A friend's daughter got addicted because of them. We decided to go after these dealers. I got hold of the drugs they were stashing and destroyed them, and they came after us. It won't happen again; those two dealers are at this moment being picked up by the police."

He could feel her eyes burning into his, digging for the truth. He could tell she was no pushover, and he was tempted to avert his eyes from hers, but he knew that if he did that, it would be a dead giveaway.

She finally looked away and said, "So what's the misunderstanding?"

"They thought we still had the drugs."

CHAPTER 26

One good thing about Nancy not being there was that Eddie no longer needed to answer her nagging questions. But he still missed her. She had been one of his possessions. She gave him the security he craved. It was this that controlled his desire for killing, his need for control over other humans. He got most of that from her. Yes, she was often uncontrollable, but when he won, that elated him beyond his satisfaction. Her mobile was still lying on the kitchen table. He picked it up. He scrolled through the numbers, found the one he was after, and pressed the call icon. He wasn't expecting a reply and wasn't disappointed when it never happened. He pulled the gun and the extra rounds from the drawer and fumbled with it, practising his speed and aiming at objects on the wall. If only he could fire off a few shots instead of just simulating. It came to him in a flash, and he jogged his memory back to scar-faced Raymond Gibb. Then a few things fell into place. That big stranger he suspected Nancy to be with must have visited the witch next door.

"What the fuck do you want?" she croaked through the narrow slit between the door and the frame. He kicked the door open, and she yelped when it hit her. Eddie hefted the pistol up to her face.

"I want a word with you."

"Help!" she screamed, but in that place, it fell on deaf ears. She felt herself being pushed into her house and forced down onto a chair.

"Who was that big guy who came about a week or so ago asking about Raymond?"

"I don't know who he was. He never gave his name."

"Fucking liar!" he shouted and slapped her on the side of her head.

"I don't know his name," she croaked, "but I've seen him going to your house a few times when you weren't there. Heard him and that woman you're living with at it."

This time in a jealous rage, he slammed the handle of the pistol down on her forehead. The impact sent her head back. Her mouth drooped open, and her dentures fell onto her chest. If he had killed her, it was his first accidental killing, and he felt no thrill from it. In fact, for the first time, a wave of panic rushed through him.

It was different this time. He would have to get rid of the body—not an easy task when living in a block of flats. He grabbed her shoulders and shook her but got no response. Slapping her face got no results either. From her kitchen, he brought a bowl of cold water and threw it at her face. Still no reaction. He noticed a dark-blue lump had developed on the place where he had hit her with the butt of his pistol. It was about the size of a golf ball. Her grey eyes stared at him, and this frightened him, sending him dashing for the door. Luckily, the key was in the keyhole. He pulled it out and locked the door behind him.

Slumped out on his sofa breathing deeply, his mind raced. He tried to think of a way to smuggle her body down the stairs and across to his car without being spotted. Then where to dump it? A sudden idea struck him that would eliminate the need to dump the witch's body. One problem solved. She wasn't a heavily built woman, but he still couldn't picture himself carrying her down all those stairs, and the risk of meeting someone was too high, with the type of creeps that lived there. Most of them were addicts or alcoholics, roaming about all night and sleeping it off during the day.

The idea he had come from a movie he remembered watching where the perpetrator dissected his victims and disposed of the body parts through the drainage system. But the only place he could dispose of the body would be down the toilet, and that would be too risky. They normally got blocked even under normal use. Conforming to the movie, he dumped the witch's body in her bath, slit her jugular, and left her to bleed out. He had no inkling how long that would take, so he decided to leave her overnight and come back in the morning. He was feeling disappointed at how slow the blood flowed. He'd thought it would squirt out like it had with some of his other victims. He left quietly and met two laughing young girls on their way past. *Interesting,* he thought. *Wonder where they are heading?* Before entering his own flat, he eyed them knocking on the door at the end of the corridor. Another young girl opened it, and they all cheered their greetings and disappeared inside. *A party,* he mused. *Wonder if they would accept a gate crasher?*

He felt hunger pangs in his gut but couldn't be bothered to cook, so he phoned for a delivery, hoping that it would be the young boy he had noticed delivering in the neighbourhood—a nice change from all the females on his recent list. *No, no, don't be stupid, Eddie,* he thought. *Deal with what you've planned first.* He grinned and switched on the television, turning to the news channel. He watched it to the end. Nothing was reported about the two girls he had murdered in Scotland. He jumped up and kicked the small table next to Nancy's chair. Surely, they must have found the one he dumped not far off the road on the Ayrshire moor.

It was the same young boy who came to the door with his food. Eddie smiled, gave him a good tip, and sent him on his way grinning. *Lucky boy*, he ruminated as he ate the food. *Maybe when I have this mess cleared, you might not be so lucky.*

The waste bin in the kitchen was full, and normally it was his job to empty it, but not anymore, not now that Nancy's wasn't there to remind him about it. So, the wrapping of his meal got tossed on the floor. Thinking of her and the big man she had run off with brought the gun to the forefront of his mind. He pulled open the utensil drawer, lifted it out, and began fondling it, thinking, *She must come for her clothes and car sometime, but not before I dump that witch's body in it.* After a few more dummy practices with the pistol, he turned towards the open drawer. Facing him was a large kitchen knife. He held it up, saw his reflection on the blade, and instantly thought of the party going on down the hallway. *With all those girls, a male gate crasher might be welcome … Control, control. Keep control of yourself. Too much to do to even think about it. Lucky bitches, but maybe someday they will have another party.*

Now where did Nancy keep her sleeping pills? He couldn't find them in the kitchen or in any of the drawers in the living room. Success came when he searched in her bedside cabinet. He found a full packet, lay down on her bed, and swallowed a few.

Eddie had tucked his hand under the pillow still holding the gun. He thought he had dozed off for a moment, but when he happened to look at the clock on the cabinet next to the bed, he realised he had fallen asleep. *That can't be right,* he thought. Then he realised that it was daylight instead of the lamps that illuminated the room. He swung his legs out of the bed and tried to stand up but had to sit back down. He couldn't maintain his balance. His head was spinning, and he was seeing everything in double. When he lay flat with his head on the pillow, the ceiling started spinning. He closed his eye to stop it, but the spinning continued.

Must have been a dream, he mused as he glanced around the room, noticing that the only light was from the lamps at the side of the bed. He sat up. *Or was it?* The clock at the side of the bed had jumped another ten hours. *What fucking day is it?* He sprang out of the bed and stood for a moment—no dizziness or double vision. He let out a sigh of relief and reached under the pillow for the gun. His legs felt wobbly as he went into the kitchen with the intention of putting the gun back in the drawer. His eyes fell on the large knife, and the memory of the body lying in the bath next door returned to him.

Bin liners. I need lots of them. I need to triple them to stop the blood from dripping out. He rummaged through the utensils for a meat cleaver or a knife with a serrated edge to saw through her bones. He found both and grinned, thankful that Nancy had stocked the kitchen with all the required tools. His euphoria soon diminished when he couldn't find any bin liners. He hadn't planned on going out to buy them, and doing so would take up too much time, as he would have to go to a DIY shop to get decent heavy gauged ones. The bin liners would have to wait, he decided, and with the knives hidden under his jacket, he unlocked the door. The blood hadn't even covered the bottom of the bath. This puzzled him. In the film, the body had completely drained. To be on the safe side, he did what the perpetrator had done and stripped naked. Where to start was a problem.

The movie never showed that. He decided to start at her feet and remembered to run the cold water to drain all the mess away.

Barton had spent the last twenty-four hours taking care of Nancy. Twice he had phoned Marlin to make sure she wasn't going to come home early. He received an incoming call from Billy, who wanted to know if Barton had any idea where Hatchet Face was. Crapper, Billy had named him.

"Did you send him and another goon to Hamilton's flat?" Barton asked.

Billy denied it and wanted to know why he was asking.

"When I went back there to get that stuff you were missing," Barton was glad he wasn't face to face with him, for he was sure Billy would spot the lie, by studying his body language, and hoped he hadn't detccted any hasitation in his voice. "The place was crawling with policemen." He continued.

The phone went silent for a while. "What makes you think Crapper was involved with the incident at Hamilton's flat?" Billie had come back after obviously ruminating over the information.

"He had been following me for some time in a big white Range Rover. In the end, they came to my house looking for that stuff, him and another goon."

"Did they get it?"

"I didn't have it. They didn't believe me, so they got rough, pulled a gun out and wrecked my place looking for it. I managed to get away. The next thing I saw was a squad of police cars flying into the street."

The call ended abruptly as usual, and for once, Barton was glad of it. He turned to go into the bedroom, and Nancy was standing, propped up against the living room doorpost, holding her side.

"What are you doing? You shouldn't be up yet."

"Those pills you gave me seem to be helping slightly." She stumbled forward and supported herself on the back of the sofa.

"Just one more day in bed and you'll be able to get about better." He eased her around, heading back to the bedroom.

She resisted. "I need the toilet. I think I can manage to wipe myself now. Just help me get there."

He helped her in and sat her on the bowl and then left, but he didn't close the door. He got settled on Marlin's sofa, listening in case Nancy had problems getting back onto her feet. His mobile sounded again. The name that came up on the screen sent a chill through him. This could only mean trouble. The only time the dapper little man called was when he was desperate for answers.

"Barton." The high-pitched military voice rang crisp in his ear. "What have you been up to, dear boy?"

"Nothing much," Barton lied. He jumped up when he heard the toilet flush. Still holding his phone to his ear, he ran and caught Nancy struggling to get back into the bedroom.

"Not what I've been hearing," Crow shouted.

With the phone jammed between his shoulder and his ear, he hefted Nancy onto the bed. "What have you been hearing?" he managed to say before his mobile fell onto the bed. He got the phone picked up and back at his ear. "Sorry about that. Just dropped my phone."

"Are you in bed with a woman at this time of day?"

"No, not exactly. I missed what you had said there."

"My associate tells me you killed one of his best men, one I recruited for him."

"If you don't mind me asking, who's your associate? Then I'll know if I did or not."

"You know better than to ask that."

"If it was a goon called Crapper, that was an accident."

The line went dead, and he was left staring at it, thinking you're just like Billy.

"One of your gangster friends?" Nancy said, interrupting his train of thought.

Barton grinned down at her. She looked beautiful lying there with her hair spread across the pillow, her watery blue eyes staring into his unblinkingly.

"Just a police friend asking about the man they found unconscious in my house." It was one of those moments that brought his mother's words back to him—ones that had often rung in his mind: When too many lies are told, one lie always leads to many more until you start to believe them.

Nancy painfully turned her head from side to side, her eyes taking in the contents of the room. "This is a lovely house. You friend has good taste. When are they due back?"

"I'm not sure yet. Maybe a few more days."

"Where are you going to take me when that happens?"

"A bed and breakfast or a hotel, until I find a flat. I was about to move out of that house anyway, so I'm not too put out about it getting trashed."

"Are you not bothered about your clothes and belongings?"

Barton shrugged his shoulders. "There wasn't anything of great value in it."

"When I can get about better, I would like to collect my clothes and belongings and my car." She turned to face him and noticed that he had averted his eyes. "What's wrong, Richard? Eddie will be at work. We'll have plenty of time to get my things together."

"I'm not worried about Eddie; I'm worried he may have reported you missing to the police. Then they'd be keeping an eye on the area."

"Don't worry about that. He'll think I've left because of his assault on me. He's confident I'll return and that he'll grovel and all will get back to normal. He doesn't know about you."

"He must know you're with someone. He's phoned my mobile twice. I never answered. It was your phone he was using."

She attempted to get up, groaned in pain, and lay back down. "Could you get more of those pills? I've only two left."

"That's not a problem. Just watch you don't get addicted to them."

She grinned. "I'll be careful. And could you get me some sleeping pills?"

"No way. You can't mix those tablets with sleeping pills."

She closed her eyes and turned her head. "I can't sleep."

"I'll see what I can do," he replied, and he left her, closing the room door behind him.

She must have swallowed about ten of those pills. He remembered that the packet had contained twelve. He checked to make sure the cocaine bags were still under the passenger's seat before starting his car up. He only got about half a mile along the road before his phone sounded. He saw Marlin's name on the fascia and pulled to the side of the road.

"Hi, Marlin. What's wrong?"

"I'm on my way home," she replied. "I forgot my parents had a holiday planned. They said I could stay until they returned, but I told them no. And anyway, I'm missing you. Will you be there when I get back to help me unpack?"

"That's great news," he replied, hoping she hadn't detected the hesitation in his voice. "What time will you be arriving?"

"If the traffic stays light, it should take me about three hours from here."

"Where are you just now?"

"I'm in Watford Gap services."

"You take your time and drive carefully."

With the help of Google, he found a local B & B and phoned up to book a room for a few days. He explained to the woman who answered that his friend had had an accident and was unfit to travel but should be well enough in a few days, if she could rest up for that time. The first hour was taken up with getting Nancy out of Marlin's house and settled in the B & B. He left her lying on the bed and told her he was going back to the house to clean things up for his friend's return.

He just managed to get things back to the way they'd been when he heard her car pull into the driveway. She was all hugs and kisses when they got her car unpacked and her child into his pen.

"Someone's been in here," she claimed as they entered her bedroom.

He smiled and put his arm around her waist. "That was me. I came round early and did some dusting and cleaning for you. I guessed you'd be tired after that long drive. I'll order a meal and get it delivered."

She giggled. "Well, you guessed wrong. I'm not that tired," she said and pushed him onto the bed.

CHAPTER 27

The knife with the serrated edge snapped at his first attempt to saw through the witch's ankle bone. His hands were sticky and bloody, and he had splatters on his arms and chest. He cursed and threw the knife against the wall. *I need to get a proper saw, maybe even a hacksaw.* He couldn't remember seeing anything like that in his house. *Will have to go to the ironmonger's, get decent bags at the same time, but not from the same shop. Can't be too careful.*

This was turning out to be more complicated than he had anticipated. He had to wash the blood from his arms and chest in the hand basin, after which he couldn't find a towel to dry himself, and he had to dress while still wet. When the corridor was devoid of neighbours, he dashed into his own flat and got into dry clothing.

He secretly grinned as he passed Nancy's car on his way to his own. *You and your boyfriend won't be very pleased at the surprise you're going to find in the boot.*

To be sure he could do the job properly, he purchased a pack of throwaway wood saws and a hacksaw with a spare set of blades. It would come in handy if another situation occurred, and he was sure it would when he dealt with that big stranger and Nancy. He bought extra rolls of heavy-gauge bin liners and was confident that things were beginning to work out now. On his way home, he pulled into the car park at the offices where he'd used to work, staying out of sight of the offices. Debra would have another car or a courtesy vehicle, but he guessed that if she did, she would park it in the same place. A time check told him she was due out for her lunch break any minute. True to form, there she was, and as an extra bonus, she was accompanied by Chambers, the man who'd sacked him. *Two lucky people for now, but your times will come as soon as the immediate jobs are done.* He lowered his body until he could watch them and not be seen. He wasn't sure if he was shocked or angry at what he witnessed when they got into the car. Chambers leaned over and embraced her, and then they started kissing. And it was no pet kiss. They started slobbering and tonguing each other. Eddie thought that at any moment they would strip off, but it didn't go that far. Chambers got out the car and darted back to his office. After a minute, Debra got out and walked to the cafe for her lunch. Was this the real reason he got sacked? He had suspected she was after a promotion but hadn't been sure she was after his job. Maybe Chambers offered it to her to get into her knickers. Even more reason to deal with them. He grinned as he started up his car and drove past her as she headed down the street.

He took one of the wood saws out of the packet and brought that and the hacksaw next door to finish his work on the dead witch. He gasped and almost fainted when he got to the bath and found it was empty—no trace of blood, nothing to indicated that a body had been lying there. In a panic, he rushed out and back into his own flat. He flopped himself down on the sofa. He dropped the keys to his door a couple of time. He couldn't hold them; his hands were shaking too much. He was certain she was dead. She must have been dead. How could she have stood the pain of him trying to cut into her ankles and the gash he had made on her neck? She must be dead. He needed to be sick and rushed to the toilet.

When he had emptied the contents of his stomach and washed his face in the handbasin, he turned to dry himself and saw the witch's body in his own bath. He covered his face with his hands and screamed. He could feel the warm urine running down his legs, and his heart was pounding in his chest. Everything seemed to be happening in slow motion for a moment. Then just as quickly, they sped up. The room was spinning around him, and he couldn't feel his legs beneath him. He began to fall into a black, bottomless pit, down and down, twisting and turning, never coming to stop.

"Stop shaking me!" he heard himself shout, but the shaking never stopped. He threw his arms up. His first thought was of Nancy waking him up for school. "I don't want to go!" he shouted again. This time his eyes flickered into a blinding light. He turned away from it and then heard the voice close to his face. It dawned on him where he was and what he had done. Slowly, his focus returned. The face that looked down at him was familiar. He could never forget that ugly scar, starting from his left eye and going all the way to the corner of his mouth.

Raymond Gibb grabbed him by the collar of his jacket and lifted him off the floor. He dragged him out of the toilet and threw him onto the sofa.

"I knew it had to be you who killed her."

"Killed who?" Eddie said, trying to edge himself away from Gibb's face.

Gibb took a step back and grimaced. "You did me a favour. I was planning to bump her off, had it all worked out when I was in the nick. Now you've saved me the trouble." He strolled around the back of the sofa, stopped, and looked down at him. "In a couple of hours, the coppers are going to be calling on me to make sure I comply with my house confinement. Had they found her body, I would have been dragged back inside and charged with her murder."

Eddie, now feeling more relaxed, sat up and watched Gibb getting settled into Nancy's seat.

"When did you get out?"

"This morning," Gibb replied. "Do you have any snout?"

"I don't smoke, but my mother does. I'll see if she has left any in the kitchen." On wobbly legs, Eddie opened the cutlery drawer and pocketed the pistol. He stuck his head through the living room door. "Nothing in there. I'll try her bedroom."

"By the way," Gibbs said, holding up the magazine as Eddie was about to walk out, "you've no ammo, so you can put the gun back. I'm going next door to wait for the coppers. I'll take this with me." He got onto his feet and squeezed past Eddie. "You can start cutting her body up. I'll be back when they leave."

"You'll be in trouble if the police do a body search on you," Eddie called after him.

Halfway out the door, Gibb stopped and smiled. "They won't find this." He patted his pocket and closed the door behind him.

Eddie lobbed the pistol down onto the sofa and sat next to it. *That's two people who know I'm a murdered, two people who will have to get put down. Gibb turning up means a lot of changes have to be made. Why is everything going belly up suddenly?* A search of Nancy's bedside cabinet exposed a few packets of cigarettes and the packet of sleeping pills. He began to hatch a plan to dispose of Gibb, but not here. Too close to home. He would have to get him away from here, and he's too heavy to carry. How to get this scar- faced guy to travel with him? Since he was a con, money could be a way of enticing him, or even drugs. He could concoct a story about knowing where a stash of drugs was hidden. The trouble with these ideas was that Gibb was no pushover; Eddie would need to be convincing and have a viable reason for taking him along.

Gibb barged into the toilet while Eddie was in the shower.

"What's the panic?" Eddie asked, pulling back the curtains and stepping out. He wrapped a towel around his waist.

"No panic," Gibb replied. "Just wondered how you were getting on."

Eddie nodded towards the bath. "All bagged up and ready to go."

Gibb followed his gaze. "That's a lot of bags for a small woman."

"Had to cut her up into small pieces. Easier to carry that way."

"What do you plan to do with them?"

My mother has buggered off with a man but hasn't collected her car yet, so I intend to dump them in the boot, let the bitch worry about them."

Gibb stood in the living room watching Eddie get dressed. "You'll have to wait until it's dark before you think about carrying those bags down to the car park."

"Do you want to give me a hand?"

"No fucking way, man. If the coppers get wind of me acting suspicious, they'll be jumping on me in a matter of minutes."

"I'll make it worth your while." Eddie grinned when he noticed Gibb's eyes light up.

"That's going to be expensive, considering I could get nicked and this time locked away for conspiracy to murder. That brings me to another question: Why did you kill her?"

Eddie shrugged his shoulders. "I didn't mean to kill her. She must have a thin skull."

"How much is my help worth to you?"

"Don't worry, you'll be well paid. I know where a stash of cocaine in hidden. Must be worth half a million. And I need your help to get it."

This time Gibb's whole demeanour lit up. "I want half of it."

"Agreed," Eddie said. "We just have to find a buyer."

"That won't be a problem. I know where to flog it. But that's going to cost you extra."

"No way." Eddie shook his head. "We split the expenses up equally. If you don't like it, I'll get somebody else."

Gibb grabbed Eddie's collar and pulled his face closer. "You're a naive little fucker. You are in no position to negotiate. You murdered my partner; I'm a witness to that. All it would take is an anonymous phone call to the police."

"That's blackmail."

Gibb burst into laughter and pointed to the toilet. "That's murder. A bit more serious. I don't think the coppers would be interested in a blackmailer when they've just nabbed a murderer."

"You're a dirty bastard."

"I know what I am, but after this, I'll be a rich dirty bastard." He released Eddie's jacket and pushed him down onto the sofa. "You can carry the bags down on your own," he said on his way out the door. "I'll be back later, and you can take me to where the drugs are stashed."

Eddie grinned when the door closed. He had noticed that Gibb was wearing an ankle tag and knew it would have to be removed before he left the flats, but he was confident Gibb would do that. The trouble was that when he murdered Scar Face, the brace would be left in his flat and the police would check on him, finding only the tag. He would have to be quick to get back, grab it, and throw it in the canal. That would be a good five-mile drive at speed before the police alert went off and they came looking for him.

CHAPTER 28

After Barton and Marlin had enjoyed the meal he had ordered and downed of few cups of coffee, Barton got up and told her he had work to do for a friend.

"I'll be back as soon as I finish."

They kissed at the door, and she stood there until he drove off. He waved, and she returned the gesture. He drove past his own house slowly to see if the police were still watching the place. No constables were visible outside, but his front room light was on, and he assumed they were inside. If Crapper, aka to him as Hatchet Face, was the one Crow had been talking about when he said someone had been killed, then his house would be a murder scene.

Nancy was sitting up in bed talking to the owner of the bed and breakfast. They both glanced at him as he entered the room. The owner—a woman in her fifties, Barton guessed—smiled and excused herself.

When the door closed behind her, he said, "You're looking much better."

"I might look it, but I don't feel it," Nancy replied. She took a long look into his eyes before continuing. "Where are you going to sleep tonight? You look shattered."

Barton felt a slight pang of guilt knowing that his looks weren't from the lack of sleep but from spending the last two hours in bed with Marlin. "Don't worry about me. I'll find someplace."

"That nice lady offered to get a single bed brought in, if you want."

"That's nice of her, but I wouldn't want to put her to any trouble."

"She assured me it wouldn't be."

"Well, if she's sure, that'd be great. I'll pay her extra." He stood up. "Where's the toilet?"

Nancy grinned. "Speaking of which, could you take me there? I haven't been since the last time you took me."

When he heard the toilet flush, he helped her back into bed and then returned to the toilet to phone Marlin. She responded quickly and cheerily.

"I'm sorry," he said, "looks like I could be here for the rest of the night."

Her voice dropped. "Oh, well, if you have to."

"You know it's important. I'd give anything to be with you tonight after being without you for a week. I promise you it's a one off. It'll never happen again."

"He must be a good friend, whoever he is."

"He is, and I owe him a big favour."

He cut the contact and flushed the toilet in time to catch the owner carrying in the single bed. He quickly rushed over to helped her, and they manoeuvred the bed through the door. She seemed quite a pleasant, talkative person.

"Since my husband passed away, I've had to do all this kind of work on my own," she complained breathlessly and set about making the bed.

Barton assisted her and asked, "If it's no trouble, could I have a cup of tea please?"

Together they glanced down at Nancy and noticed she had fallen asleep. She must have taken the sleeping pills, Barton decided.

"Come down to the kitchen," the owner said. "I'll make us a brew."

"How long has it been since your husband passed away?" Barton casually asked during their conversation whilst drinking tea and eating some sticky buns.

She opened a pack of cigarettes and held it out to him, but he shook his head.

"You don't mind if I do?"

Barton shook his head again.

"My Albert passed away five years ago. It's been hard trying to keep this business going on my own."

She lit her smoke with a plastic lighter. "Oh! By the way, my name is Brenda."

She held out her hand, and Barton took it. She held his hand for a long moment and smiled. Barton recognised the invitation and decided to take advantage of it.

"Must have been hard for you in this big house on your own?"

She nodded. "Would you like to see round it?"

"I would love to."

She led him into a large lounge that, in his opinion, was overfurnished with dated decoration. A smaller lounge came next looking much the same with dust on top of the furnishing. Next they descended the stairs and entered a bedroom.

"This is my room," she said, standing much too close to him.

He took her hand, and she responded by pulling him onto the bed. Two hours later, he awoke with her arm across his chest. He tried to ease himself away from her, but she tightened her grip and pulled him back onto her. There was no way Barton could resist, and this time she took charge and jumped on top. He cooperated with her every demand and played along with her rhythm. Afterwards, they lay naked on top of the bed, and he started to see why her Albert had passed away before his time. She snorted a few times, and then the snorting became snoring. As time went on, the noise she was making became unbearable. His lack of sleep had sharpened his temper to the point where he could stand her snoring no longer, and he elbowed her on the side of the head. The noise stopped. After a couple of minutes, he couldn't hear her breathing. He held his own breath and listened. No sound. He sat up and put his ear to her mouth. He heard nothing and couldn't feel her breath on the side of his face. He shook her. Still no response. He jumped out of the bed in a panic when he realised she could be dead.

Nancy was still in a deep sleep when he got into the single bed. After swallowing two of the sleeping pills he had brought in for her, he still found it difficult to fall over. How could Brenda be dead? He hadn't hit her that hard. Maybe, he fretted it wasn't how hard the blow had been but where it had been. A voice seemed to come from a distance, sounding shallow with an echo. Then it came closer, and the echo had gone. He felt something on his shoulder. He shot bolt upright in time to see Nancy step away from his swinging arms. She was holding her side and whimpered in pain at her sudden movement.

"Do you have to lash out every time someone disturbs you?" she whimpered.

The fog left from the sleeping pills hadn't cleared from his head, and it took a few minutes to pass completely. He sensed her standing close by, gazing down at him.

"Sorry, I couldn't sleep, so I popped a couple of those pills."

"I know how you feel," she replied. "Where did you get them?"

He ignored her question and said, "Nice to see you can get up on your own."

"I didn't get up on my own. Brenda helped me."

He was on the point of asking who the hell Brenda was when it all came back to him. He swung his legs out of the bed and stood up, still in the nude.

"Say that again."

Nancy repeated herself, and he slapped his forehead. *Cracking up. I'm cracking up.* He turned away from her and noticed his clothes folded over a chair at the other side of the bed. He wanted to ask how they got there but thought better of it. They both turned when the door opened, and Brenda edged herself in carrying a tray of food.

"Good morning," Brenda greeted him as she breezed in, leaving the tray on the bedside cabinet. "I don't normally do bedroom services, but under the circumstanced, I thought I would make an exception."

She smiled on her way out without giving Barton a second glance.

He stared at the door long after it had been closed. It had to have been a dream brought on by those pills. Nancy's question earlier about where he'd gotten them came to the forefront of his mind.

"You seem to be at a loss," she said, interrupting his thoughts.

He turned and began getting dressed. "Those sleeping pills, don't take any more of them. I'll kill that bastard Franny when I see him. He told me they were genuine prescription medicine."

"Well, they certainly help me get to sleep."

"Any other side effects?" Barton asked, pulling up his jeans.

Nancy opened her mouth to reply but was interrupted when a loud scream came from another room. Barton rushed out and was almost knocked off his feet by Brenda running towards the stairs.

"What's wrong?" he shouted.

She stopped. "Do you have your phone on you? I've just found my twin sister lying in her bed. I can't get any response from her. I think she dead."

Barton held her his mobile and stood beside her as she dialled for the emergency services. When she handed it back to him, he said, "Show me where she is, and I'll have a look. I've done some first aid courses. Maybe I can resuscitate her."

Barton followed her to the bedside and was shocked by how similar they looked it was like looking at Brenda's reflection. he put his finger to the woman's jugular vein and shook his head.

"You must be identical twins."

Brenda nodded. "Her name's Linda. A lot of people get us mixed up. Even my husband had difficulty telling us apart. She's the black sheep of the family. Is she gone?"

"Looks like it. Better wait for the medics for an official report."

She slumped down on the chair where Barton had left his clothes and stared at him with tear-filled eyes.

"I know you were in here last night with her. I lifted your things and brought them into your room. I didn't disturb her. Thought she was still asleep. This has happened before with other men. She pretends she's me to seduce them. She's mentally unsound and has been on drugs most of her life. Don't worry, I won't say anything to your partner or wife or whatever she is."

"It must have been your sister who was talking to Nancy when I came in last night?"

"It certainly wasn't me."

"When I left her, she was snoring her head off. That's why I got up and got into that single bed. That must have been your sister I helped carry the bed into the room."

She slowly rose off the seat. "We better get downstairs and wait for the emergency services to arrive."

Barton followed her down the stairs. "Did she have any other medical problems?" he asked as they entered the lounge.

They sat in silence for a while, both dwelling on their own thoughts. Barton finally said he needed the toilet and got up and walked out. Before he flushed, he phoned Billy.

"I need help," he said, speaking softly, and waited for a reply. "What kind of help?" came the belated reply.

"I was sleeping with a woman last night, and when I woke up in the morning, she was dead." He heard Billy repeat his words to whoever was in the office with him, and the sound of guttural laughter from what must have been a group of men rang in his ears.

"So, you fucked this woman to death?" More background laughter. "What do you want me to do about it?"

"I didn't fuck her to death. I accidently hit her with my elbow. Her sister found her the next morning.

"And you think the sister will point a finger at you to the law? My advice to you is to fuck the sister and make sure she keeps her mouth shut. If you're as good at the sex game as your reputation makes me believe, that won't be a hard job for you."

"Thanks for nothing," Barton replied, and this time *he* cut the connection. He flushed the toilet and returned to Brenda in the lounge. She was wiping her tears with a tissue, and he sat beside her and put his arms around her shoulders.

He had no intention of trying to seduce her; it all just seemed to happen there on the sofa, as if it were the right thing to do in these circumstances. They lay there together half naked. Suddenly she jumped up and scrambled to get herself dressed.

"That's them at the door," she cried, running out of the room.

Barton got himself sorted out and found her talking to a couple of paramedics in the hallway.

"I think she made a mistake with her meds or something when she got into bed," he heard her explain. Barton caught himself thinking, Billy you're a genius, as he joined them climbing the stairs.

CHAPTER 29

One by one, Eddie had carried the heavy bin bags down the stairs and stashed them in the boot of Nancy's car. This time when he flopped down on her bed, he was careful of how many sleeping pills he swallowed. He didn't fall asleep as quickly as he wanted, but he had to resist taking more, knowing that Gibb could bang on his door at any time.

The suddenness of the collar of his shirt being pulled jerked Eddie's head backward and shocked him out of his drug-induced sleep. He felt himself being pulled out of bed and dumped onto the floor. He threw a few wild punches, but all he hit was Gibb's arms. He found himself staring into bloodshot eyes that were no more than a few inches from his.

"What do you think you're doing?" Eddie cried.

"Time to move, you little shit."

Eddie felt himself being dragged to his feet and slapped across his face. "Move where?"

"You know where. Get your car keys."

Eddie dug into his pocket and held them up. "Now what?"

This earned him another slap, an eye-watering thump. He staggered back and fell on the bed, gazing up at Gibb while holding his stinging cheek.

"What's all the rough treatment for?"

"We're going to get those drugs now. I've got a punter for them, so get your arse moving."

"And if I refuse?"

"Then I'll fucking kill you."

"Do that and you'll never get them."

"A smart little arse, eh? I'm not stupid enough to end your stupid miserable life without finding out where the drugs are first, and by the time I'm finished with you, you'll be glad to tell me."

Eddie noticed an opportunity. He knew if it failed, he was as good as dead. Gibb was standing over him with his legs apart. Luckily Scar Face never saw it coming. Eddie shot his foot up as fast as he could, striking Gibb's crotch. Gibb screamed and buckled over onto the floor. Eddie ran into the kitchen drawer and grabbed a knife. He then rushed back in and stabbed it into the back of Scar Face's neck. He felt the point of the blade snap through Gibb's spine below his skull. When he extracted it a gush of blood followed with the power of a garden hose. Eddie's face was in direct line with the stream, and he was blinded by it.

He dropped the knife and wiped the blood out of his eyes. He was horrified at the amount of it on his arms and chest. The carpet was drenched; he could feel it squelch under his feet. Another unplanned killing, another body to get rid of. Bloody hell, what could be done about all this mess? More panic struck him when he noticed Gibb was still wearing the ankle bracelet. Was this an oversight, or was it Gibb's way of getting Eddie nabbed by the police, since Gibb knew that when he left the flat, he would get traced?

More blood started to seep from Gibb's ankles when Eddie hacked at the bracelet. Normally the sight of blood excited him, but now he felt sick. Even the bracelet was soaked in it. Before, he'd been willing Nancy and her lover to arrive, now it was the last thing he wanted to happen.

Gibb's feet dragged the hallway carpet along with them when Eddie pulled him into the toilet; then the carpet got stuck on the toilet door. He dropped the body. Letting the head thump on the floor and landing a good hard kick to Scar Face's ribs seemed to ease his stress. Gibb, Eddie estimated, must be about fifteen stone. How the fuck was he, with his eight-stone clerk's body, going to get him into the bathtub? He decided to delimb the corpse and then decapitate it. It should be a lot lighter. He wasn't too bothered about the toilet floor. It was laminated and should be easy to clean.

Before he got started, he searched in Gibb's pockets for the magazine for the pistol and began to panic more when he failed to find it. He remembered how confident Gibb had been saying the police wouldn't find it. From under the kitchen sink, where he had hidden the tools and the bin bags, he pulled out the wood saw and the hacksaw and noticed he had failed to clean the gore and bone fragments from the teeth. How could he have overlooked such a thing? he wondered as he approached Gibb's corpse. It was at that moment that it dawned on him that he still had the key to Gibb's flat. It was in the first pocket he dug his hands into. Things were starting to look good. Making sure that the corridor was clear, he darted into Gibb's flat. If the police had done a search in Gibb's flat, Gibb would have been landed right in it; it took Eddie only five minutes to find the magazine inside a pair of old trainers. How stupid could he have been? That was one of the first places an expert would look. Another check of the corridor and he was soon looking down at the scar on Gibb's corpse, wondering who could have done that to him. Determined not to separate the magazine from the pistol, he rammed it into the handle.

By the time he got to Gibb's other leg, he had to change the saw. It was taking too long to get through the thicker bones. He discovered that unlike with the witch, he had to elevate Gibb's heavier body to successful saw all the way though. He did this by hefting the torso over the side of the bath and using a chair to support the legs. To avoid slipping on the bloody floor, he spread towels over it. As long as Gibb's ankle bracelet was still in the flats, he guessed the police wouldn't pay a visit for a few days, giving him time to get rid of the remains. The last of the black bin liners had been used, but he still had Gibb's entrails lying on the bottom of the bath. He decided that some parts of the body wouldn't be as wet as others, like the pieces of limbs. Up to this point he had tripled the bags against leakage. Now he peeled off the third bag from the ones where he thought it wasn't necessary.

When the last bag got dumped into the bath, he showered and got dressed. The job of cleaning up would have to wait. Time to eat, he decided. He locked the doors on it all and headed for a restaurant.

"What's going on out there?" Nancy asked, attempting to get up off the pillow.

"Nothing to worry about," Barton said.

"What do you mean, nothing to worry about?" she said. "I heard an ambulance outside, and the next I heard was footsteps running up the stairs. What's going on, Richard?"

"It's Brenda's sister. Something went wrong with her."

"What?"

"I'm not sure. It seems she was on medication and may have taken an overdose."

"I need the toilet. Will it be OK for us to go there?"

"If you can hold on for a few minutes, they're about to carry her down to the ambulance."

This, he knew, wasn't going to happen soon. After the paramedics had arrived, the police had knocked on the door. They had asked him and Brenda a lot of questions, finishing their investigation with the other guests. They'd still been searching about when he entered the room Nancy was in, and he didn't want them to see her being assisted about, looking obviously injured. He opened the room door a crack and saw Brenda talking to a suited man. Barton could tell he was police. He was saying something about an autopsy, and Barton saw Brenda nod. She walked the detective to the door and headed up the stairs. Barton stepped out to meet her, closing the door behind him.

"What's happening?"

"The police seem happy it was an overdose."

He felt the tension slip from his body, and with a deep sigh, he said, "Thanks for not getting me involved."

She smiled up at him and reached her hand out, running her fingers over his designer stubble. "But you are involved. You involved when we made love in my lounge."

He took her hand away from his face and edged closer to her. Their lips brushed softly, and he quietly said, "I don't mind being involved with you," deep down thinking, *Do I have a choice? It's a clever way of blackmailing me; it'll be fun playing along with her.*

"We need to be careful," he said, pointing his thumb at the room Nancy was sleeping in.

She was a handsome woman, just a few inches short of himself, with wide-set, startlingly blue eyes and shoulder-length wavy brown hair. The one difference he noticed between her and her twin sister was that Brenda had a fuller breast.

"How long have you two been together?" she asked, leaning her head on his shoulder.

"Just a couple of weeks."

"So, it can't be anything too serious?"

"I'm not too sure about that. I find her attractive," he said, but his mind wasn't on this conversation. He was wondering what kind of woman Brenda must be. Her twin sister had just been lifted away in a body bag to the morgue, and he was getting the impression that Brenda wasn't the grieving sister she'd first appeared to be. He eased himself away from her, but she pulled him back. He didn't resist.

She tightened her arm around his and said, "We could run this business together. I need a man about this place. Things are looking good. Getting plenty of guests in all the year round. We could have a good life together."

"That sounds cosy." He smiled and eased his arm away. "You'll have to give me time to get a few things sorted, and it wouldn't look good, me moving in so soon after your sister's untimely death."

"Who's going to notice?" she said, shrugging her shoulders.

He took two steps up the stairs, turned, and looked down at her. "The police, for a start."

Nancy was sitting on the edge of the bed when he walked in. "Nice to see you up," he said.

She attempted to get onto her feet, but the effort caused too much pain, and she fell back down. "I need the toilet, or I'll wet this bed."

He eased her arm over his shoulder and lifted her onto her feet. It was no easy task, descending the stairs one step at a time. At the first landing, Brenda appeared and rushed up to help. Barton left them at the toilet door as Brenda slammed it on his face. Soon the door opened again, and they struggled out.

"I need to go out for a while," he said. "Could she sit in your lounge till I get back?"

Brenda smiled. "Of course she can. That's what it there for."

Nancy gave him a sidelong glance. "How long are you going to be this time?"

He heard her question but went out the door without giving an answer. He didn't have one to offer. After the stale air in that big house, the air outside was so cool and refreshing to breathe. He felt giddy for a moment. The cocaine was still safely packed under the passenger's seat. He soon got on his way, glad to be away from that place. Marlin was pushing her baby's buggy up the driveway when he pulled up at the kerb.

"Been out, have you?"

She smiled. "Doing a little shopping. Have you had a busy night?"

Barton nearly choked at the irony of her question. He smiled. "You could say that." He lifted the buggy up the steps with her, and the little chap inside giggled up at him. "He's in a good mood today." He smiled down at the child.

"Maybe he's glad to see you."

"I hope so. He's going to have to get used to me." He lifted the infant out the buggy and was thanked with a whack on his nose with a plastic toy.

She turned away, giggling to herself. "Sorry about that," she managed to say.

Barton couldn't help but join in with her laughter. "That's a fine welcome. I wonder what would have happened if he *hadn't* been pleased to see me."

As they sat in her kitchen drinking black coffee, because she'd forgotten to get milk, she was telling him about her parents and what they'd done during her visit. When she was finished, the crunch came.

"What did you get up to?"

Keep it simple and easy to remember was the first thought that came to mind. "Nothing much. Just a little business here and there."

"I don't mean to hassle you, Richard, but if we are to live together, I would like to know what business you're into. You don't need to go into details. Just give me a rough Idea, in case one of my friends ask."

Keep it simple, son. Keep it simple. "I organise security jobs; I'm involved in training people for them."

She smiled and nodded. "That's good enough for me. Explains why you have to go out at night."

He reached his hand across the table and placed it on top of hers. "I don't need to go out tonight."

Eddie regretted having decided to go to the nearest cafe. He had ordered fish and chips. The fish was dried up inside the batter, and the chips were almost cold. Afterward, he drove around the town to pass the time, being reluctant to go back and face Gibb's remains. He always found it easy to think while driving. He couldn't divert his thoughts away from Nancy, wondering where she could be, what was she doing, whether she had feelings for that big ape. He patted his jacket pocket for reassurance from the pistol tucked in there. He'd soon put an end to that big stranger. There was always a chance that he might just see him driving about with her sitting beside him. Eddie felt sure he could identify his car. After an hour, he gave up and decided to pull into the car park where he'd once worked and see what Debra was up to. Maybe he'd get lucky and see her and Chambers together again. He checked the time. She would be finishing off her day's work and would soon rush out to her vehicle to beat the rush hour traffic.

Dead on time, Debra came trotting out with an armful of papers. She threw the documents in the rear seats and jumped in behind the wheel. Soon she drove out onto the main street. Eddie gave her a few minutes and then followed. *You're a lucky girl, Debra. If I hadn't so many things to clear up, this would have been your last day on this planet.* He revelled in the thought of catching her and Chambers together one day soon. He patted his pocket and felt the solid weight of the pistol. *A job for you.*

Reluctantly, he turned off the main drag and headed for home. He tried to get into his thinking mode but couldn't come up with a safe way to get rid of Gibb's dissected body. He was overcome with relief to see Nancy's car still parked in the same place. He pulled into his usual space—didn't want any of his neighbouring creeps wondering why he had changed. The last thing he wanted was attention.

The parents of one for the girls he had murdered in Scotland was on television appealing to the public for any information of her whereabouts. He was slouched back on the sofa with his feet up, drinking from a beer can that had sat open for a week. His eyes lit up when he saw the couple, and he jumped to his feet and did a silly dance, turning the volume up. They went on to say that their daughter and her friend had left to go to a concert in Scotland and hadn't returned home. Now that his spirits had been lifted and things were not looking as bad as they'd seemed, an idea occurred to him that made him feel even better: smaller plastic bags, the type used in shopping. He could wrap the body parts in foil and place them in the shopping bags, not too much at a time. Then he could carry them out to his car, just one bag a day. That shouldn't arouse suspicion if he did this at different times. The big question was, how much foil and how many bags would it take?

He returned to his position on the sofa, A female reporter was reading from a script handed to her about the killings in Sandbach services, saying that the police thought it was gang related. He sprung up and turned the television off, punching the air and doing another dance.

"I just can't do anything wrong," he shouted at the telly. He was singing "Too clever for them" as he entered the toilet and almost slipped on the body sludge on the floor. He lifted out the top black bag and tried to judge how much foil in would take to wrap up the contents. Would it arouse suspicion going into a shop and buying so much? Another thought struck him: would he have time to get it all cleared out of the flat before it started to smell and the neighbours started to wonder where the odour was coming from?

The Asian woman behind to counter smiled as he dropped twelve packs of foil in front of her. "You do much cook today?" she asked in a heavily accented voice.

Eddie returned her smile and nodded. "Could you give me a dozen of your carrier bags please?"

"Maybe I sell you a box filled," she suggested, still holding her smile.

"That will be great," he replied as she bent over and hefted the box onto the counter. He had driven all the way to the outskirts of the city as a precaution.

As he waited at a set of traffic lights, his thoughts drifted to that ankle bracelet Gibb had worn, and it dawned on him that Scar Face would have been able to get out at certain times of the day. That would be the perfect time to dump it somewhere. He went on to wonder if it could be traced under water and decided to take the chance if he could find a place in the canal deep enough without having to hire a boat. Nancy's car hadn't been moved, and he was pleased with that. He sniffed around the rear of it but couldn't smell anything. Maybe the plastic bags concealed it. But he was getting concerned that if she didn't turn up soon and drive it away, he would have to do it.

Pulling on Nancy's rubber gloves, he opened the first bag without removing it from the bath so as to avoid further mess. Piece by piece, he wrapped the contents in the foil and put the packages into one of the shopping bags. After checking that there were no drips, he carried the bag down to his car and dumped it into the boot. This was going to take forever at one bag a day, so tomorrow it would have to be two bags, and so on. The first place that came to mind for dumping the bags was the Manchester Ship Canal. It was the nearest, and it was deep enough. His main fear was whether he would be able to find some stones or rocks in the dark to put inside the bags to make sure that air inside them didn't cause them to float. He thought about making holes in the bags, but drips from them might land on the canal banks, and dogs might sniff at them and alert their owners.

He switched off his light before driving into the car park; he didn't want the neighbours coming to their windows to see who was driving in at two in the morning. Before he got out, he made sure the interior light didn't come on when he opened the car door. Keeping to the shadows, he made his way inside.

There was no need for sleeping pills. He got in, had a quick wash, and lay out on the sofa. The sun woke him the next morning, shining through the window directly into his eyes. He felt as if he had just slept for a minute. Black coffee was all he had for breakfast. He couldn't face cooking anything. His body ached from the heavy work of cutting the bodies up and carrying them. It had been a long and wet trudge along the canal bank from where he'd parked. He estimated that he would have to do another ten trips before he had gotten rid of the remains. The urgency was the tag and how frequently the police made their checks. The more he thought about this, the more he began to panic. He didn't want to panic; that was when mistakes were made. Before he could get rid of the bracelet, he would have to dump the body parts. That would mean carrying two or three grocery bags at a time, and he'd need to carry the last lot out during the day and include Gibb's ankle bracelet.

"Where are you, Nancy?" He shouted when he had loaded his dirty clothes into the washing machine and couldn't work out the correct setting. After a few tries, he gave up, slammed the machine door shut, and strutted into the living room, dumping himself down on the sofa. He turned the television on more for company than to watch. His adrenaline was in overdrive, and he couldn't settle. He was soon back on his feet, knowing now that time wasn't on his side.

The toilet was beginning to smell of human excretion. He stripped off all his clothes and started to cut the body parts into smaller pieces. The smell was getting stronger with every bag he opened. He didn't have much in his stomach, but he still retched a few times before he had finally wrapped the last piece—Gibb's head—in the foil. He opened the toilet window and let the fresh air blow on his face. The shock came when he went to open the kitchen window and saw a convoy of police cars charging into the car park. He jumped back out of sight, ran to his front door, and locked it. He hid in Nancy's bedroom and squeezed himself into the built-in wardrobe, crouching down and pulling all her clothes over him. He listened for the inevitable banging on the door.

Junior was up before them, his wailing disturbing the peace of the morning. Marlin swung her legs off the bed, wrapping the duvet around herself and leaving Barton lying naked. He grabbed a corner and pulled it back. Laughing, they started a tug of war, and in the end, he let her win.

By the time he got up and dressed, she had the child fed, washed, and changed. "What plans do you have for today?" he asked.

She placed the baby in its pen. "I've arranged to meet some friends for lunch."

"I'll get out before you leave."

"You don't have to. You have a key; you can come and go as you please. This is your home now, if you want."

"You know that's what I want."

"Do you want some breakfast?"

He nodded and followed her into the kitchen. "Just a cup of tea and a slice of toast," he said and sat down at the table.

His phone sounded as he kissed her at the door. He left her standing there, waving, as he got into his car. He held his phone tightly to his ear so she couldn't hear what was being said. Billy was shouting at him.

"Are you any closer to finding that bastard who killed my daughter?"

Barton managed to edge a few words in. "I'm getting there."

"A little bird informs me that the police have a suspect and are watching him. You get in there first, or I want my money back."

"Did your little bird tell you who the suspect is?"

"Not until the coppers are sure they have the right man."

"Not even a little hint?"

"Not yet," Billy replied after having a few words with someone in the background. "Any sign of that missing cocaine?"

"As I told you, when I went back to get it, the police were all over the place, so I legged it out of there. The next I knew, that guy Crapper and another goon jumped me at my house. They wrecked my place, supposedly searching for your cocaine. I need another place to stay. The coppers will be watching my house."

A long moment of silence followed before Billy came back and said, "Come to the shop. Make it look like you're putting a bet on. I'll leave the keys to my daughter's house with big Gunther behind the counter."

"Thanks," Barton replied. "The moment you hear who that suspect is, let me know."

Nancy was sitting at the breakfast table talking to another guest. They eyed him as he entered. It was obvious she was still in pain by the expression she showed. He lifted a chair and placed it next to her.

"How are you feeling this morning?" he asked, the seat creaking in protest.

"Still very sore. Brenda and this gentleman helped me down the stairs." She glanced at the overnervy little man sitting opposite.

Barton spared him a glance and a grimace and then clasped his hand over Nancy's. "I've got a place for us to stay for a while." He couldn't decide what the look she gave him meant. He had hoped she would be pleased, but she was she wasn't showing it. "We can go and pick up the keys today and move in."

"I would like to get a change of clothes. I feel dirty. Haven't changed my underwear for three days."

The little man cleared his throat and stood up, his face glowing with embarrassment. "If you'll excuse me, I'll get on my way." He hastily left the room, closing the door.

"Nor have you been able to wipe your arse," Barton added.

"That's not funny." She withdrew he hand.

"Give me your sizes, and I'll get you some new stuff."

"You're going to look a right fanny buying woman's underwear."

"I could ask Brenda to come and pick it for you."

"Ask Brenda what?" Brenda interrupted carrying a mug of tea to a guest sitting at another table. When she had delivered the mug, she came over and repeated herself. "Ask me what?"

"Nancy hadn't time to pick up her suitcase, and she wants some clean underwear. I was wondering if you could come along with me and help pick some for her."

"Please, if you don't mind," Nancy said.

Brenda laughed. "Why? Are you too shy?" She slapped Barton on the shoulder.

Barton smiled back at her. "No, it's not a thing I do often. I wouldn't know what to look for."

"A big boy like you doesn't know what a pair of ladies' knickers look like?" Brenda continued laughing. "I've a few things to do first, but then I'll come with you." She headed back to her kitchen grinning and shaking her head.

"Do you need the toilet?" he asked Nancy, putting his arm around her shoulders.

"I'm fine," she said. "If you could help me into the lounge, though, I'll watch the telly while you two are out."

All he needed to do was help her off the chair, and she managed to drag herself into the lounge. But she needed help to sit down on the sofa.

"That's an improvement sant," he said, grinning.

All she did in response was nod and pick up the remote. She scrolled through the channels, avoiding looking at him. He got the feeling she wasn't too happy with him. He understood why she would be upset about the battle at his house if she wasn't used to that kind of thing. How could he make her understand that it was for her benefit? The cash he could get for the bags of cocaine would get them a decent deposit on a mortgage.

His phone sounded, and Brenda walked in at the same time. He pointed to his mobile and put it to his ear. She nodded back, and he walked out to the hallway. Billy's name showed up on the screen.

"Hi, what's wrong?" he said before Billy got a word in.

"What's wrong, he asked," Billy shouted. "I'll tell you what's wrong. The fucking law's after you. They found your prints on a piece of gnome that was used to smash Crapper's head in, and it's your name is on the rent agreement on that house. You're their number one suspect. How do you intend to get that sorted out?"

"I thought they were burglars, so I tried to defend myself and my property. I didn't mean to kill him."

"And you think the police are going to swallow that? You fled the scene of the crime, according to my informer."

"You weren't expecting me to hang around to answer their questions, were you?"

Billy did his usual trick when faced with a question he had no answer for and cut the connection. Barton tucked his phone back in his pocket and pushed open the door. Brenda joined him. She wanted to use her car, and Barton was glad of that, in case the police had his registration number.

"Where are we going?" he asked.

She started her car up and smiled at him. "I know a nice little shop that stocks what you're after."

"Not too expensive, I hope?"

"It won't cost you anything."

"Where is it?"

"It's right here." She placed her hand on her crotch and drove off.

CHAPTER 31

Eddie had no idea how long he had been crouched in the wardrobe. If the police had banged on his door, he'd never heard them. He pushed the door open a crack. The bedroom was in darkness. Had he fallen asleep? It had been late afternoon when he'd crawled in here. When he tried to get up, pain engulfed his entire body. He wanted to scream but thought better of it. The police could still be in the building. On his hands and knees, he crawled over to Nancy's bed and, using it for support, lifted himself onto his feet. His legs were like jelly as he made his way to the kitchen. He had to grope in the dark, not daring to put the lights on.

The police cars were gone; only the resident's vehicles remained, the dim light from the only lamp standard reflecting off the metal bodies. He moved closer to the open window and could see no signs of life. He gazed intently into the shadows behind the cars. This brought on a flashback to when he'd observed the big stranger prowling in that area.

Surely Nancy wouldn't leave him for a big ape like that.

The stench from the toilet was getting stronger as he passed the open door, heading back to the bedroom. Earlier in the wardrobe, before he must have dozed off, an idea had come to him, and now he decided to carry it through. Who would suspect anything wrong with a woman carrying grocery bags to a car?

The shortest of Nancy's skirts hung well past his knees, but that didn't bother him. What did, though, was her brassiere. She was ample breasted and broader in the back than he was. After numerous attempts, he finally solved the problem, padding it with the spare bin liners. Putting on some makeup took a bit of practice. Then came the big worry: his hair was short, and Nancy had never had a spare piece like he had noticed on one of his victims. He found a head scarf stuffed in the pocket of one of her jackets. He grinned and held it to the light, thinking, *You'll do just fine.* He wrapped it around his head and admired his work in the mirror, smiling. *Hope one of those perverts who live in this block of flats don't try to rape me.* He patted his pocket feeling the pistol. *They'll be in for shock if they do.*

He was still giggling to himself when he lifted two shopping bags out of the bath. He held them aloft to make sure there were no drips falling from them. He made a final check out the kitchen window to check there was no one hanging about in the car park, and then off he went carrying a bag in each hand.

This was a longer drive, but it would be worth it. It also meant a long walk to the banks of the River Ribble over some marshy ground. He knew this area well from his childhood. He'd often come there looking for mushrooms. He knew the deepest points where the tide was strongest. He had no problems finding his way under a full moon, and the sides of the river were laden with huge pebbles, which he scooped into the bags on top of the body parts.

Turning off his lights, he quietly drove back to his parking place and bounded up the stairs to his flat. As he was about to turn the key in the door, a gaggle of female laughter burst from the flat at the end of the corridor. He remembered the same giggling from the last time he saw girls enter. This time, they were leaving. Before he entered his flat, he took a mental picture of the three girls, deciding that the next time they showed up here, he would follow them to their homes and find where they worked (if they did work) and where they socialised. Then he'd make himself familiar to them. He might even get to join them at their parties.

He lay down on Nancy's bed. He could still smell her perfume on the pillows. Sleep didn't come. His mind was on the three girls and how he could separate them. They were lovely creatures. One was a little overweight but still beautiful. He reached for the sleeping pills, and his mind turned to the bags of body parts in his bath. He pressed one pill out of the card and put it on his tongue. The ankle bracelet was still a problem. He'd have to dispose of it during the daytime. Anther pill accompanied the first. He'd go to the canal again, but in a different place. Could he risk putting it into one of the bags? He took pill number three and then, to finish off, another, downing them without a drink.

At first it seemed like a bright beam was burning into his eyes, penetrating his closed lids like a blinding pink sheet. He rolled over, but still the light shone at him. He blinked quickly and finally opened his eyes. It was daylight. The sun was beaming directly through the window and into his face. When he turned, it reflected off the dressing table mirror. He sprang out of the bed. His head started spinning, and he had to sit back down on it. The spinning didn't stop, and he thought his body was beginning to float around the room. Panic set in, but he remembered taking the pills and lay back down, hoping it would pass.

It did pass, and so did the hours. When he woke, the room was in darkness. This time, he rose out of the bed slowly. No spinning or floating. The smell hit him, and he brought the contents of his stomach up into the bowl. Then ran out, holding his mouth and gagging all the way. He swallowed down glasses of water, trying to rid himself of the taste in his mouth.

He slumped down on the sofa, weighing his options, and decide he had only two: The first was to risk taking what was left in the bath out at once. The second was to just bugger off and abandon his house. Get lost in another city. Change his identity. He had quite a lot of funds in his account and should be able to pay for false papers if need be. He stood up. *No! Why should I run? Nancy must come back for her belongings, and the big ape will be with her.* He patted his pocket, feeling for the gun, and realised he still had Nancy's clothes on. He was about to go and change but stopped and about- turned. *No*, he decided, *any blood or stains that come from the bags will be on her clothing and cause more confusion for the police.*

At two-hour intervals, he carried two bags to his car, and it was well into the late morning hours when he dumped the last of the bags into the boot. To drive to the canal would take too long, and it would be nearly daylight when he got there—too big a risk of being spotted by early morning dog walkers. As he closed the boot door, he noticed that the wheely bins had been pushed out to the pickup point. He grinned at the outrageous idea that came into his head and decided he might just get away with it if he scattered the remains wide enough. Maybe about every hundred bins, he could drop a bag in and cover it up with the garbage already in there.

As he dropped the last of the ten bags into a bin, a police car pulled up beside him, and the constable wound down the window and asked what he was doing.

"I dropped something in my bin by mistake, and I'm searching for it."

The constable grinned. "Good luck with that, madam," he said and drove off.

Luckily, Eddie hadn't buried the bag too far into the garbage and soon retrieved it. He couldn't leave it in there for them to identify him, even though he was wearing women's clothes. They would soon discover his disguise when they investigated further. That said, he was hoping the body parts would never be discovered but just dumped in the refuse tip and buried.

"It took you both some time to get me new underwear," Nancy complained.

"We didn't know your taste or your size. Had to guess," Brenda said.

Barton held out the shopping bag. "Hope it's to your taste."

"Anything would have done as long as it was clean." Nancy searched in the bag. "Not bad," she commented when she pulled out a pack of pants. "Not too sure about the bras." She held one to her chest. "Cups look small, despite what the label says."

"Do you need help to change?" Brenda asked.

Nancy shook her head and looked at Barton. "Just help me upstairs."

He left her to change and joined Brenda in the lounge. She was seated on the sofa and patted the cushion next to her. He sat on it, and she drew closer and clasped a hand on his knee.

"We could have a good life together," she said.

"I know," he replied. "Give me time to get Nancy settled, and we can get things sorted out. But I must tell you, I've got a job to do. It won't feel right depending on you."

"You won't be depending on me. You'll be doing jobs around the house; you'll be earning your keep. You get Nancy settled, if that's what you want. I'll have to get my sister's funeral sorted out, by which time things will be fine for you to move in."

That won't happen soon, Barton assured himself, remembering how long Billy had to wait to get his daughter's body back. This would give him time to get Nancy moved in and spend some time with Marlin. Maybe by then, the plans in Brenda's head would have changed.

"I'll move Nancy out tomorrow." He smiled at her and put his hand on top of hers that were now on his knee.

She returned his smile, withdrew her hand from his, and pulled his head closer. They kissed hungrily.

He hesitated. "What about your other guests? They might walk in." "They're all away, out for the day."

The worries of Nancy, Marlin, and even the bags of cocaine disappeared from his thoughts as they made love on that sofa. She was wild and hungry, even though they had done it an hour ago in her car. They lay on the sofa, panting and smiling as if the world outside didn't exist. A sudden noise from upstairs disturbed them in their tranquillity, and they both jumped up and scrambled to get dressed. Brenda had only her trousers and pants to pull up and was out the door and rushing up the stairs before Barton had his jeans pulled up and secured. When he walked through the door, Brenda was helping Nancy back into bed.

"What's happened?" he said, rushing over to help.

"I thought I would try to go to the toilet on my own," Nancy replied. "Sorry, I knocked over the lamp, and when I leaned over to pick it up, I took a dizzy turn and fell."

Brenda picked up the fallen lamp and said, "I don't think she's ready to travel."

"I'll be fine," Nancy assured her.

"It's not far, and I'll be careful with her," Barton said.

"Would you like me to come along and help?"

"I wouldn't want to put you to all that trouble when you've a business to run," Nancy said.

"She's right," Barton quickly cut in. The last thing he needed was for Brenda to know where he was planning to stay with Nancy. "You stay and look after your guests, and as soon as I get her settled, I'll come back and pay the bill. Or if you prefer, I'll pay you now."

She turned on him with a sharp expression, eyes narrowed, and was about to snap at him but changed her mind and let the tension slump from her body. She could see what he was up to but let it go for now.

"If that's what you want, you can come back tomorrow and pay the bill."

"That's fine," he said. "I need to get some work done, so I'll be back at breakfast time to pick her up."

Brenda followed him down the stairs and gripped his elbow as he was about to open the door. "Get back here as soon as you drop her off."

He kissed her lightly on the lips, ignoring her threatening attitude. "I wouldn't miss the opportunity you have offered me for the world."

"You'd better not. A phone call to the police is all it would take to make them look more closely at my sister's autopsy."

Halfway out the door, Barton grinned at her. "That's no way to start our future together."

He was glad to be outside and breathing fresh air. In his car, he called Marlin, and as usual, her enthusiastic response to him pricked at his conscience. She wanted to know where he was and when he would be home.

"I'll be with you soon, honey," he said.

"Give me a time, and I'll make us something to eat."

"I'll be on my way in a few minutes."

As he was about to start his car, his phone sounded, and Billy's name showed up.

"Hi, Billy. To what do I owe the honour of this call?"

"A little bird tells me the coppers have a suspect for my Amanda's murder. Make sure you get him here before they decide to make an arrest."

"Did your little bird tell you where I can get my hands on this suspect?"

Billy read the address out to him and cut the call. Barton didn't even have time to get his pen out of his pocket, never mind write the address down. Fortunately, he remembered, because he had visited the street before when he had been to see Don Kilby. He started to wonder if it could be Don who was the suspect. Surely not. He was a nasty little man who specialised in selling dodgy mobile phones. He wasn't big enough to tackle Billy's daughter. She was a big, healthy fitness fanatic. Don was small and unfit, smoked like a burning tyre, and was a boozer of cheap wine.

"Who is it?" came a squeaky voice from the other side of the door.

"It's me. Barton."

"What do you want?"

"Just a couple of words with you Don."

"What about?" he asked and opened the door.

"I heard the coppers hauled you in about that murder a few weeks ago in the park."

"What's that got to do with you?"

"Nothing. I heard they were watching you, that you were a prime suspect."

"Well, I'm not anymore. They let me go, couldn't prove anything. I had an alibi that checked out."

"A gentleman I know wants to buy a lot of mobiles. I recommended you." Barton noticed his ears prick up and his little eyes widened.

"What gentleman?" Don gave him a brown-toothed grin.

"If you come with me, I'll introduce you."

"How many phones does he want?"

Barton shrugged his shoulders. "I don't know. You'll have to ask him."

Don stepped back, closing the door at the same time. "Something doesn't sound right. Why would somebody want to buy a lot of old mobiles?"

Barton put his foot in the door, grabbed his collar, and dragged him out. Don started screaming and received a punch to the mouth. He fell at Barton's feet and got dragged and dumped into the boot of Barton's car.

Before pulling away, Barton phoned Billy and arranged to meet him at the old building again. He was having difficulty hearing what Billy was saying for the noise Don started making in the boot. He jumped out, opened the boot, and landed a few more punches to Don's head. That soon shut him up.

The same two goons came out the door of the old building. Barton lifted the boot and watched them carry Don's limp body through the door. Billy came striding out as they passed. He said a few words and then approached Barton.

"Did he say anything?" Billy asked.

Barton shook his head. "Said he had an alibi that checked out."

"Well, a good kicking won't do him any harm, and it'll send out the message not to mess with me." He turned to walk away, stopped, and shot Barton a sharp look. "Any sign of that missing cocaine?"

Barton shrugged his shoulders and shook his head and watched Billy return to the building.

Back in his car, he called Marlin. She sounded disappointed he hadn't arrived at her home.

"I'm so sorry," he said. "One of my trainees had an accident, and I had to take him to hospital."

A long silence followed before she replied saying she was about to make something to eat.

"I'll be there in under half an hour."

"Just in time," she announced and threw her arms around his neck. "I was getting worried you'd be held up again. I've made us something special. Took ages to prepare."

Barton grinned and sniffed. "Mm! It smells delicious. If it tastes as good as it smells, I'll marry you tonight."

He followed her into the kitchen, both of them laughing at his comment and as he sat down at the table. He regretted saying it while at the same time wishing it could happen. She was a lovely woman and a lovely person, far too good for him. He cursed himself for developing a fondness for her baby. He soon scoffed down the food she had prepared. He hadn't realised how hungry he'd been. He could feel her watching him getting stuck into the meal. *This is the life I wish I could have,* he caught himself thinking when they sat on the sofa with mugs of coffee. She had recorded a film and got it going as they sat back, arms around each other, to watch it. The baby disturbed the moment.

"Sorry about that," she said. She made to get up but felt his hand holding her back.

"I'll go and see want he wants." Before she could protest, he was on his feet sanding heading for the child's room. The youngster was crying but stopped when Barton turned the light on. "What is it baby?" he said. The child grinned up at him, and Barton could see the start of a tooth coming though. He picked the baby up and walked back into the living room. "I think he's having trouble with his mouth."

Marlin reached into a baby bag she kept under the pram and held him a tube of paste. "Rub this on his gums."

Barton got his finger bitten with the new tooth. "I think he's trying it out," he said, smiling, and held his finger up.

She laughed. "Sorry. I meant to warn you." She got up and took the child from him and returned him to his room.

Sitting on the sofa alone with his thoughts, Barton wondered whether he could really settle down to this kind of life. A part of him was saying yes until the memory of his past came to the fore and the light at the end of the tunnel flickered and died. How could he tell her without hurting her, maybe even destroying her? She had been hurt enough, first by thinking her husband had left her for another woman and then by discovering it was for another man. Then she'd gotten the text message about his suicide. What would she do if she discovered he had been partly responsible his death?

CHAPTER 32

Nancy's car still hadn't been moved, and he was glad of that. It meant she hadn't turned up for her belongings while he was out. But he still had one more job to do, and it was the riskiest one. The ankle bracelet had to be moved to an area where the police were likely to think that Gibb was out shopping or doing some other vital errand, but it still had to be difficult to find. His first thought of lobbing it into the canal was no good. The law would come out there looking for him, wanting to know why he was so far away from his home. Putting it into one of the wheely bins would be stupid. They would come looking for him there and then start a search, and the chance that they would dig up some of the body parts was too big a risk. He would have to dump it somewhere else, a place where Gibb might dump it before absconding.

The smell hit him the moment he stepped inside. He wished he had made a better job of cleaning up. *Disinfectant,* he thought. *Nancy must have some in one of the cupboards.* He found three different kinds plus an array of air fresheners. He used a whole container scrubbing out the bath and splashed half of another over the floor, spreading it with a mop. He almost choked himself with air freshener spraying it all around the flat. The final idea came to him as he sat on the sofa watching the television. The scene he was watching was of a highspeed bullet train. It was from a documentary he had little interest in, but it gave birth to the idea, and he complimented himself on the thought. After a final sniff around the flat, he dashed out and down to his car still wearing Nancy's clothes with the ankle bracelet in his pocket.

After a half-hour drive, he arrived at the station, bought a ticket, and boarded. He got off at Preston, leaving the ankle bracelet under the seat. He stood on the platform and waved the train goodbye, acting like a few others standing close by. The return train wasn't due for another hour, so he decided to head for the nearest cafe. He had been walking for quite a ways before he found a restaurant that didn't look too expensive. On his way, he had bought a newspaper. This was not one of his habits, but he decided to read it to pass the time while also hiding his identity. By the looks he'd been getting on the train, he could tell he didn't look much like a woman, with his short-cropped red hair. He had forgotten the headscarf. The last thing he needed was to be distinguishable. He continued reading his paper on the return journey. The carriage was almost empty, and he'd chosen to sit as far away from the other passengers as possible. He studied the situation-vacant section on the page before the sports column, and one job drew his attention, a job he knew he could handle and, with his qualifications and experience, was certain to get it. He punched the number into his mobile and got an interview for the next day. Behind the newspaper, a broad grin spread across his face. There must be scores of girls working there, he though. Maybe a few young men and, to change his modus operandi, a few mature men.

It dawned on him after he had got into his flat and sat down to watch television that he hadn't checked if Nancy's car was still parked in the same place. His mind had been so full of the job interview the next morning that he'd paid no attention to the things he considered a priority. Her car wasn't visible from the kitchen window, so he decided he would have to go down and check. As he got to his feet, a news flash came on the television. He hadn't picked up what had been reported, nor was he interested. What caught his attention was the prison photo of Gibb. The report said that members of the public should not approach this man, as he could be armed and dangerous. Eddie had a good laugh at that as he headed down to the car park, thinking, *Not anymore, he's not.*

The smell hit him before he approached the vehicle. In a panic, he ran back up to the flat and picked up her keys. He also remembered to scoop up her headscarf, wrapping it around his head as he ran back down the stairs. When he stepped out of the door, he stopped in his tracks. Two of the residents were standing close to Nancy's car and seemed to be having a conversation about the vehicle, given the way they were gazing at it and pointing. Eddie was about to dart back inside when he noticed one of them looking in his direction. Left with no other choice, he strolled towards Nancy's car and strode past them, trying to ignore them as he got inside. The strength of the odour made him gag, and he swiftly operated to window switch before starting the engine up.

One of the men stepped over—a dirty little man with greasy hair. "What's that smell?" he shouted.

Eddie grinned. "Rotten eggs. Forgot about them. On my way to get it cleaned up." *Or your nose is too near your arse,* he thought but dared not say. Without waiting for a reaction, he slipped the car into gear and pulled away. Through his rear-view mirror, he saw the two men make their way into the building, still discussing the smell, it seemed from the gestures they were making. He drove through the town centre, with all the widows open, wondering whether to dump the car or lob the bags out somewhere in the countryside, doing the same as he had with the other remains and scattering them about a mile apart from each other.

He had clocked up seventy miles of country lanes before he tossed the last bin bag into a pond. The stench hadn't diminished when he returned to the car, and he kept the windows open all the way back.

The air fresheners and disinfectant, he hadn't used in the flat might get rid of it. He packed the containers and air fresheners in one of the remaining shopping bags and bounded down the stairs. The acrid smell of human remains had almost gone but was now replaced by the eye-stinging, breath-catching odours of disinfectant and the fumes from the spray cans.

He sat in his usual position on the sofa with a satisfied grin, commending himself on a job well done. Now he could concentrate on the job interview in the morning. He needed to leave an hour early, giving himself time in case of heavy traffic. With all his qualifications, he was hoping he wouldn't need a reference. After a shower, he got into his own clothes and opened a tin of beans. Too hungry to heat them up, he scarfed them down straight out of the tin. He had placed the pistol on the arm of the sofa and started toying with it, aiming and mock shooting at characters on the television and hoping for Nancy and her big ape of a lover to arrive. He froze when the picture of the girl he had picked up the day Debra's car had gone off the road appeared on the screen. She had been reported missing a few days previous, and her body had been discovered in a wooded area near the village of Whitworth, near Rochdale.

There was no mention of how she had been killed, and he felt slightly disappointed. He wanted his technique to be known to the public, how he'd used different methods and various locations and genders. He wanted to stand out from other serial killers he had read about. He wanted it to be noted how he had outwitted the police for so long. As he lay fully clothed on Nancy's bed with two of her sleeping pills in one hand and the gun in the other, he grinned to himself. Life was looking good for a change. He let the pills drop on the floor. *Won't be needing them tonight. Tonight I'll sleep well.*

Brenda was helping Nancy down the stairs when he entered through the front door. Barton bounded up and took over, and Brenda skipped down and held the door for them. She caught Barton's eye as he passed. She didn't need to say a word; he knew what that look meant. Nancy was moving a lot better and managed to help herself get seated, but he had to fasten her safety belt. When he got in beside her, she turned her head away from him, as though looking out her side window.

"What's the matter now?" he asked, in the process of starting the engine. She gave no response. He wondered if she had heard and was about to repeat himself when she turned on him.

"Do you know that woman?" she demanded.

He slipped the car into gear and moved off. "Not any better than you."

"She seems to know you quite well."

He held his reply as he manoeuvred the car around a roadworks. "I can't understand why. I've only spoken to her in a general manner, nothing personal."

"That's not the impression she gave me."

"Well, I don't know what you two have been talking about, but I can assure you, I don't know her any better than you."

They sat in heavy silence, and he was getting the vibe that she didn't believe him. She didn't betray a hint of curiosity when he pulled up at the bookmaker's shop but instead turned her head back to the window. She was still wearing that stern expression when he stepped out the door and headed towards his car. She was facing him but looking past him. He dumped himself down next to her and slapped his hand on the steering wheel. This got an instant reaction.

"What the fuck's going on inside that head of yours?"

She stared into his eyes and shook her head. "Are you another gambler?"

He grinned and gave her a throaty giggle. "I'm not a gambler. I was in there picking up the keys to that house."

He got out, trotted up the drive, and unlocked the door. She was halfway out of the car by the time he got back. He rushed over and held her while she regained balance.

"I've no idea what this house is like, so I'll sit you down and explore it."

Fortunately, the house was on the ground floor, no stairs to climb to get inside, but there was an upper floor. It seemed the house had been converted into flats and then later sold as a self- contained house. He liked the layout and wondered if Billy might rent it to him on a long-term basis.

"I need the toilet," she said when he returned to the living room. "Get me to the door, and I'll manage the rest myself."

"Will you be wanting a shower or a bath later?" he said, helping her into the toilet.

"Oh yes, please. If you can get me into the shower, I think I can manage."

"Give me a call when you're finished, and I'll come and get you into the shower. I've put fresh linen on the bed, if you want to go there after you're finished. There's a television in the bedroom. I know it's early, but I have to go out and don't know when I'll get back."

He waited in the living room while she tended herself. He got seated on the sofa and turned the television on. The early news was on, and without paying too much attention, he sat there listening for her to call. The figure that came on the screen dressed in prison overalls gave him a jolt. He had seen that name somewhere recently, but at that moment he couldn't think where. He heard Nancy call from the toilet, and that's when it struck home: Raymond Gibb was one of the names on Billy's list. He'd lived next door to Nancy. He jumped up off the sofa and caught her attempting to dress herself. He quickly assisted and got her into the bedroom.

After he had got her settled in the bed and handed her the remote for the television, he said, "That guy who lived next door to you has escaped from the nick. Gibb, his name is. It's on the news. They say he could be armed and dangerous. Did you have anything to do with him—I mean, as a neighbour?"

She deliberately averted her eyes from him, fiddling with the remote and gazing at the screen. "I only saw him once. It was when he was getting lifted by the police, and that was from the kitchen window."

"How about your son? Did he have any dealings with him?"

She turned around and glared at him. "Where's this leading?"

He shook his head. "Nowhere. I just wondered if, being a neighbour, you had spoken to him."

She returned her attention to the screen and shook her head. "Eddie was shit scared of him and avoided him." She pointed the remote and pressed. The television came to life at the news channel. The female presenter was holding up an ankle bracelet, saying that the one found under a seat in a train in Glasgow by a young boy was similar. According to police reports, the wearer had absconded, and members of the public should not approach him. Next, an identity photo came on screen showing a man of about forty with dirty black hair and a distinguish scar that ran from his eye down his cheek to his mouth.

"A nasty-looking fucker." She cowered back. "I've been living next door to that."

Barton stood at the door. "What do you fancy for eating? I'll bring something back with me."

Still gazing at the screen, she shook her head. "You decide."

He slowly shook his head and walked out. He locked the outside door, remembering that Gibb was on the loose and knowing that this would be an ideal place to break into and to get some easy cash.

Brenda beat him to the door and opened it while his hand was still outstretched, reaching for the handle.

"You took your time," she snarled. She turned and strutted up the passage.

"Had things to do," he said, following her into the lounge.

She plopped herself down on the sofa and patted the cushion next to her. "Next time, get back when I tell you."

He didn't sit down beside her. Instead, he walked over, kicked her in the ankle bone, reached out, and grabbed her hair. She screamed at both the pains. His face was an inch from hers.

"Don't fuck with me," he shouted. "You want to phone the cops? You do that, and your days are numbered. I'm from a big organisation that could either grind your business into nothing or explode it to the extent of it becoming a national enterprise. The choice is yours." He released his grip on her hair and pushed her head back against the back of the sofa, at the same time pulling her jeans down and ripping open her blouse. She didn't fight back and embraced his effort, hungrily pulling him into her.

"Hope you're like that all the time," she said with a wide grin, pulling her jeans up and trying to repair her blouse.

"If that's the way you like it, that's the way it will be."

She stood up and brought herself up to his height, standing on her toes. She grasped the collar of his leather jacket with both hands, kissed him hard, and looked into his eyes. "That's the way it better be."

He pushed her and held her at shoulder's length. "I've got work to do. I'll be back when it's finished."

She swiped his arms away. "I told you, you don't need to work."

"I told you, I'm with a big organisation. I've no choice. If I don't do the job, they'll come after me."

"What organisation are you talking about?"

He headed for the door and said, "Trust me, you don't want to know." He closed the door, still seeing the image of her standing there, gazing with her mouth wide open.

He had an inkling that she would be spying on him through her window, so he quickly got the car on the move and pulled into a car park close to the town centre, where he phoned Billy.

"Have you been watching the news?" he said before Billy had a chance to speak.

"What about it?" Billy's voice crackled through the static.

"One of the names on your list has absconded from the law, and there's a nationwide search for him."

"So, what's that got to do with me?"

"Well, I'm thinking that if you're a known associate of Gibb's, the police might want to question you to find out if you know of his whereabouts."

Two or three minutes of silence followed, and Barton was beginning to wonder if they were still connected. Then in the background, he heard a door closing and voices mumbling, but he couldn't make out what was being said.

"Do you think you could find this guy Gibb?" Billy's voice boomed unexpectedly.

"If the police can't find him, what chance have I got?"

"Because you're not restricted to obeying the fucking law. You can break a few bones to get the information. If you need help, give me a call."

Nancy was sitting up in bed engrossed in the television. If she heard him enter, she never acknowledged it.

"You're looking better," he said, leaning over to kiss her head. "I've got some food. Hope you like it." He handed her the bag, but she ignored him, so he left the food on the bed. "I wish I knew what's annoying you."

He sat on the chair close to her, and still she didn't look his way. He jumped up, knocking the chair backwards, and it crashed to the floor. This got her attention. She Jumped and screamed as a bolt of pain shot through the left side of her body. Then she slumped back onto the pillow.

"I hate my life," she whimpered. "It's been nothing but hurt and punishment. My husband was a violent, drunken gambler. Every time he lost, I got the brunt of it, me and the child. No wonder Eddie grew up the way he did."

Barton picked up the chair and instantly thought of the hoodie when she mentioned the name. "I'll make us a brew. We can eat some of that food, and we can talk afterwards." He left her searching through the bag and went into the kitchen. He found tea bags but no milk. "Can you drink tea without milk?" He shouted through to her. When he got no response, he took it as a yes.

He almost dropped the two cups of tea when he turned and saw her standing at the kitchen door. "What do you think you're doing? You should be in bed." He put the cups on the table and reached over to her.

"We need to talk," she said as he eased her down on a chair beside the kitchen table.

"No," he said, "we need to eat first, get your energy back up." He darted out and returned with the bag of food.

They ate in silence and downed it with the tea, which was now cold, with no milk or sugar. Nancy liked her tea sweetened, and she cringed at the taste but drank it down, as the food he had brought was spicy.

"Can we talk now?" she asked.

Barton swallowed the dregs from his cup. "If that's what you want."

"What reason did you have for turning up at the block of flats where we live?"

The question took him by surprise, and he hesitated before replying, not that he had anything to hide about that visit. It was just so unexpected. "Why do you ask?"

She shrugged her shoulders and regretted doing so, wincing in pain. "Richard, I need an answer and an honest one."

Barton was still confused and wondered where her line of questioning was leading. "I came looking for that guy who lives next door to you."

The tension in her face and body seemed to relax, and she smiled and reached her hand across the table onto his.

"What did you think I came to your flats for?"

She smiled. "It's not important now. I just wondered."

It was important enough for you to ask, Barton thought, *but maybe not enough to dwell on*. He got onto his feet and helped her back into the bedroom.

After she got into a comfortable position in the bed, she turned to him and said, "I've become very fond of you, Richard, but at the same time, I'm frightened of you. Maybe it's the kind of life I've lived. I just think that every man has a dark side to him—well, every man I've been involved with."

Barton wasn't listening. His mind had wandered to the conversation he'd had with Billy, and he decided the best place to start looking for Gibb would be at his home. He knew he would have to be careful, since the police would be keeping an eye on the place in case he should return. But the only person he could get any information from was that old witch he lived with.

CHAPTER 33

With a final polish and a dust over, Eddie squeezed his feet into his new shoes and laced them up loosely, hoping they had stopped pinching. He took a last glance in the mirror at his best suit—still fitted perfectly. The creases were razor sharp, thanks to Nancy. The nice, crisp white shirt had been neatly folded in his drawer. He had selected a blue-and-red-striped tie. He almost asked Nancy for her opinion but then remembered she wasn't there. Was that a tear in his eye? Surely not. Just a piece of dust or something on the surface of the mirror. He finished with a final spray of deodorant, the one that she had bought him last Christmas, and remembered he had scorned her for paying so much for it. If she had been here to see him, her heart would have been bursting with pride. He pondered for a moment, wondering if he should call that number, but just as quickly, he dismissed the idea.

The only blemish in the clear blue sky was the vapour trail of a plane high above. The sun reflected off the roofs of the cars. He was feeling good and knew he looked good. He caught the eye of two woman who turned their heads in approval. The attractive black girl stood up from behind her desk at reception. Eddie could only gaze at her. He decided she must be about six feet four and had to crane his neck to look into her eyes.

"I have an appointment with a Mrs Birckenhall. My name is Fisher."

He grinned up at her, and she smiled, exposing a set of pure-white teeth with a large space between the two front ones.

"Come this way, Mr Fisher." She stretched out a long arm in the direction of a long corridor.

He walked beside her along the passageway, feeling dwarfed, his head just above the level of her elbows. All the while, his thoughts were on bringing this beautiful black woman down to his size, one day meeting her on a quiet road and dealing with her in his specialised way. She abruptly stopped and opened a door.

Eddie was slow on the uptake and had to turn and walk back a few steps. She ushered him into a large, plush office. Behind a long desk hung a portrait of an obese man, one of those annoying pictures where the eyes of the subject followed you no matter where you stood. She told him to take a seat in front of the desk, saying that someone would be with him shortly. Eddie hoped so. He couldn't stand those eyes staring at him.

The first to enter was a slim, mature woman with white hair tied up at the back of her head. She was followed by a short, dumpy bald man with bottle-bottom glasses. Next came a tall, gangly gaunt man, who in Eddie estimations would have looked more at home on a farm. After a quick introduction, they got seated. The woman in the middle held out her hand and asked for his qualification certificates. The two men leaned over and studied the papers with the woman.

The bald-headed man said, "In your own words, could you tell us why you left your previous employment with Pritchard Finances?"

All eyes were on him, and he grinned." I didn't leave. I was fired because my car broke down on the motorway and I didn't get to a meeting on time."

They each fired questions at him, and he had all the answers ready. The interview lasted for well over an hour, and he could see they were getting tired of quizzing him. The woman folded her laptop and stood up. She held out her hand and thanked him for his time, as did her two associates, and as usual told him they would be in touch.

On his way past reception, he saw the tall black girl talking to a group of youths. This delighted Eddie, who could imagine bumping them off one at a time over the space of a few months, provided he got the job. The tall black girl broke away from the group and approached him.

"That was a long interview," she said grinning. "A good sign. You could be successful."

He returned her grin. "I hope so, eh! I didn't get your name."

She continued to grin. "I didn't give you my name. If you get the job, I'll give you it."

Eddie pulled into the car park of his old office and parked in his usual place behind the building. In two minutes, Debra would be rushing out the office, heading for the cafe to get lunch. Debra was a creature of habit, and he was hoping that her boss, Chambers, would be accompanying her. If not, he had worked out a plan he knew wouldn't fail. She was on her own. Eddie got out of his car and followed her. She was a smart walker, and he was breathing heavily when he sat opposite her.

"Mr Fisher!" she exclaimed. "This is a surprise. I didn't expect to see you in here again."

Eddie gave her one of his best smiles. "I was driving past and saw you come in. I thought I'd say hello."

"Have you found another job yet?"

He nodded and waved to the waitress. "What are you having?"

"My usual," Debra said. "They know what to bring."

"As a matter of fact, I have found another job. That's what I was hoping to have a word with you about." The waitress arrived, and he ordered a coffee before turning back to Debra. "I know what's going on with you and Chambers," he leaned over the table and said quietly.

Debra jerked back in her seat, her eyes widened. "What do you mean you know what's going on with me and Mr Chambers?"

"He's fucking you."

She jumped up, knocking her food over, and stormed out. On the way, she bumped into the waitress carrying a tray, knocking it from her grip and causing the contents to fall to the floor. Eddie had anticipated this would happen and soon caught up with her. He grabbed her arm and pulled her into an abandoned shop door. He kneed her in the groin, and she buckled over, gasping for breath.

"You tell Chambers that when the company I've applied for a job at contacts him for a reference, he better make it a good one, or his wife and your partner will get to know about your dirty little affair."

He was well on his way to his car before Debra had recovered. When he drove past, a few pedestrians had gathered around the shop door. One man had his hand on her back, and a woman was holding a tissue to Debra's forehead. He grinned but at the same time hoped he hadn't hurt her too much so that she would be fit enough to deliver his message to her boss in time. He was held up at the cursed level crossing. The queue in front consisted, he reckoned, of about fifty vehicles. The gates should have been about to go up. When they did eventually, he had to rouse himself from a momentary doze with the help of a chorus of horns blasting from behind. Cars were coming through from the other side mush faster than the ones he was following. One of the vehicles caught his attention. He was sure he had seen it before. A glance at the driver convinced him he was right. He could never mistake that big ape with his long black hair bunched up at the back and the thick designer stubble. It was the bastard that Nancy had left him for. He almost ran into the car in front of him trying to squint back to see if she was in the car with him. It was a bloody missed opportunity. He cursed as he pulled into his usual parking space at his home block of flats. Nancy's car was in the same place where he had left it. He knew it hadn't been moved, as he had planted an empty match box at the rear offside wheel, and it was still intact. The vision of the big ape sitting snuggly in his car was still with him when he got changed and settled in the living room. If the traffic hadn't been so busy, he could have turned around at the roundabout and followed him. But he was satisfied that he knew they were still in town. Where? It would only be a matter of time before he spotted that car parked somewhere. Until word came back about this new job, he made it his mission to drive around all the streets until he found it.

Barton parked his car a few streets away from the block of flats. He waited for a while until a group of people came past walking in that direction. He made sure they were heading for the front entrance and started walking behind. Nancy's car was in the same position, but two vehicles up from it was another car with two men sitting in the front seats, all eyes. He knew straight away they were the law, but it was too late to turn back. That would only look suspicious to them. Two of the group in front turned to the left, while the others took to the stairs. He chose to follow and got out at the floor where Gibb lived. He made a quick retreat when the female constable came out of Gibb's door.

Jumping down the stairs taking them two at a time, he soon found himself at the main door. Had the glass been still in place instead of the plywood board, he would have seen the two plain-clothed detectives heading in his direction. It was too late to turn back, and he had to brave it out and walk past them, avoiding eye contact. He could feel their eyes on his back, and he quickened his pace slightly.

"Excuse me, sir," a voice came from behind.

Without stopping, Barton looked back to see the two men walking towards him. He stopped and turned. "Can I help you, sirs?" he asked.

They showed their ID cards, and one held up a photo in front of Barton's eyes. "Have you seen this man going about this area?"

Barton stepped closer and studied the photo. "I haven't seen him about here, but wasn't he the one in that picture on the news?"

"That's right, sir," he said putting the photo back in his pocket. "Do you live here, sir?"

"No, just visiting a friend who wasn't at home,"

"Can you tell us what flat your friend lives in?" the other detective stepped forward and asked.

"Can't remember the number, but it's on the fifth floor. Third door on the right."

"Do you come here very often?" the one with the photo asked.

After the barrage of questions was over, Barton briskly walked to his car. He couldn't get away quick enough. Before starting the vehicle, he phoned Marlin, saying he was on his way. She informed him that she was shopping and would get back as soon as she could.

He arrived at Marlin's house a lot later than he had anticipated because of the hold up at the level crossing. She drove her car into the drive as he was unlocking her front door. He left the door open and darted over to help with grocery bags and the baby buggy.

"Have you had a good day, honey?" he asked as he followed her inside.

"Just the usual," she replied with a deep sigh. "You don't seem to keep regular hours where you work."

"The hazards of the job."

After she had attended to her child and put the groceries away, she sat beside him on the sofa, rested her chin on her hand, and gave him a troubled look. "Richard, I don't know how to put this to you, but I'm a bit short of money. That's why I went to London, to see if I could borrow from my parents. They're not very well off and could only give me what they could afford.

He smiled, took her hand away from her chin, already holding the other. He clasped them between his. "Don't worry, sweetheart. I'll sort it all out for you. Just give me your bank account number, and I'll transfer some cash into your account. Why didn't you tell me earlier?"

"I was embarrassed to."

"That's nonsense. I'm living with you; I'm entitled to support you."

The moment she had mentioned money, he'd instantly thought of the drugs hidden in his car. He hadn't checked they were still there the last trip out.

She smiled and threw her arms around him. "You're a life saver." She got up. "What would you like to eat?"

"I'll let you surprise me," he replied and pulled his mobile out his pocket. "I'll transfer some cash over now. Write your details and number down on a piece of paper."

He hated himself for making her believe he could help, when in truth he didn't have any cash in his account. He fumbled about on his phone. She came back from the kitchen, where she kept paper and pens, and handed him her bank details.

He waited until she was out the room and shouted, "I'm having a problem with my account details. I think I've entered the wrong password. I'll need to go to the bank and get it sorted out."

"That's OK," she called back. "I've been having a few problems with my account. Maybe that's the reason."

"I'll go to the bank first thing in the morning," he said walking into the kitchen beside her. She was bent over, sorting out the laundry from the basket. He placed his hand gently on her hips, and she got up, turned, and smiled, still holding dirty baby clothes. "I think I should go and withdraw some cash from the machine until I get the bank problem sorted. How much will you need to tide you over?"

She threw the baby clothes back in the basket. "My mortgage is due. It needs to be paid by tomorrow. That's five hundred. If you can get that, it will be OK for now."

"I'll go and get that now," he said. "But don't rush to make dinner. I have to go into the city first. Got something I must do."

She smiled and nodded. "Give me a call when you're on the way back, and I'll get it started."

Under the driver's seat of his car, the envelope Billy had handed him lay tucked safely under the carpet. He counted out the five hundred and returned it. Next, he checked the bags of cocaine and grinned when they were still safe and intact. Without taking them from under the seat, he felt the seal ties with his fingers. He didn't want the dampness the get in. Marlin waved at him from the window as he pulled away. He returned the gesture and edged into the rush hour traffic. He wished he could have phoned Nancy first, but she hadn't her phone. She had left it behind in their rush to get her into hospital. All he could do until he got there was hope she'd managed to get herself to the toilet.

She was on her way to the toilet when Barton opened the door. She was using the walls of the passageway to support herself. When she tried to turn towards him, she lost her balance and slid to the floor. He eased her back onto her feet, listening to her wincing with pain.

"You're not helping yourself, trying to be independent."

"I'm desperate. Get me there quick before I have an accident."

He helped her into the toilet and left her. "Shout when you're finished or if you need help."

He sat down in the sofa and turned the television to the news channel, hoping to get more information on Gibb. He didn't want to learn that the law had caught up with him. However, either he'd missed the report, or the police were keeping quiet about it. What did come up was the parents of a girl whose body had been found near the village of Whitworth asking for anyone who'd noticed any stranger or vehicles in the area acting suspicious to contact the police. Barton became interested, as he had been brought up there before his parents moved to the city.

The sound of harsh intake of breath from behind made him turn to see Nancy standing at the door. He jumped up, thinking she had hurt herself.

"Why didn't you shout for me to help you?"

"I'm fine," she insisted. "I haven't hurt myself." With his help, he eased herself onto the sofa.

"I thought you had injured yourself," he said, sitting down beside her. He could tell she had had a shock; her face was ashen, and her body trembled. "What's wrong?" He took her hand, feeling it shake in his. He began to wonder how long she had been standing at the door. "Was it that news coverage that shocked you?"

She nodded. "I hate to see that happening to young girls."

"Do you know the girl or maybe her parents? Is that what got you upset like this?"

"No, I just hate to see a young girl murdered like that, a young life ended so quickly."

He had often seen this on the news and noted people's reactions. Some were disgusted, others angry, and others saddened by it. But he'd never observed a reaction like the one Nancy was having unless the victim was family or a close friend.

"It's got to be something more than just seeing another young girl murdered to get you into a state like this."

"I'll be fine in a minute or so. Just let me be."

He didn't want to leave it like that; he could feel there was more to it. One giveaway on her part was that if she was so upset about the girl, why hadn't she shed a tear? He decided to change the subject.

"I was at your home flat today looking for Gibb. The place was crawling with police."

If she had been shocked before, she looked a lot worse now. He got up and walked around the back of the sofa.

"It's OK. Your Eddie wasn't there, and if he had been, there were too many policemen about for him to start something."

"I'm feeling sick. Help me to the toilet," she cried, trying to get up.

This time he had to almost carry her. She trembled so much that he had to squeeze her in his arms to stop her from falling. He stood outside the toilet door listening to her retching. After a while, all went silent. He wondered what she was doing. Not washing herself; he would have been able to hear the water running. The silence continued until he was forced to knock.

"Are you OK in there?"

The door burst open, and she staggered out into his arms. This time he had to pick her up and carry to the bedroom.

"What's the matter with you?" he asked, placing her on top of the bed.

Her head lolled to the side, and her eyes were heavy, the pupils almost disappearing under her top eyelid. Her mouth drooped. He took hold of her chin and turned her head to face him. He knew right away what was wrong. He rushed into the toilet and found two empty pill containers. One, he read, was pain killers; the other, sleeping pills. How many she had swallowed? He had no way of knowing. The only person he could think of to help was Billy, for there was no way he could take her to a hospital. Too many questions would be asked. The one that would cause the most trouble would be, where had he gotten the pills? Billy's recommendation was one he wasn't sure of.

"Pump some salt and water into her," he said.

"What if she drowns or chokes to death?"

"Get a rubber tube, put it down her throat, and pour it in to her. Have a bowl ready, for she will be sick."

Barton could tell by the delays between his answers that Billy was repeating something someone else was saying and guessed his wife, Gail, was advising him what to say. He remembered Billy telling him once that his wife had been a nurse.

He searched the house but failed to find a rubber or plastic tube. *Improvise* was a word from his days in the army, a word that had served him well a few times since then. But first, he decided to try the finger-down-the-throat method.

CHAPTER 34

One advantage Eddie had, although it was a small one, was that he knew which direction the big ape was traveling, but a glance at the street map showed a large residential area. It could take months to find the place where he and Nancy were staying, and would the big ape's car be parked there when he passed? Still, he decided he wasn't going to find them sitting in the house hoping they might turn up.

He locked his flat, smiled and waved to the female officer standing at Gibb's door, and pranced down the corridor feeling her eyes piercing the back of his neck. He grinned at her again as he opened the door leading to the stairs. He dashed down the steps, taking them two at a time, glad when he reached the bottom and was outside heading for his car. Before he got the engine started, he noticed two men sitting in a vehicle at the far end of the parking area. It was the way their eyes followed him that alerted him and made him suspect that they were police. He avoided eye contact with them as he drove past but constantly

"

glanced at his rear-view mirror to see if they were following. An plan instantly dawned on him for if they did pursue; he would drive all the way round the roundabout and head back. Fortunately, when he got there, he could see no sign of them.

The nearest filling station was busy, and he had to sacrifice a half hour before filling his fuel tank to the top. Darkness fell quickly, as the day had been overcast. The streetlamps came on, and still he failed the find the big stranger's car. As a consolation, he spotted a young boy at the roadside trying to fix his cycle. Eddie pulled up beyond him and walked back.

"Having some trouble?" he asked, noting that the boy wasn't as young as he'd first thought.

The young man stood up. "I think I've punctured my front tyre. I tried to fix it, but it still wouldn't blow up. I think I'll have to leg it home."

"It's getting dark," Eddie explained. "It'll be dangerous walking this road. Where do you live?"

"About two miles from here on Warton Avenue."

"I'm heading past that way, if you want a lift. The boot of my car is big enough to hold your bike if we take the wheels off."

The young man smiled. "Thank you, mister."

In a few moments, he had the wheels off, and together they got it tucked in the boot. Studying the young man's physique, Eddie decided he was well formed and fit. He would have to take him from behind with the crowbar. He didn't want to shoot him in case the shot could be heard. All the way on the drive, Eddie conversed with him. He discovered that his father was in the local police force. Inside, Eddie grinned, thinking, *This is going to be a challenge—one of the best yet.*

"I have to make a small detour to deliver a package to a friend; it won't take a minute."

"No problem," the young man replied.

Eddie had used this road every day going to and from work and was familiar with a few narrow lanes leading off to urban estates. He had often used them in search of a victim. The one he chose was ideal, as it had a two-mile stretch with no houses and conifer trees on both sides. All he had to do was hope no cars came along.

"Did you hear that?" he said to his passenger. In the dim light, he saw the young man shake his head. "I think something is rattling about in the boot. Best see what it is. Don't want to damage your bike."

He pulled over and got out of the car and then opened the boot lid. He returned to the passenger door, opening it. "I think something is jammed in the spoke of you bike," he said, holding up the crowbar. "If you can hold your bike, I'll lever it out."

The young man only managed to get halfway out the door when the crowbar smashed down on the back of his head. Eddie watched him fall to the ground, but he wasn't dead. He tried to get up, so Eddie again brought the crowbar down. This time he had a clearer view and was more accurate with his strike. There was no doubt this time; the young man was dead. He dragged the body in amongst the trees and then dumped the bike on top of him. Now the disappointment of not finding the big stranger's car didn't feel so bad. He turned up the radio and drove home, singing along to the music.

Barton turned Nancy on her side and put his finger down her throat. He got the expected reaction, but nothing came up. Then he remembered her being sick and thought maybe she had nothing left to bring up. His next call for help was to Brenda. This was his last resort. He would first ask for the tubes before asking her to come here. She didn't think she had tubes in her house and quickly volunteered to help.

"I'll come and collect you," Barton quickly offered.

She was standing at her door when he pulled up. She jumped in and said, "Tell me what happened."

Barton explained all that had happened and told her where he'd gotten the medication from.

"Let's hope we get there in time. What was she like when you left her?"

"I tried to make her sick and bring the contents of her stomach up, but nothing came up."

"What drove her to do such a stupid thing?"

"I'm not sure. She got upset over a news item about a young girl's body being found. said she needed to be sick."

"You took her to the toilet and left her there?"

No, I stood outside the door and heard her being sick. Then things went quiet. The next thing I knew, she was falling out the toilet door into my arms."

"Sounds to me like a cry for help. If she was determined to end it, she wouldn't have opened the door to you."

Nancy was lying in the same position he had left her in. He rushed to her and felt her jugular vein.

"Are you any good a CPR?" he cried to Brenda. "I can't get a pulse."

Brenda shook her head. "Just the basics. I thought you army guys got trained to do that."

"Like you, only the basics."

"We'll have to call an ambulance." She pulled her mobile from her pocket.

Barton grabbed her hand. "We can't. How can we explain where she got the pills from?"

"You'll just have to tell them you don't know."

That wasn't Barton's concern, although he pretended it was. This house was the dwelling of a murdered girl and also the unofficial home of a police detective who had committed suicide. There would have to be a media uproar and a lot of investigation. That he couldn't let happen.

"It's not going to be as simple as that. This house belongs to a friend of mine. His daughter was found murdered in the park a few weeks ago. She lived here. Her boyfriend committed suicide a few days later. That's going to create a lot of police attention."

"Why?" Brenda asked with a look of concern. She stepped away from the bed and stood close to him, gazing into his brown eyes.

"Well for starters, the boyfriend was a policeman."

She turned and looked at Nancy on the bed. "I'm sure she's gone."

He tried again to find a pulse but failed. Then he stood up looked at Brenda. "I think you're right." After moments silence, he said, "I'd best take you home. Don't want you involved in this."

She nodded. "What are you going to do?"

"I'll think of something."

"Do you want to come in for a coffee or something?" Brenda asked when he pulled up at her gate.

He grinned. "I wouldn't mind the 'or something' part."

She grinned widely, grasped his collar, and pulled him over to kiss his cheek. "You go and get that mess sorted out first, and then we can get the 'or something' sorted out," She giggled and jumped out the car.

He drove away, leaving her standing at the gate waving. His mind started churning over the things Nancy had said as he drove through the streets back to the house where he had left her. He was still pondering over her words as he stopped outside the front door. The statement she'd made about it being no wonder Eddie had turned out the way he was … was she just referring to the kicking he had given her, or was there more she wasn't telling? Why go to the length of suicide over the death of a girl she didn't know?

He avoided going into the room where she lay and went straight to the toilet. Laying on the tap on the wash basin was a sheet of toilet paper. He was about to crumple it up and flush it away when he noticed writing on it—just a few simple words that explained why she had committed suicide. Now it made sense. His first reaction was to phone Billy.

Billy was a bit disgruntled about being disturbed and wasn't bashful at letting Barton know, but when he learned about Barton's suspicions, he became more interested and fell silent.

When Barton had finished, Billy said, "So, you've been fucking the mother of the guy who could have murdered my daughter?"

"I wouldn't quite put it like that. I've just discovered this, and I'm not a hundred per cent sure it was him."

"You got the note from his fucking mother. What more do you need? Get out there, hunt the bastard down, and bring him to me."

As usual, the phone call got cut. Hunting this Eddie down wasn't the problem; Barton knew that the little hoodie would return to his home. The problem was that the area was crawling with police. He would have to hang about close to that block of flats without arousing suspicion. His only hope was that they would find Gibb and call their observations off.

One of Billy's orders was to get Nancy's body off of his property before one of the neighbours started complaining about the smell. Well, Barton decided that if Billy wanted the hoodie, he'd get his mother as well. Before he left, he checked to make sure all the windows were secure and turned off the heating to delay decomposition. Then he locked the door on his way out. He started his car and phoned Marlin, telling her he was on his way over. He got her usual, overwhelming response, that girlish musical tone she used when she was excited.

"How soon can you be here? I'll get dinner on," she chirped.

"I'll be with you in about half an hour, depending on traffic."

On the drive to her house, he ran through all the ways he could think of to finish with her without hurting her. When he pulled up at her door, he still hadn't found a way.

She ran down the passageway and threw herself into his arms. They kissed hungrily for a while until she eased herself away and said, "Dinner's almost ready." Then she turned and trotted into the kitchen.

He followed her and handed her the envelope. "I think that should cover your mortgage."

She took it from him, shook her head, and corrected him. "Not just my mortgage. Our mortgage."

That stung his conscience, and he didn't know where to look. Luckily, she placed his meal down in front of him and gave him a welcome distraction.

"You seem distracted," she said as she took the seat opposite him. "Is everything alright with you?"

He smiled and picked up his utensils. "Just a few work problems, nothing to get too concerned about." He could tell she wasn't convinced based on the expression on her face. "I'll soon get it sorted."

After the meal, she tended to her child, Barton got settled on the sofa, got the telly going, and without realising it, dozed off. He jumped when her hand rested on his shoulder, and she stepped back, shocked.

"Sorry," he said. "A bad dream."

"No need to apologise. It's my fault. I should have spoken to you before putting my hand on your shoulder. I was wondering if you were working tonight."

He nodded and glanced at his watch. "Is that the time?" he jumped to his feet. "Sorry, sweetheart, I have to get a move on; was that enough cash to cover the mortgage?"

"More than enough. Thank you." She got up and walked him to the door. "Will I see you in the morning?

He nodded and kissed her. Then he ran down the path and charged out the gate. As usual, she waved from the window as he pulled away in his car.

Driving along the now quietened street, he wondered if it would be worth the risk to do a recce of the car park at the block of flats where Eddie, the hoodie, lived. It was on his way to Brenda's house, so he decided, what the hell. He parked a few streets away and walked the rest of the way. Keeping to the shadows, he edged his way behind some conifer trees. From there he could see most of the vehicles. Some looked as though they had been abandoned, but the one with the policemen sitting in it was not there, unless they had changed their position and were no longer in his field of vision, which was, in his opinion, a good possibility. He decided it wasn't worth the risk of them nabbing him again and creeped his way back to his vehicle. Once clear, he risked a look back to convince himself that the coppers had moved to another position. That was when the hoodie appeared, walking towards his car. Barton couldn't believe his luck, but there was nothing he could do with the police maybe watching and his car too far away to give chase.

Feeling unsettled after the excitement with the young man, Eddie couldn't sit still in the house watching boring program on the television and decided to go searching for the big ape's car. He headed in the direction he'd seen him drive earlier. It was all down to chance, but you never won if you didn't try. He eliminated the street close to where he had spotted the stranger driving past and ended up at the outskirts of town.

The first few streets he recced were mostly big affluent houses and bungalows with double garages at the side. As he got nearer the town centre, the dwellings were mostly terraced blocks with cars parked all along one side of the road, making it difficult to spot the vehicle in question. After two hours, he gave up and decided the best time would be in daylight. Most people would be at work then, leaving the streets with less vehicles.

Once again, he got stopped at the level crossing. The lights began flashing as he approached, and the barriers came down. He began drumming his fingers on the steering wheel to the time of the music on the radio. He was getting impatient. Four bloody minutes and still no sign of a train. Three minutes later, by his watch, it flew past like a bullet. He waited another two before the barriers lifted. He was shocked at the backup of cars and buses that came through from the other side of the track. There must have been something big going on in town or a hold-up farther along the road.

He approached a police cordon and was diverted to the other side of the road. He drove past police cars and paramedic vehicles and could see in the distance along the narrow lane where he had murdered the young man. An ambulance had reversed in and was parked at the spot where he'd dragged the body into the trees.

A glimmer of panic rushed through him, but it was soon replaced with delight—delight that he could commit a brutal murder and drive past just a few metres from the scene. Suddenly the music from the radio lightened his mood. He was enjoying the moment and began singing along.

Hunger pangs started to nag. He couldn't remember when he'd last eaten. He began searching for a cafe or restaurant. Driving along the main street, he could see plenty of potential victims standing outside the pubs smoking, but he had had enough for one day. Best not to do too many in the one neighbourhood. Anyway, his plans for his next victims were already set in his mind. All he had to do was find where that car was parked.

The lights of a Chinese restaurant caught his eye, and he pulled into the car park. A young Chinese girl took his order. He thought she didn't look old enough to be working in a restaurant. She was a pretty girl with a permanent smile. He had never killed a Chinese girl. He'd done an Indian woman and a black man. Maybe soon he could chance his luck.

After the meal, which he ravenously wolfed down, she placed a cup of black coffee in front of him. He thanked her and paid his bill, and she delayed a moment longer than he expected. He gently placed his hand on hers.

"You're so beautiful."

"Thank you, sir," she replied, and she dropped a piece of paper in front of him before she headed off through a door at the back.

He got up and discreetly picked up the paper. He slipped it into his pocket, and before opening the door, he glanced back, seeing that she was at another table. She glanced at him and nodded. When he looked at the paper, all that was written on it was a mobile number. Sitting in his car, he entered the number into his own mobile before driving off.

His mind was full of thoughts about that pretty Chinese girl. Maybe he wouldn't kill her. There was something about her that appealed to him and gave him that familiar tingling flutter he'd used to get when he looked at Nancy. Could she take Nancy's place in his life? It was a thing worth thinking about. He must get to know her first. His thoughts were still with her as he opened the door to his flat. As he was about to step inside, two men in suites approached him from behind.

"Excuse me, sir," one of them said.

Eddie jumped in surprise and almost fell in the door. He felt strong hands grip his arms to steady him.

"Sorry about that, sir," the one with the glasses said. "Were making enquiries about your neighbour. Have you noticed him going about?"

Eddie shook his head. "In a place like this, it's best not to interfere with the neighbours."

"We understand that, sir," the first man's colleague interrupted. "You'll have seen on the news that he has absconded, cutting off his tag. He could be armed and dangerous. For your own protection, if you have any idea of his whereabouts, I'd advise you to let us know."

"I will." Eddie grinned and was about to step through the door when he felt himself being held back. He turned and was staring into the eyes behind the glasses.

"Did you know the woman who lived in the flat next door?"

Eddie shook his head. "Didn't know there was a woman living in there."

"According to what we have learned, there was, and there doesn't appear to be any sign of her either," the spectacled detective went on.

Eddie shrugged his shoulders. "As I said, I didn't have anything to do with them."

"Can I have your name please, sir?" the other detective said, a pen and notebook in his hands.

Eddie sighed with relief when he finally got the door closed on them. He slumped down on the sofa and swallowed some of Nancy's sleeping pills.

He jumped out of his sleep with a start. He heard banging coming from somewhere. "Go away," he said in a voice that sounded distant, but the banging persisted. He rolled off the sofa and staggered to the door. The two detectives were standing, smiling at him. "What now?" he asked. "You got me out of bed."

"In bed with your clothes on?" the detective with the glasses said with a wide grin.

"Fell asleep on the sofa. Too tired to shower and change."

"Just one more question, sir, and we'll not bother you again. Forensic has found blood in the bath next door. Did you hear any kind disturbance?" the detective asked.

Eddie shook his head. "I'm not in much. It could have happened when I was out."

"But you would have heard it if you were in?" his colleague said.

"I can't answer that. I wasn't here."

"The reason I ask is that if you'd heard, then the neighbour at the other side would have heard also."

"Have you asked them?"

"Can't get an answer from that door," the spectacled detective replied.

"Sorry, I can't help you officers, but I have to get back to sleep. I have an early start tomorrow.

They nodded and walked away. Eddie hastily closed the door. He checked his watch and for the first time realised he had been asleep for six hours. *Have those two been hanging around all this time?* he wondered as he got himself resettled back on the sofa. The lovely Chinese girl was the first image that came to his mind's eye. She was so pure and beautiful. To kill her would be the worst thing he could ever do. He would phone that number first thing when he woke.

With a mug of coffee in front of him on the kitchen table, he ran through his contact numbers. Having found hers, he was about to make contact when someone banged on his door again. He raced up the passageway cursing and swearing. *Fucking*

Tweedledee and Tweedledum, likely. He yanked the door open and was surprised to see a girl in uniform. He gave her one of his best smiles.

"What can I do for you, Constable?"

She fished a notebook out of her breast pocket and read out the registration and description of Nancy's car. "I've had a complaint of a powerful odour coming from it."

"Sorry," Eddie said, and he tried to look as if he was. "Our pet had the runs. He was at the end of his life, and we had to get him put so sleep. Bowel cancer. Haven't had time to get it valeted."

She spent a few minutes writing it all down and said, "That's fine, sir. Try to get it done as soon as possible."

"I will do, Officer."

He watched her walk towards the door at the end of the passage and then rushed for the kitchen window to check she wasn't sniffing around the vehicle. Panic was starting to build up. If she could distinguish that smell and knew about the woman next door being missing and the traces of blood found in the bath, it would just be a matter of time before they came back with forensic scientists wanting to check inside the car. *Get rid of it* was the only thought that came to him, but where? How, without being seen driving it away in daylight? It was too late to wait for darkness. They could be back banging on his door long before that.

He downed the dregs of the coffee that was now cold and cringed. That's when the idea came to him: use Nancy's car to find the big ape and when he was finished, dump it down that ravine where Debra had lost control of her car when he'd cut the brake lines. He'd need to make sure that nosey farmer was not around. That thought brought on the memory of his application for the new job. He wondered if Debra had passed on the message to her boss/lover. *I'll deal with them later.*

Nancy's car smelled fine. He only caught a slight whiff now and then when he pulled up at traffic lights. The report must have gone in before he'd gotten rid of the cut-up remains of the witch's body. Nevertheless, he drove with the widows open. This time, he started searching at the other end of town. On the outskirts, houses were well spread out and surrounded by trees. Each had a long driveway and a double garage. No vehicles were parked on the streets. One house caught his attention. It had a sign at the gate saying it was a B & B. The driveway was packed with cars all the way to the back of the building. This, he decided, would be the kind of place where they would stay until they found something more permanent.

CHAPTER 35

Brenda was busy emptying her dishwasher when Barton walked into the kitchen and kissed the back of her neck. She jumped and almost dropped an armful of crockery.

"Bloody hell, I almost shit myself," she howled. "Give me some warning the next time." She burst into laughter.

Barton laughed along with her and then offered to help. "I'll put them away if you show me where they go," he said pointing at the dishes in her hand.

"The dish rack's behind you." She dropped them into his hands and gathered out another armful before he returned. "Well done. You haven't broken any."

"I'm not that clumsy," he protested.

"That's good." She grinned. "This'll be part of your job."

After they had finished with the dishes, he opened the kitchen door and checked that none of the guests were within hearing distance. He closed it softly and said, "I need your help to get rid of Nancy's body."

Brenda took a hasty step back and held up her hands. "No way. I'm not getting involved."

"But you are involved. You were there when we found her, and we never phoned for an ambulance or informed the police. That makes you a party to a crime."

She slumped down on the nearest chair. "I've enough on my hands at the moment. They haven't released my sister's body, and I don't know when to arrange a funeral for her."

"This won't take long," he assured her. "I just need you to help support her body out of that house. We'll walk her as if she's had too much to drink in case someone happens to witness us. After that, I'll drop you off, and that will be the end of it for you. When I've done what I've planned, I'll come straight back to you. We can wait until they release your sister's body, and then we can make the arrangements." He gazed into her eyes, waiting for a reaction, but realised her mind was somewhere else.

"If I can remember right," she said thoughtfully, "there's a wheelchair in my garage. We can dig it out, and you can use that. Then you won't need my help."

Barton gave the idea some thought, trying to picture himself placing Nancy's body into the chair and then getting her into his car. Having an extra pair of hands when getting her out of the car at his destination would be better, but she wasn't willing to help.

"Well, I suppose that will have to do," he said, and held out his hand. "Do you have the keys to the garage?"

She nodded and said, "I'll get them and help you find it."

When they pushed up the roller door, Barton could see she why she'd offered to help. The place was packed full of cardboard boxes, discarded furniture, and even an old piano buried under doll houses and children's toys and cycles.

"How far in is it buried?"

She shrugged her shoulders and chuckled. "I don't know."

An hour later, when they had all the contents out of the garage and stacked in the gravel back yard, they finally found it against the back wall. Barton pulled it out and found that the wheels were seized, the tyres were flat, rust pimples were showing through the chrome frame, and the padded seat had fungi on it.

"It's going to take a week to get this thing workable."

Brenda laughed and walked away. "That's why I employ you," she cried over her shoulder.

When she had disappeared around the corner of the building, he sent a two-fingered gesture after her.

Left on his own, it took him well over an hour to get the gravel yard cleared and everything back in place. The day was wearing on, but that didn't bother him. His plan was to transport the body at night. The chair became more of a problem. He had to strip the wheel off and oil the ball bearings, repair the flat tyres, and wash it down with hot, soapy water. Luckily, it folded up easily, and he got it into the boot of his car.

"I'll be back later," he told Brenda. He got a small wave from her and left her tending to customers in the lounge. Before he set off, he called Marlin to say he was on his way over.

Marlin was at the door before he had a chance to open it. She threw her arms around his neck, and they kissed hungrily. He edged her inside, and they ended up in her bedroom. They lay naked on top of the bed, grinning and breathing heavily.

"Where have you been?" she finally asked. "I was expecting you back hours ago."

"A few jobs came up. That's what it's like in this business, no set hours of work."

He had no doubt about how he felt for her. That was what was frightening him. How was he going to tell her that soon they would have to end the relationship? If he was honest with himself, it was the last thing he wanted to do. This was the life he'd wanted when he'd gotten demobbed from the forces—to settle down and have a family. Now he was past the point of no return with criminal organisations. She swung her legs out of the bed, disturbing his train of thought. He reached and caught her hand and pulled her back in. Their faces were so close that the point of their noses touched.

"In all my life," he said, "I don't think I've ever been so happy."

She kissed him and got up. "I feel the same way."

He got up and joined her, and they got dressed together. "I've got a job to do later, but I'll be back as soon as it's finished."

"Can you stay the night with me?" She turned before opening the bedroom door.

"I'll try to get away," he replied and followed her into the kitchen, where she started preparing a meal. He sat himself down on one of the chairs, leaned his arms on the table, and admired her as she worked on vegetables.

She suddenly turned. "I wish I knew where I stood with you, Richard.

He got up, took the knife out of her hand, and held her, gazing into her tear-filled blue eyes. "I wish I knew myself. I know what I want, and I'm determined to get it."

"What is it you want?"

"At this moment, to spend the rest of my life with you."

She stepped away from him retrieved the knife, returning to her vegetables. "What does that mean, 'at this moment'?"

"The way I feel when I'm with you."

"And when you're not with me?"

"It's the same. It's just that my job involves a lot of stressful decisions. I just can't let my concentration wander."

She smiled to herself. It was just the answer she was wanting. She returned to sit at the table with him and said, "As long as you're not taking advantage of me, using me until someone better comes along."

He reached over and took her hand. "There is no one better than you."

This won't be a good area for a strange car parked on the street. The occupants in these houses will report it, and a police car will be around to investigate in a matter of minutes, Eddie thought. He turned left at the end of the street stopped, deciding to spend half an hour to see if the big stranger would drive out onto the main road. His success depended on which direction the big man turned. If he made a right, Eddie would have to find a place to turn around and lose valuable time, running the risk of losing him in the traffic. But all this depended on the stranger actually being in that B & B.

Time was up, and it was getting dark. The traffic was slackening off, and he decided to head for home. Nancy's car was smelling a lot better now, so if the police started sniffing about it, they would be disappointed. He parked her car in the same spot, trying to make it look as though it hadn't been moved. He was surprised to discover that the police were no longer snooping around the area. They must have decided Gibb wasn't worth the manpower and that he might turn up eventually for his belongings. If only they knew they would have a long wait. The door to Gibb's flat was cordoned off with blue- and-white tape.

Sitting in his regular position on the sofa with a mug of black coffee, because he had run out of milk, he got the television going and turned to the news. The first thing that came up was about Gibb. The broadcaster was saying that the police suspected him of killing his partner, hiding the body, and absconding.

Eddie couldn't help bursting into laughter. Those two murders had happened too close to home, and he didn't mind someone else getting the credit.

The next report made him jump up and boost the volume. The same presenter was reporting that a man's head had been discovered wrapped in foil when a wheely bin was hit by a speeding car. It was when the occupant of the house went to pick the garbage off the street that it was discovered. A positive identity had not yet been established, and a spokesman for the police wouldn't comment on it, saying it was early days yet.

The scene was close to the place where the police car had stopped and asked what he was doing. Luckily, he had been wearing Nancy's clothes, and the officer had addressed him as *madam*. He grinned. They'd be looking for that woman when they got their investigations in place.

He sunk back down on the sofa and began thinking about the report. He decided the police must know who that decapitated head belonged to. No way could they not identify that face with that long scar. So why hadn't they come out with it? Could they be hanging on until they found his partner before announcing having identified them both. That was going to take them a long time.

He jumped again when his phone sounded. He couldn't identify the number and cautiously answered.

"Mr Fisher?" the voice asked.

"Who's calling?"

After announcing his name and company, the speaker informed Eddie that his application for the position of assistant sales director had been successful and asked him to report to the receptionist on Monday at 09.00. Eddie switched his mobile off, jumped to his feet, and punched the air. "Great!" he shouted to himself as he gazed at his reflection in the mirror on the wall opposite. That gave him a week to find that big stranger and Nancy. A week to plan how to get rid of their bodies. He would have to take them away from there and dump them miles apart.

Using Nancy's car to track them down didn't seem such a good idea anymore. She would instantly recognise it if she was traveling with him. He decided to head into the nearest car hire firm first thing in the morning and get one.

Groggy after another night of drug-induced sleep, he staggered to the toilet and vomited the contents of his stomach. After an ice-cold shower, he still didn't feel any fresher. He tried to shave, but his hands shook too much. His whole body trembled out of control. Panic was taking over, an attack like he hadn't had for years. Bloody pills. He picked up the packet from the living room floor and was shocked to find that there was only half a card left in the packet. He ripped the tablets out and flushed them down the toilet.

He couldn't focus on the face of his watch and fumbled his way to the kitchen. The big clock on the wall was showing six thirty. Too early, he decided and headed back to the sofa. After what seemed to be only a few minutes, he was aroused with banging. Feeling a lot fresher, he rushed to the front door and found nobody there, but when he glanced at Gibb's door, he saw three men in overalls were boarding the door up. Back in the kitchen, he glanced again at the clock and thought it had jumped two hours. It couldn't be right. His mouth felt like sandpaper and tasted like shit, but a mug of black coffee flushed it away. The only thing he hadn't thought about buying was tooth paste and mouthwash. *First thing to buy*, he thought as he was getting dressed. Clean clothes were another thing he was running low on. He must phone that lovely Chinese girl. She'd attend to these things if he could persuade her to move in. If she refused, well, on her back be it.

By the time he drove away in the hired car, an hour had flown past. "Bloody paperwork," he cursed as he started his search of the streets. He started with that B & B, and that took up another hour without success. He had gotten out the car and walked around the building, but most of the vehicles had gone. All the vehicles that had been parked on the streets were gone, their owners probably at work. He saw a cafe at the side of the street and fancied a decent cup of tea and something quick to eat. When he stepped out of the hired car to go in, however, he saw the big stranger driving past. He noticed that Nancy wasn't with him. He dived back in the vehicle and chased after him. Fortunately he was facing in the same direction this time.

For a moment, he thought he had lost him, but then he noticed the big stranger turning left at a traffic light. Eddie had to make a last- minute swerve and got a chorus of horns blasting from behind. He didn't have to drive far along the street before he saw the vehicle pull in and park in front of a two-storey building. He drove past slowly and parked a few yards farther along, from where he could observe through his rear-view mirror.

The stranger got out his car and opened the boot lid. He hauled out a wheelchair, unfolded it, and wheeled it into the house. *What the fuck are you up to?* Eddie pondered, and he started to wonder if this was where the big stranger and Nancy were living. That being the case, he would have to make a change to his plans. He couldn't start shooting at them here without arousing the neighbours.

He got the hired car started up. At least now he knew where they were. He could start making other plans. As he was about to engage the clutch, he took a last glance in mirror. That's when he saw the big stranger pushing the wheelchair towards his car. When he came under the glow of the street light, Eddie could make out a figure slumped backwards in the chair. As they got closer to their car, there was no mistaking who that figure in the wheelchair was. Eddie could hardly believe his luck. Now he had them both together. He watched the big man heave her into the back seat and then fold the chair and dump it back in the boot.

He ducked down into the foot well in case the big man recognised him on his way past. Then he gave them a few minutes before pursuing them. He cursed at the junction, where he had to wait for a truck to pass; the driver was in no hurry. Finally, when the truck pulled off into a lay-by, he was able to get up some speed. Then the cursed barriers at the level crossing were down. There was only one car in front of him, and so remembering the length of time he'd waited the last time, he decided to take the chance.

This was one of the older crossings with only a half barrier. He swerved out past the car in front and drove around it. The last thing Eddie's eyes took in was a passenger train about ten feet away from him traveling at sixty-three miles per hour.

CHAPTER 36

Barton and Marlin observed the usual routine. They kissed at the door, and she rushed to the widow to wave as he drove away. He had a good look around his car before getting in. The tartan throw he had covered Nancy's body with hadn't been disturbed, not that he had been expecting it to have been. It was just a habit he had developed from his military days: always check the vehicle before getting in and starting it.

The drive through town was, as usual, chock-a-block with traffic and pedestrians. All the traffic lights were against him. The only thing on his side were the gates at the level crossing, and he'd just managed to get clear of them when he heard the warning bell and saw the barriers drop through his rear-view mirror. When he heard the train rushing past behind him, he thought, *That was quick. Not much warning this morning.* He heard the squeal of the brakes from the train but didn't give it a second thought.

He pulled up at the park gates under overhanging beech trees. This was the back entrance, and it was only used by joggers and the occasional dog walker. This morning being damp with drizzle, the area was deserted. He had changed his mind about doing this in the dark and instead spent the night with Marlin.

He took a short stroll to the gateway to check that there was no one in the park heading his way. All was clear, so he quickly dashed back to get the chair out of the boot and ready. He shot another glance in all directions first before he dragged her body out of the rear door and got her propped up on the wheelchair and covered her with the tartan throw. Again, he was fortunate. The bench he had planned to leave her on was deserted, and no one was around. *Well,* he reassured himself as he sat her on it, *at least this way she'll get a decent burial.* He folded the chair, wrapped the throw around it, and pushed it to his car.

When he entered the front door of the B & B, he could hear a vacuum cleaner in operation upstairs. He loped up and found Brenda working on the carpets in one of the rooms. He located the socket and switched it off. She swung round, puzzled at why the machine had stopped, and then saw him standing a few feet away.

"I put the chair back in the garage," he said and handed her the key.

"What did you do with that poor woman's body?" she asked, pushing the vacuum to the side.

"Don't worry about that. I put her where she will be found soon so her body will be put to rest with a decent burial."

He learned from Brenda that all the guests were out, and they decided to spend some time together in her bed. An hour later, they decided to have something to eat.

"All this sex makes me hungry," she said, grinning, and she placed a bowl of salad down on the kitchen table in front of him.

"The exercise will do us good," Barton replied when she placed a plate of cold ham in front of him as well and sat down opposite him with one for herself. "How about your sister's body? Have they given you any info about when they will release it?"

She shook her head and began lifting salad out of the bowl. "They're not a hundred percent sure what drugs she had taken. They say they have more test to do."

After the meal, they sat on the sofa in the lounge drinking coffee. Barton picked up the remote and got the television going.

"You're a telly fan, I see," she said with a quiet giggle and moved up closer to him.

They sat through a film, and then the news came on. He was about to change the channel when the news showed footage of a train that had crashed into a car. Later they discovered that the driver of the car had driven around the barriers.

"What bloody idiot would do a thing like that?" Brenda said. "I've always said there should be a double barrier there."

The presenter went on to report that the vehicle was a hired car and that the person who'd hired it had been identified. The police have named him as a Mr Eddie Fisher. Barton almost spilled his coffee down his shirt with the shock. The report went on to say that as yet, no trace of the hirer's remains have been found.

"What's the matter?" Brenda cried.

Barton placed his cup on the table at the side of the sofa. "That's Nancy's son, the one who gave her a kicking."

The scene showed the remains of the car that had been lifted off the rails by a mobile crane. It looked as though it had been through a crusher. Although he was expecting something to come on about Nancy's body being found in the park, he realised that the train crash would be the main story and another body found wouldn't take priority at this time.

"That's a bit of a shocker," Brenda said. "Coincidences do happen at the most tragic times."

When they announced the time of the incident, Barton realised that he had driven over that level crossing about the same time and remembered thinking at the time that the train had been quicker than normal at reaching it. He remembered the sound of the train brakes being applied, although at the time he'd thought nothing of it. And what of the hired car? Why had Eddie had to hire a vehicle when he had a bloody good car of his own? Plus Nancy's was sitting parked up.

Later, while lying in bed with Brenda snoring next to him, his mind was racing, thinking over the events. Suddenly he sat up like he had just been jabbed with a taser, as it had dawned on him that the little hoodie shit had been following him. He'd hired that car so he wouldn't be recognised. Nancy had said "No wonder Eddie turned out the way he has." What had he turned out like? Was he the reason she'd overdosed?

He could lie still no longer. His mind was awash with unanswered questions and muddled theories. His memory took him back to the day after Billy's daughter had been murdered when he'd seen Nancy in the park close to the place where her body had been found. What was that all about? Why had she been there? She hadn't come across as the type of sick site tourists who visits disaster areas.

He headed downstairs and put the kettle on, deciding to mull it all over with a coffee. Brenda walked in behind him.

"Now there stands a worried-looking man," she said as she sat down at the table. "I'll have one too, if you're making it."

He could feel her eyes on him as he prepared the two cups. "What make you so sure I'm worried?"

"For a start, why are you up at this time of the morning? Why have you been fidgeting about all night in bed? To me that's as good a sign as any."

"It's the shock of two people I knew ending their lives in such a short time."

"I know how that feels. I've just lost my sister and can't get her body to put her to rest."

He handed her a coffee and sat next to her. "I hope the police don't discover that Nancy died in that flat.

"I bloody hope not. Did you make sure nobody saw you put her body on that bench?"

"That's not what I worried about. It's how many of your guests saw her here."

"Let's hope that that disaster at the level crossing gets priority in the news and the discovery of the body of a woman who had overdosed on a park bench will slip away unnoticed."

They sat for a while watching early-morning television, not really concentrating. Then she jumped up.

"I have to do breakfast. I've got two businessmen who want an early start. You can help if you want."

He grimaced and shrugged his shoulders. "I'm not a very good cook."

"I'll find something for you to do. It'll help take your mind off the problem."

He got up and followed her into the kitchen and sat down at the table, watching her prepare and cook the food.

"You're not going to be much help sitting there," she said without looking round. "Go into the fridge, get the milk out, and fill up the jugs."

After the early breakfast, they retired to the sofa in the lounge and sat with two other guests watching the morning news. The train crash was still the top story, and soon after they talked about it, a high-ranking police officer came on saying that a weapon had miraculously been found in good condition in the wreck of the car. This weapon, he went on to say, had instantly been sent for testing at ballistics and had been found to be the same weapon that had been used to murder the couple in Sandbach services on the M6.

Barton stood and nodded for Brenda to follow him out the room. "I need to go make an urgent call," he explained as he headed for the front door.

"Can't you make it from the kitchen? Nobody will hear you."

He opened the door and said, "No, because the moment I make the call, I'll have to go."

It was a strange voice that answered Billy's mobile.

"Can I have a word with Billy?"

When Billy finally came on, Barton spoke before Billy had a chance to. "We need to talk. But not on the phone."

"Why what's wrong?" Billy barked. "Where can we meet?"

A long pause followed, and then Billy came on saying, "Do you know my shop on Market Street?"

"I'll find it."

"Meet me there in an hour."

Knowing the parking problems in Market Street, Barton left in plenty of time and was glad he had done so, for he had to walk about a quarter of a mile. He found Billy and two other men in a small box room with a desk that didn't leave room for much else. They stood huddled together smoking, and Barton soon started coughing and wiping his stinging eyes. He had deliberately left the door open, and the two men got the message and left.

Billy sat sideways on the edge of the desk and said, "So, what's the big secret?"

"I think I've discovered who killed your daughter."

"You *think* you've discovered? I told you the last time to be sure before bringing the person to me."

"That's the problem. I can't. He could be already dead." Barton went through all the details of his suspicions while Billy smoked one cigarette after another.

"So, what you're telling me is, you were fucking the mother of the guy who murdered my daughter, and it took you all this time find out?"

"Yes, well, it wasn't as simple as you make it out to be."

Billy stumped his smoke out on a tin ash tray on the desk and stood up. "I saw that train crash on the news, and all I can say is, the lucky bastard got the quick way out." He edged his way out through the door, saying, "You owe me. I paid you to bring the bastard to me, and you didn't."

Barton followed him out through the shop and onto the street, where Billy's Range Rover and driver were waiting. The huge, black vehicle had hardly gone a hundred yards when Barton's phone sounded. Brenda's name came on the screen.

"What's wrong Brenda?"

She took a moment to answer. "Richard, get over here please, as quick as you can."

The call was cut short. *That sounds like more trouble,* he thought, and he made his way back to his car.

He couldn't get turned into the street; it had been cordoned off with blue-and-white tape, and two constables were standing in the middle of the road diverting traffic. Like the rest of the drivers, he slowed down to rubberneck and saw the street was crowded with police vehicles, blue lights flashing the full length of it. The shock came when he noticed that Brenda's B & B was the centre of the show. Uniformed, armed police were standing at the gate. Barton decided this was no place for him to hang about and drove on past.

He decided to go back to the flat Billy had loaned him. He didn't want the distraction of Marlin; he needed to do some serious thinking. He flopped down on an easy chair, finding it difficult to think clearly. The nagging question was why the police were at the B & B. Could they have been looking for him, had Brenda committed a crime, or—and he hoped that this was it—were they looking for one of her guests? The latter would make sense of her unexpected call. He recalled there being some weird-looking characters among them.

His phone sounded again. He didn't recognise the number but reluctantly answered it.

"Richard!" Brenda sounded distraught. "I'm in the police station. They say my sister had been poisoned."

"How could that have happened?" Barton was being careful with his words in case the call was being recorded.

"I don't know. They say it was rat poison. I don't have that in my house."

"Where did it come from, then?"

"I don't know. Maybe one of the guests brought it in."

"What do you want me to do?"

The call got cut short, and he was left staring at his mobile and wondering if he should use redial. Then, after a moment of panic, he thought better of it. Although Brenda wouldn't know where he was, the chance of the police tracing the signal was a risk he wasn't going to take.

His next call was to Marlin telling her he was on his way. Within a matter of minutes, he was in his car and driving. She was, as usual, delighted to see him and threw her arms around his neck. She stepped back and stared at him, wondering why he wasn't responding to her embrace.

"You look troubled," she said. "Has something happened at work?"

He nodded slightly. "You could say that." He walked past her into the living room and got seated on the sofa.

She followed him and sat next to him, putting her hand on his arm. "Would you like to talk about it?"

He picked up the remote. "It's nothing for you to worry about. You've got enough on your plate."

"Don't be like this, Richard. Your problems are mine. We live together; we should share problems."

He placed his hand over hers. "Honest, darling, it's nothing."

With his other hand, he turned on the television, hoping to get some answers from the news. But so far, there was nothing about Brenda's sister. All he got was the mindboggling Brexit negotiations. They watched it to the end in silence, and still there was nothing.

He had another restless night, worrying what had gone down at Brenda's and how much she had she told the police of his involvement. How could the poison have been given to Linda, and how could it have been administered without her tasting it? She would have died painfully, screaming the place down. Somehow, he had to get to Brenda without the police's knowledge. He knew they could only hold her for forty-eight hours if they haven't charged her with anything.

Barton and Marlin woke up together listening to the child crying in the next room. He jumped out of bed first and got his jeans on. By the time he had pulled his shirt on, she was up and in beside the child. He joined her in the kitchen, where she was bathing him and getting soaked by his splashing while he giggled at her.

"The poor wee chap's got a tooth coming though. Must be painful. He has been crying for the past few nights," she said.

Marlin was at the window waving as he drove off. He didn't like leaving her alone with her upset child, but he had to know what was going on with Brenda. In his usual side-street parking place, he called Billy.

"What is it this time, Barton?" Billy barked.

"I've a good idea where those bags have been hidden. You know the ones I mean."

"Well, go and get them and bring them back to the warehouse."

"I'll do that, but first, I need you to get your legal team to go to the police and say they are representing a Mrs Brenda Morgan."

"Who's that?"

"A woman I know who is being accused of poisoning her sister."

"Why?"

"Because I need to know what she has told the police."

"Why? Are you involved in it somewhere?"

"She owns a B & B, and I was living there when we discovered the body. The last thing I need is to be dragged in as a witness."

After a time of grumbling and cursing, Billy finally said, "OK, I'll get that sorted out while you pick up those bags."

Barton decided to kill some time for an hour, firstly so Billy would think he was picking the bags up somewhere and secondly to give his legal team time to get established in the police station. When he finally pulled into the yard in front of the old building, Billy was standing talking to four men. They turned when he pulled up a few yards away, and they all burst into a fit of laughter. He got out of the car carrying the two bags and handed them to Billy, who was still in a state of uncontrollable laughter.

"Are you going to let me in on the joke?" Barton asked, holding out his hands.

Billy handed the bags to one of the men and turned back to Barton, wiping tears of laughter from his eyes.

"You," he sniggered. "You—" Again he couldn't get the words out, and the guys at his back were almost bent over in fits. "You've … been fucking the wrong woman," he finally burst out.

"What are you talking about?"

Billy, now a bit more under control, said, "The woman you thought was Brenda was actually her twin sister Linda." It appears that this Linda had been a naughty girl in the past, and the police had her fingerprints on record. She confessed to poisoning her identical twin so she could take over the business. Your name hasn't been mentioned so far, but my advice is for you to lie low for a while."

Marlin's mobile rang out. A recorded voice on the line informed Barton that this person was not available to take the call. Three times Barton tried, only to get the same response.

"Come on, Marlin. Pick up your phone," he shouted.

The thought of having to tell her that their relationship would have to end, that he would have to leave this area, was causing him a great deal of anguish. His first thought was to phone her and tell her—the cowardly way. The selfish way. But how could he look into those beautiful blue eyes and see the hurt he would cause? He started up his car, and after a time of thinking hard to come up with an way to tell her that wasn't hurtful, he decided just to turn up at her house and face her.

He pulled up in front of her house and noticed that only the dim light from the living room was on. Unusual, he thought. Normally at this time she would be bathing her baby, and most of the lights in the house would be on. He was still not sure how he was going to tell her. He sat just staring at the window, his mind in turmoil. Finally, after some long, dragging minutes, he decided just to brave it out. Her car was parked in her driveway, so she must be in. He headed for the front door and knocked. No response. Again he knocked, this time harder. Still there was no sound from inside. Then he remembered he had a key. He opened the door softly in case she had decided to bathe and bed the baby early. He didn't want to disturb him.

The living room door was ajar and the light from the table lamp was shining through. Wearing his best grin, he walked in expectin to find her maybe to be feeding her baby. He got two steps inside and froze. Marlin's naked body lay on the sheepskin rug in front of the sofa. Her torso had been mutilated by what appeared to have been multiple stab wounds. Her eyes were wide and staring at the ceiling. The rug beneath her that had once been white was now red with her blood. It took time for his brain to register what he was looking at.

Being careful not to leave any trace of himself, he stepped closer and could see the stab wounds on her chest and neck. Her stomach had been slit open, and its contents were beside her on the rug. Barton couldn't control the revulsion churning inside him, and he scrambled to the toilet. When he had no more sickness to bring up, he turned to wash his hands and face. Reaching for a towel, he noticed the bath had been filled. The child lay face up, submerged in the clear water, his mouth and eyes wide open.

He spent the next hour cleaning up any trace of himself around her home and found her mobile behind the sofa. He dialled the emergency services on it and sneaked out, hoping that he hadn't been spotted by the neighbours. As he sat in his car, he destroyed her phone and vowed to get the bastard who did this, even if it took the rest of his life to do so. Then he drove off at a crawl with no lights on.

End.

9 781961 438545